THE DEVIL IS A PART-TIMER!

9

SATOSHI WAGAHARA

ILLUSTRATED BY
■ 029 (ONIKU)

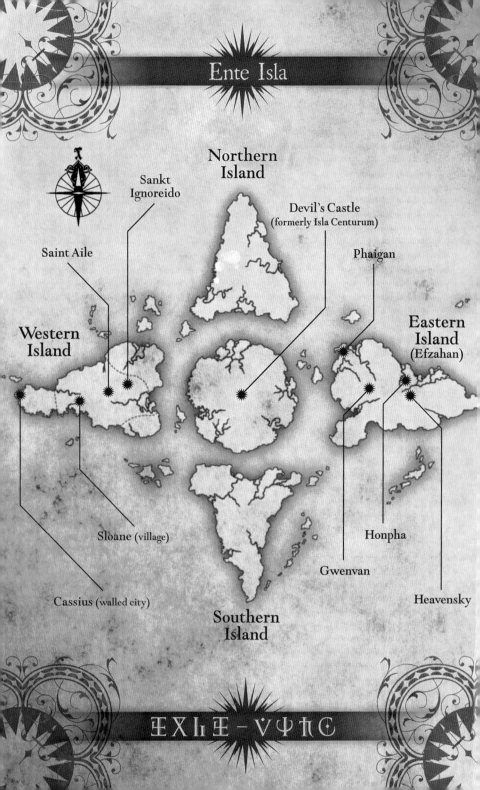

Ente Isla

Northern Island

Sankt Ignoreido

Saint Aile

Devil's Castle
(formerly Isla Centurum)

Phaigan

Western Island

Eastern Island
(Efzahan)

Sloane (village)

Honpha

Gwenvan

Cassius (walled city)

Southern Island

Heavensky

RÉSUMÉ

"Me-and Maou are same, soul and body!!"

NAME

Acieth Alla (TSUBASA SATO) —MAou

Looks About ~15!~

We'd better look into her birthday. —Chiho

AGE　**GENDER**

ADDRESS

...AZuKA #201

SASAZuKA...X-X, SHIBuYA-Ku, TOKYO

← Inside Maou! —Acieth　　Acieth↑← ...to take this more seriously! —Chiho

TELEPHONE NUMBER

I want one. ← HE...

PAST EXPERIENCE

None. ← Same as...

Isn't...? —Chiho

...you not ...compared to ...ly a newborn?

QUALIFICATIONS/CERTIFICATIONS

I want a driver's license! ← NO!

Acieth Alla

(Tsubasa Sato)

Alas Ramus's younger sister and another personification of the Sephirah Yesod. A free spirit, she speaks Japanese in a not-quite-native fashion. During the battle at Chiho's high school, she fused with the Devil King and manifested herself into the same shape as the Better Half.

THE OTHER WAY AROUND!
...AOu

COMMUTE TI...

We're together all the time! ↙

FAMILY/DEPE...

MA...

NAME OF GUARDIAN

HIROSHI SATO

STOP IT! —MAou

NAME		
Emeralda Etuva —Yusa		
DATE OF BIRTH	AGE	GENDER
Ignora 1213, summer		
ADDRESS		GE Emi
Secretary's Offi		
Holy Magic Ad		—Emi
WHY DOES		
AND ASH		
TELEPHO		
080-		

AST EXPERIENCE

223, Month of the Wing	joined Palace Magic
225, Month of the Tree	top graduate, Pala
233, Month of the Wing	joined Sant Aile Holy Magic Admin... tudent...
Month of the	ecretary, Holy M
hy're you ex	

"Careful with your S-Holy Energy β intake, all riiiight?" Emi

UALIFICATIONS/CERTIFICATIONS
alace sorcerer, holy magic doctorate, flu

KILLS/HOBBIES
ating

EAS
st happena

Emeralda Etuva

The official court sorcerer of Saint Aile, the Church's capital, on Ente Isla's Western Island. She was once a traveling companion of the Hero, and her calm and gentle personality masks her tremendous power as a magic user. Loves sweets, despite being more mature in years than Emi.

NAME

Sariel Mitsuki Sarue

DATE OF BIRTH

love has

AGE

no

GENDER

no time

ADDRESS

My Future Palace of
Heaven's Chateau
X-X-X Hat...

TELEP

0'80 -

"Such...
such beauty...
M-my
goddesssssss!!!"

PAST EXPERIENCE

My time in heaven do

20XX   rated Sentucky F   Chi

Future 1   heart with   ddess

Future 2   Mg   d SFC merg   team

Future 3   a lif   with love await

Future 4   a lif   with love c

QUALIFICATIONS/CERTIFICATION

sales agent (level 2), bookkeeping (level
Handwriting Exam level (1B), Evangelist o

SKILLS/HOBBI

romanti   Mayum

The Archangel Sariel

(Mitsuki Sarue)

An archangel who posed as the
manager of a Sentucky Fried Chicken
franchise to seize Emi's holy sword.
After tasting defeat at the hands of the
Devil King, he fell deeply in love with
Kisaki, visiting the MgRonald she runs
daily until she finally banned him from
the premises. It looks like he has
been given a reprieve
for now, but...

DEP

0 min.   ed for futu

SATOSHI WAGAHARA
ILLUSTRATED BY ■ 029 (ONIKU)

YEN ON
NEW YORK

THE DEVIL IS A PART-TIMER!, Volume 9
SATOSHI WAGAHARA, ILLUSTRATION BY 029 (ONIKU)

Translation by Kevin Gifford
Cover art by 029 (oniku)

HATARAKU MAOUSAMA!, Volume 9
© SATOSHI WAGAHARA 2013
All rights reserved.
Edited by ASCII MEDIA WORKS
First published in 2013 by KADOKAWA CORPORATION, Tokyo.
English translation rights arranged with KADOKAWA CORPORATION,
Tokyo, through Tuttle-Mori Agency, Inc., Tokyo.

English translation © 2017 by Yen Press, LLC

Yen On
1290 Avenue of the Americas
New York, NY 10104

Visit us at yenpress.com
facebook.com/yenpress
twitter.com/yenpress
yenpress.tumblr.com
instagram.com/yenpress

First Yen On Edition: December 2017

Yen On is an imprint of Yen Press, LLC.
The Yen On name and logo are trademarks of Yen Press, LLC.

The publisher is not responsible for websites (or their
content) that are not owned by the publisher.

Library of Congress Cataloging-in-Publication Data
Names: Wagahara, Satoshi. | 029 (Light novel
illustrator) illustrator. | Gifford, Kevin, translator.
Title: The devil is a part-timer! / Satoshi Wagahara ;
illustration by 029 (oniku) ; translation by Kevin
Gifford.
Other titles: Hataraku Maousama!. English
Description: First Yen On edition. | New York, NY :
Yen On, 2015-
Identifiers: LCCN 2015028390 |
ISBN 9780316383127 (v. 1 : pbk.) |
ISBN 9780316385015 (v. 2 : pbk.) |
ISBN 9780316385022 (v. 3 : pbk.) |
ISBN 9780316385039 (v. 4 : pbk.) |
ISBN 9780316385046 (v. 5 : pbk.) |
ISBN 9780316385060 (v. 6 : pbk.) |
ISBN 9780316469364 (v. 7 : pbk.) |
ISBN 9780316473910 (v. 8 : pbk.) |
ISBN 9780316474184 (v. 9 : pbk.)
Subjects: | CYAC: Fantasy.
Classification: LCC PZ7.1.W34 Ha 2015 | DDC
[Fic]—dc23
LC record available at
http://lccn.loc.gov/2015028390

ISBNs: 978-0-316-47418-4 (paperback)
978-0-316-47419-1 (ebook)

1 3 5 7 9 10 8 6 4 2

LSC-C

Printed in the United States of America

PROLOGUE

The grand empire of Efzahan held firm control over all the land that composed Ente Isla's Eastern Island. It was ruled by the Azure Emperor, the absolute font of all power in the land, and this emperor lived in a castle and surrounding city that visually expressed all of his majesty—all the glory that allowed a single nation to so effectively control such a great expanse. Such was the impression it gave visitors from all of Ente Isla that it came to be known as Heavensky—as vast as the blue sky that extended from horizon to horizon across the earth.

This land, this Efzahan, once suffered just as painfully under the iron rule of the Devil King's Army as the rest of Ente Isla. But even Alciel, the Great Demon General who had led the demon horde's conquest of Eastern Island, found himself taken aback by the vast, sheer beauty of this city, enough so that holding Heavensky Keep and the emperor's family within his grasp was a source of honest pride to him.

"Like, is all of that true? I know it's written in that history text-book they cobbled together after the invasion, but..."

A castle as vast as Heavensky was all but doomed to be complex and mazelike inside. And within an upper chamber, one only the nobility was allowed to step into, a brawny man in a spotless toga over a cheap T-shirt with "I LUV LA" on it had his audience's attention.

"I mean, not to cast aspersions, but you don't seem like the type of guy who's into all this lavishness. Like, you really didn't mind spending the fortune it must cost to maintain all this? This place has gotta have a huge cleaning bill."

An equally brawny companion in a full suit of armor accompanied him, but the person in the toga was addressing a third man, one who was currently using this armored companion's shoulder for support.

"..."

The man, dressed in simple, modest clothing, showed no sign of responding to the question—or to much else at the moment, given his lack of consciousness.

"Still not awake, huh? Guess we did ask a lot outta him... Hey, can you at least tie him back on the throne for me? And when he wakes up, try not to manhandle him again; call me instead. Let him have whatever kinda tantrum he wants 'til I show up."

"Lord Gabriel, may I ask who this man is? What does he have to do with the Great Demon General Alciel?"

The man called Gabriel chuckled a bit as he shook his head. "It's better if you don't know. It'll just make more work for me if you do. I'd have to transform him myself, and I'd really like to avoid that pain in the ass if I could."

The armored man furrowed his brows at this reply.

"My lord, if I may, I am one of the proud Knights of the Inlain Azure Scarves, the most prestigious of the Eight Scarves of Efzahan. There is nothing you could tell me that would prevent me from carrying out my mission, sir."

"Oh? Well, if you insist. That guy draped over your shoulder? That's your Great Demon General Alciel, so... Oh, see? See? Can you stand up properly, please?"

Despite all the lofty words of a few seconds ago, the armored man was now on the floor, the unconscious man's arm still around him.

"I've got a safety valve in place to seal off his demonic force, but I think he's gonna shake that off with a quickness once he wakes up. That's why I want you to tell me first... Ah, this is no good. This is exactly why I didn't want to tell anyone."

The courageous Knight of the Inlain Azure Scarves was racked with fear, his eyes darting and unfocused.

"Man, I wanna show you guys exactly who you're so afraid of.

We're talking about a guy who spends five minutes at the grocery store agonizing over whether to buy a six- or a twelve-pack of eggs. Here...we go!"

Gabriel plucked the unconscious Alciel—known in another world as Shirou Ashiya—away from the incapacitated knight, heaved him over a shoulder, and stomped off and upward, farther into Heavensky's higher reaches. It didn't take him long to reach the castle's throne room.

Normally the Azure Emperor, the sole icon of power in this great land, would be conducting his political affairs in this chamber—instead, the throne was about to support Shirou Ashiya, the Devil King's house-husband dressed from head to toe in discount off-the-rack UniClo clothing.

"Bet this brings back some memories for you, huh?" Gabriel asked as he deposited Ashiya upon the throne in the middle of the vast, temple-like room, almost large enough to be a stadium. "But from here on out this joint's gonna play home to an event you're probably even more familiar with, so enjoy yourself, okay?"

He grinned.

"I'd love to mess around with that little situation a little, you can trust me on that. But nobody likes it when someone tries to clone a big hit, yeah?"

Gabriel shrugged to himself. As he did, the ornate chamber, packed with furniture and décor from the world's finest craftsmen, suddenly echoed with a harsh, electronic sound.

"Oops, there it is," he muttered as he reached into his toga. It was a ringtone—from an unlisted number, the screen said.

"Who's it gonna be—someone top-level? Or maybe the big man 'imself, huh?"

He didn't try to hide his excitement as he tapped at the screen.

"Yello, do you have ten-pound balls? Oh, wait, I mean, is your refrigerator running? ...Sorry, sorry, I just always wanted to say that. Yeah, this is Gabriel."

The joke apparently flew right over the head of the caller. His ranting through the earpiece could easily have been heard from an observer ten feet away.

"Oh, hey, how'd you know I was on the Eastern Island? ...Huh? Him? Hee-hee, nice! I always knew he had a good head on his shoulders... Hmm? Ohh, now you know I can't say that quite yet. But, yeah, I'm definitely here, and... Ahh, I guess I might as well admit it: Emilia's gonna be paying a visit soon, too."

Gabriel paused. There was no need to hurry this call along. He was too busy savoring the irate reaction from across the line.

THE DEVIL DEVISES A FULL MILITARY EXPEDITION

The other side picked up on the fourth ring.

"Oh, hey, Kawacchi! You okay to talk for a sec? Great. So, um, sorry to spring this on you, but what do you think about swapping shifts three days from now? Yeah. Um, it doesn't have to be the whole thing. Like, even half would help me out a ton. Day, evening, whatever... Oh, you will? Cool, thanks! I'll make it up to you later, okay? ...Huh? Aw, man, no way—you're gonna have to ask her yourself, dude. I couldn't really, like... Yeah. Sure, okay. Thanks again! I really mean it... Okay, sure, see you..."

He ended the call, then wrote "OK" on a particular square of the shift schedule that was laid out on the low *kotatsu* table.

"Cool. Now who's left...? I already got Kato doing two days for me, so that leaves Kota and Aki and Ken... Ooh, but he said he was busy studying, so maybe not..."

A sheet of paper titled "Employee List" lay next to the schedule on the table, each name with a symbol or piece of scribbled text next to it that only the original writer could comprehend.

"After that... Eesh, and of course I had to pick up a Sunday-night shift at a time like this... Shige told me he's a no-go for weekends, and Yoko usually works shifts alongside Mitsu, so..."

The hemming and hawing continued as his eyes darted between the schedule grid and the staff list.

"...Man, looking at it like this, it's a goddamn miracle we can keep the café open, huh? I don't even know how we're gonna launch the delivery side."

He shook off the thought before it threatened to drive his concentration off track any further.

"Well, that's why I gotta get this wrapped up in a week! Uh, I don't think Ryuta can do nights..."

Suddenly, the voice of a very non-hurried woman entered his ear.

"Ooh, real tough!"

He was the only one in the room. It was unclear where the voice came from.

"Well, yes, it kind of is, okay? I have to cover for the manager most of the time if she's not there, so if I'm gone too, that means no management at all in the store!"

"Management? Why do you need management?"

"Ugh..."

Sadao Maou, the young, dark-haired man currently agonizing over his work schedule, groaned at the unseen voice that seemed to poke fun at his very psyche.

"...Look, they're called 'management' because they're supposed to be around at all times, okay? So can you shut up for a second already? I'm kinda busy here!"

"Meeeeeanie..."

"Daaahhh!"

He knew it was pointless, but Maou still rubbed the side of his head, attempting to quell the unwelcome voice inside. It had little effect. The voice cackled in laughter.

"Maou, you scare the neighbors!"

"...I just need to fill in two-and-a-half more days. Then I'm home free."

"Oh, who cares? Maou, we look for big sis, okay...?"

"...I'm gonna take a break, and then it's back to the phones! Please, someone...anyone...you gotta trade shifts with me!"

"I thought you more...commanding, Devil King. Now, very weak-sauce!"

Maou decided to ignore the slander running through his mind, whether it was intended to be so grammatically poor or not. She was only doing it, he knew, because he was engaging her. He stood up, stretched his cramped legs, and opened the door to the kitchen's refrigerator.

"Huh? Where's the Fla-Vor-Nice I had in here? I know I bought the mashed-potato flavor..."

"Oh, sorry, I eat it."

"Daaaaaammit! You can't even find those right now! They can't keep up with demand! You brat!"

Five seconds later, he was engaging her again. The pilfered frozen dessert apparently had the power to make the Lord of All Demons fly into a non-affected rage.

"Maou? Maou, are you okay? What's going on?!"

A panicked voice issued forth through the door as the furious Maou was about to bang his head against the wall. It saved him at the last minute.

"Oh, is that...you, Chi?"

"Y-yeah, um, I heard shouting from your room, so...are you all right?!"

From outside he could hear the voice of Chiho Sasaki—his coworker behind the counter, his confidant who knew about his true self and the nature of his world, and Japan's sole representative witness for the cataclysmic events happening across the universe at the moment.

"It, it's nothing. Well, no, I mean, it—it's not nothing, but it's nothing important, so... Here, lemme open up for—"

"Someone with Chiho. I feel it."

"Dahh, shut up!"

Just as Maou was about to unlock the door, he noticed the serious tone behind the voice that set off this whole inquiry in the first place. The events of the past few minutes caused him to overreact in grandiose fashion.

"Uh, um, if now isn't a good time for you, I could always come back later…"

"Huh? No, uh, sorry, Chi, it's nothing. It's not your fault or anything. Just, um, come on in!"

He opened up the door to find a fairly reluctant-looking Chiho there, his tone clearly giving her pause.

"Are…you really sure?" Chiho said, peering into the apartment.

"Uh… Hello…"

And next to her, expression equally dubious, was Rika Suzuki, looking right at Maou.

"Oh. Hey. You, um, feeling all right?"

"Yeah, more or less," Rika replied, sizing up both Chiho and Maou with her eyes. It made Chiho blush a little. "Chiho here's done a lot for me, I have to admit…"

This came as something of a surprise to Maou. The events that took place here three days ago, when Rika last paid a visit, were nothing short of disastrous. Rika wasn't as inoculated against such supernatural and violent events as Chiho was—why would she be—and having the full brunt of Ente Isla's existence thrust upon her had to be a shock. He had heard that Rika had barely left her place for the past three days. Chiho had stepped up to support her, communicating via voice and text, paying her the occasional visit to calm her frayed nerves.

"So what was all that about 'they can't keep up with demand' and stuff? Did someone eat your Fla-Vor-Nice or something?"

"Uh…"

Maou found it hard to respond. Any hope that the girls hadn't heard him was gone.

"Fla-Vor-Nice? What about that?"

"Oh, you didn't hear, Chiho? So, like, Fla-Vor-Nice is putting out these special-edition ice pops that don't taste like normal ice cream and they had, umm…potato something? And it was this huge success, and they're having trouble keeping it stocked in the grocery stores."

"Oh! Is that what it was?"

Chiho looked up in astonishment, apparently not as up on current pop-culture trends as Rika. Maou—between his sadness at the lost ice cream, his embarrassment at having his ranting heard through the door, and the ensuing Fla-Vor-Nice stealth-marketing campaign unfolding before him—silently wished he could teleport himself anywhere else but here.

"Yeah, that's great, guys, but you're here to see me, right? C'mon in. Don't have much to offer, but..."

Chiho obliged, stepping into Devil's Castle as she kept a watchful eye on Rika behind her. There was a plastic shopping bag in her hand.

"Thanks. Oh, and I got something for you here..." She seemed to be taking pains to keep her voice cheerful as she offered the bag. "I bought this on the way, so..."

"Oh, thanks... Whoa! Fla-Vor-Nice?!"

The presence of the now-legendary frozen treat in the bag made Maou shout to the heavens.

"And it's the mashed-potato flavor, too!"

"Huh? Really?" Even Rika looked surprised.

"I didn't realize it was rare or anything when I bought it," Chiho said as she pointed at the logo on the bag. "It just happened to be in the freezer at this liquor store near my place, so I figured 'why not?'"

"For real? They're apparently so popular that I haven't been able to find these anywhere lately! Thank you so much, Chi!"

"You haven't?" Chiho smiled as he watched Maou rip open one of the packets. "Well, I'm glad I made you happy!"

"Um," Rika said, still incredulous at how much this seemed to mean to Maou.

"Oh? Oh, sorry... Come in, come in," he responded, beckoning at her after realizing she was still outside. Rika stayed where she stood, returning Maou's glance.

"So...Emi and Ashiya really aren't there, huh?"

"...No. They're not," Maou said, taking care to balance the ice pop in his right hand as he solemnly shook his head. Indeed, if the mastermind of the local kitchen was still around, he would never let something as serious as a purloined dessert escape his watchful eye. Shirou Ashiya—the Great Demon General Alciel—was no longer by his superior's side, for the very first time since Maou set off to unify the disparate tribes of the demon realms. He had been taken—taken by the archangel Gabriel, a foe that Maou and Emi shared.

Losing this presence that had faithfully stayed by his side, even when he failed in his conquest and wound up marooned in Japan, felt like someone had amputated his right hand. And judging by how Gabriel put it, he, along with Emi Yusa—the Hero Emilia Justina, the eternal thorn in his side, the woman who dismantled his empire and chased him all the way to Japan to finish the job—was being held somewhere on Ente Isla.

"We didn't hear anything from Ashiya or Emi's father, and it's just been too crazy to worry about all that since, so…I asked Chiho if I could come here with her today. So I could hear the truth from you."

"The truth?"

"Well…about Suzuno, about Urushihara, about Ashiya, about you…and, really, about Emi, most of all. Chiho said you were going off to someplace-or-other the day after tomorrow to search for her."

"Oh… Why d'you ask about those other two, though?"

Maou flashed Chiho a glance. He had no way to gauge how much she'd told Rika. But Chiho just shook her head in response.

"I saw both of them disappear into that rain, jumping from roof to roof like they had superpowers or something…and then I saw you flying away from here, Maou. And then Ashiya told me that…that Emi wasn't born on Earth. Then this weird group of people seized him and…went off somewhere."

It was clear from this that neither Maou nor Crestia Bell—aka Suzuno Kamazuki, the Church cleric from Ente Isla who lived next door in Room 202 of Villa Rose Sasazuka—had rewired Rika's brain to forget any of these memories. That was the whole reason she was here now.

"So if you know something…I'd really like you to tell me. About Emi, and about my friends."

She was after the truth. The truth about Emi Yusa, her trusted friend. Maou looked at the wall separating him from Room 202 and let out a small sigh.

"All right, well…chill out a bit, all right? If you wanna know, I'd be happy to tell you. But you need to give me some time, okay? 'Cause I think it'd go a lot more smoothly if Suzuno and Amane…uh, if that girl who saved you were here, too. Once they get back, I mean."

Rika gave a resolute nod. "…Okay. I'll wait." Then she entered the room, settling down next to the low table in the middle.

"Man, nothing flaps you, huh?" Maou offered with a smile.

"Uh, hello?" Rika fired back, half-chuckling. "It was kind of traumatic. I had a fever for forty-eight hours straight once I was back home."

Maou could tell her smile was half-forced, but he figured pointing that out would be cruel.

"Is Suzuno out right now?" Chiho asked, notably less serene than Rika at the moment.

"Hmm? Yeah, she went out somewhere with Amane this morning."

"Um, to the hospital, or…?"

"Hmm? Nah." Maou shook his head, realizing what Chiho was worrying about. "That girl was practically back to normal this morning. I guess that gash wasn't anything too serious after all."

"Huhh?!" Chiho shouted in disbelief. Her shock was understandable: The next-door neighbor was an active part of the events of three days ago—and at the height of it, she had been clawed from shoulder to chest by an enormous demon as she'd attempted to protect Chiho from harm. Even if Suzuno were a high-level Church cleric with untold holy magic at her fingertips, Chiho couldn't imagine such a grave wound healing up within three days.

"Yeah, well, Amane was going on about how crazy that was, too, actually. But you know how she never fills us in on stuff, so…"

"…True." Chiho nodded.

Amane Ohguro ran a beachfront snack bar in Choshi, a fair distance northeast of Villa Rosa, that Maou and his acquaintances had temped at briefly. She was also the niece of Miki Shiba, the shadowy, corpulent lady who owned Villa Rosa and served as the landlord of

Devil's Castle. Both she and Amane seemed like they were native to Japan, but both acted as though they knew who Maou really was from the start—and Amane, for her part, had wielded powers in front of Maou that were beyond even his own imagination.

"Do you think Amane will come back here, though?" Chiho asked.

"Yeah. Her stuff's still in Suzuno's room."

Amane had spent the past three days staying in Suzuno's apartment. That did little to quell Chiho's concern. What if Amane decided to disappear without a trace again after busting out her powers, like she did in Choshi? She had yet to divulge her reasons for visiting Sasazuka in the first place, and her exact nature was still a mystery to them. Neither Maou nor Chiho felt safe in fully trusting her.

"They said they'd be back late in the afternoon, so let's just try waitin' them out for now, huh?"

"All right... Oh! I was so surprised about Suzuno that I forgot all about this. Maou?"

"Yeah?"

"Where'd that girl go?"

There was more than a trace of sternness to the question. Maou doubted he was imagining it.

"...You mean Acieth? She's here. Right here."

He pointed at his own forehead, wincing as he did. Housed inside was a voice currently pleading at him for a bite of the mashed-potato Fla-Vor-Nice he was slowly working his way through.

"There... Really, Maou?!"

"Wh-what do you want me to say? That's how the system works or whatever! She's annoying me enough in my head, but if I take her out, it's gonna be even worse. She's a hellion."

Now Chiho looked even sterner than before. It sounded too much like an excuse to her. "Well," she began, "if we're going to talk to Suzuki about this, we're going to need to talk to Acieth, too!" Her hands were on the lapel of Maou's shirt. She was placing far too much emphasis on every syllable. "Take. Her. Out. Now!"

"Aggh! Stop shaking me, Chi! I'm gonna drop this ice pop! Look, okay, okay, I'll do it! I need to concentrate, so stop shaking me! I'm not used to this yet!"

The lack of forward progress was starting to seriously agitate Chiho. Peeling her away from him, Maou turned to an empty corner of the room, supported his dazed head with one hand, and pointed forward with the other.

"Mmm...come forth, Acieth!"

As he spoke, a dull purple light shone out from Maou's body. Rika, seeing this up close, tensed up—but Chiho couldn't provide her support right now.

"Maou, I want bite, toooo!"

The light from Maou's body slowly began to gather and form a body—not in front of Maou, but behind him. She was maybe a little younger than Chiho, her silvery hair—complete with a purple whorl on one side—indicating she was plainly not from Japan.

She was now here, with them, and that wasn't really the issue right now. The issue was that she had her arms and legs entangled over Maou from behind him, in a close embrace. And that wasn't all—her mouth was wide open and making a beeline for the ice-cream pop near Maou's own face. For someone like Chiho, and all the feelings she had for him, that was far too much to let slide.

"Ah, ah, ah, Acieth, what're you doing to Maou?!"

"Ooh, um, getting some skinship with him? As a partner?"

"Agh!" Maou, despite the fact that he was the one who summoned her, acted just as shocked. "Get off me, Acieth!" She had yet to materialize in any position Maou intended—but that didn't mean it had to work like this, either.

"Oh, Maou! So bashful!"

"That's not the problem, man! You're not gettin' a single bite of this! You already ate my snacks without permission!"

"It is okay! I am the growing girl!"

"Could you at least pretend to listen to me? You're not gettin' a bite, and that's it!"

The grappling match continued between the King of All Demons and the mystery girl over some ice cream for several seconds. Then it was abruptly stopped.

"Stop! It! Right! There!"

"Whoa!"

"Aghh!"

Chiho, forcing her way between the two, pulled Acieth away from Maou's body.

"Chihoooo! Why are you doing?"

"I have another pop for you, Acieth! Just stop trying to take Maou's from him!"

"But just see people eat something, it looks…so tasty…"

"I don't care!!"

"Ooooh… All right," Acieth said as she stepped back, sufficiently cowed by Chiho's tirade—but not so much as to keep her hands away from the shopping bag with her ice-cream prize.

"Wow, Chi," an astonished Maou whispered behind Chiho, "Acieth actually listened to you."

"…Maou."

"Y-yes?!"

He didn't think Chiho would find anything wrong with the appraisal. But when he turned around, he detected something murderous to her face. He stiffened up, posture straight.

"If you keep spoiling Acieth too much, you know how jealous Alas Ramus will be once she returns. She'll hate you for it."

"Sh-she will?"

"And you, you…you just can't let that happen to you, all right? I know this is kind of a weird situation, but Acieth is a girl, all right? A girl!"

"N-no, I… Okay, maybe I could've put it nicer, but I swear, Acieth never listens to me—"

"I'm not talking about that!"

"Whuh?!"

Try as he did to plead his case, Maou began to acutely feel that he and the glaring, reddened Chiho were on nowhere near the same wavelength.

"All that…that 'getting to know' each other…in broad daylight…
That just isn't right, Maou!"

"Ch-Chi? Chi, I think you got the wrong idea, I…I'm not doing
anything like…"

"Oh, well, oh, well. That is life! Me and Maou, we same body and
heart now!"

"Nnnnhhh!!"

"Ch-Chi! Chill out! You know what she means, right?! And Acieth, I don't care how bad you are at this language—I swear you're
picking your words on purpose, aren't you?!"

Acieth seemed to be all but taunting Chiho by this point. But it
was true. They both really did occupy the same body. Acieth had
a single shock of purple in her silvery hair—the telltale sign of one
born from a Sephirah, one of the jewels that formed the world of
Ente Isla. There was another person in Maou's and Chiho's lives
with the same characteristics—Alas Ramus, the near-baby who
fused with Emilia's Better Half and treated her and the Devil
King as her own parents. And while it was hard to believe, given
their external ages, apparently Acieth was Alas Ramus's younger
sister.

Given that they were sisters, it was safe to assume Acieth had
similar abilities as her sibling. Just like with Alas Ramus and Emi,
Acieth was now fused with Maou, helping him and his friends
escape death three days ago. Which was great, but apparently this
was permanent—and like with the Hero and her "daughter," even
if Maou materialized Acieth, she was no longer able to go beyond a
certain physical distance from him.

Acieth had always been a, shall we say, sociable girl. But her behavior had undergone enormous changes before and after the fusion. To
wit, she was now physically all over him all the time—enough so
that Chiho, who never acted so blatantly jealous if another girl had
Maou's attention, just couldn't keep her cool around her.

But on the other hand:

"You are…Rika? Do you want ice cream, too?"

Now her interest was fully shifted from the pained Maou and the half-trembling Chiho. She offered a packet to Rika, who currently had nothing to do but stare at the three of them bickering with each other.

"Oh, uh, I'm fine. Thanks."

The refusal seemed to put Acieth off a little. It was unusual to see.

"Maou!" Chiho snapped.

"Y-yes?" the startled Maou said, exposed to the full brunt of Chiho's stare.

"It sure would be nice if Yusa and Ashiya came back, huh?" she droned.

"Y-yeah, I think?" Maou chirped right back.

"...You guys make no sense to me," a befuddled Rika observed.

Then Maou's phone, more than a little bit behind the times, went off.

"Oh, I got a text from Suzuno. Must be close to home."

Thirty minutes, as the text specified.

"Ooh, how good! This morning, I ask Amane, buy ice cream for me!"

"How much're you planning to eat, anyway? Don't come runnin' to me if you get a stomachache."

Maou didn't expect a response. He couldn't help but admonish her anyway.

"So when they get back, guys," he continued, grabbing the papers he had out on the table, "I guess we'll start talking about rescuing Emi, Alas Ramus, Ashiya, Emi's dad...the whole gang. I'll worry about shifts again later."

"Uh, hey..."

"Agh!"

Rika half-rose to her feet at the weak-sounding yelp that suddenly came from parts unknown. Everyone, except for Acieth, focused their eyes on the closet—just in time for it to open up an inch or so. Behind it was the Great Demon General Lucifer, better known around here as Hanzou Urushihara, the dead weight of Devil's Castle and a man who styled himself as the greatest slacker in the world.

"Dude," he moaned to the group, "I don't care if you forget about me or whatever…but try to keep it down, okay? I'm not all fixed up like Bell yet. All that shouting makes my wounds hurt still, all right?"

✳

Emi and Ashiya were marooned in Ente Isla.

Though perhaps that was not the right word: Emi, after all, had originally chased the Devil King from Ente Isla to Earth—and Ashiya had been one of the demon leaders commanding the world's conquest. If anything, Ente Isla was exactly where the two of them belonged. But, even in their native land, they were well and truly stuck.

It all started when Emi, curious about what her parents were doing on Ente Isla and what kind of past they had, decided to return home to find answers. She was the undisputed strongest human being in the universe. At the time, not even Maou, her natural enemy, could imagine her running into any kind of danger.

But Emi never came back—not even after the day she promised to return—and Alas Ramus, fused into the young woman's Better Half sword, was undoubtedly still with her. The child's fate worried Maou enough to make him fail the written exam for his motor scooter license, something he was trying to earn so he could help out with MgRonald's new delivery program.

So he marched back to the exam center in Fuchu for a retest, only to run into a strange man and his daughter: Hiroshi and Tsubasa Sato, two people who boarded Maou's bus at the space observatory in Mitaka. Despite their names, they were clearly new to Japan. Thanks to their chance encounter, Maou found himself entangled in their affairs all through his retest—but then he found out who they really were. The man was none other than Nord Justina, Emilia's father and someone thought to have died in battle against the Devil King's Army; while Tsubasa Sato was Acieth Alla, Alas Ramus's younger sister and fellow Yesod Sephirah embodiment.

Just as Maou was trying to digest all of this, a top general from the Malebranche, a nobility-level demon tribe that had been getting in

Maou's hair quite a bit as of late, appeared at Chiho's high school, forcing her to come face-to-face with him. Suzuno and Urushihara rushed to Sasahata North High School to assist, but Emi's friend Rika Suzuki accidentally saw them fly off into the air, leading her to demand an explanation from Ashiya. He'd decided he had no other choice—but just as he had begun his tale, Maou had literally flown into the room from the test center, taken there by Acieth's powers. He'd stayed only long enough to drop off Nord and fly right back out the window.

So there they had been. Three people—Rika, Ashiya, and Nord—a fairly baffling combination to see in Devil's Castle. But before they could get to the bottom of everything, Efzahan's Knights of the Inlain Azure Scarves, led by Gabriel himself, attacked Villa Rosa Sasazuka. Rika had survived unscathed—thanks to the appearance of Amane Ohguro, proprietor of Ohguro-ya in Choshi—but Gabriel had spirited away Nord and Ashiya. And over at the school, the combined powers of the Malebranche officer Libicocco and the archangel Camael had dealt both Suzuno and Urushihara grave injuries.

This was the scene that greeted Maou when he'd arrived at the school—and that was where he fused with Acieth, much as Emi fused with Alas Ramus, and then tapped into untold new powers. That provided all the edge he needed to repulse Camael and Libicocco.

But it could hardly be called a victory. Chiho, Suzuno, and Urushihara were all hurt. Ashiya and Nord had been kidnapped. And Emi and Alas Ramus were quite likely being held captive in Ente Isla. For Maou, it was nothing less than a rout.

As far as Maou was concerned, he truly was the Devil King. Room 201 in the Villa Rosa Sasazuka building was actually Devil's Castle, and the neighborhood of Sasazuka was the castle town that served it. Shirou Ashiya, Hanzou Urushihara, Chiho Sasaki, Suzuno Kamazuki, and his nemesis Emi Yusa really were his Great Demon Generals, so christened by none other than the Devil King Satan himself.

They were his team of officers, his companions, the men and

women Maou needed in order to launch a new bid at world domination. Protecting his team was a responsibility Maou took dead seriously. He had to punish the charlatans who had dared defy the true Devil King's Army. He knew he had the right team for it. And now Satan, the Devil King, was ready. It was time to sally forth from Japan, work with his companions, and prepare the New Devil King's Army for a full invasion of Ente Isla, the Land of the Holy Cross.

✳

"Oh, no way..."

Maou's eyes stared into space.

"How can this even happen?!"

"Maou..."

Chiho reflexively laid a sympathetic hand on his shoulder. The anguish in his voice was clear to her.

"But this is the reality of it," Suzuno intoned at the stupefied man before him. "One almost too cruel for you to accept, I imagine, but reality nonetheless. Such is what little power you have to work with now."

"Suzuno! You're being too hard on him!"

"Attempting to soften the blow for the Devil King will do nothing to change the facts, Chiho."

"God...dammit..."

The pain was too much for Maou. He slammed a fist against the tatami-mat floor beneath him. The thudding sound echoed throughout the apartment.

"Why...? Why...?!"

He gritted his teeth, his tragic-looking eyes ruefully turned to Suzuno as he shouted at the top of his lungs.

"Why did you score your motor-scooter license first?!!!!"

"Shut up, Maou," the honestly pained-sounding Urushihara was heard whispering from the closet. Maou was in no position to respond. He was too busy staring down Suzuno, who looked like she hadn't a care in the world. The brilliant, radiant card in her hand was a laminated license, one with Suzuno's name and photograph on it.

"I earned it because I thought that we needed it. Judging by your behavior as of late, I doubted you were capable of passing the retest before we departed."

"Yeah, but...but why did you...?!"

Maou stood up, throwing his body toward the window on the wall. He pointed a finger down at the backyard.

"Why," he cried, "did you pass that test and immediately come back home on a scooter?! You're just picking on me! You're messing with my mind, aren't you?!"

There, emitting a soft sheen in the sunlight next to Maou's Dullahan II fixie bike, was a scooter. A Honta Gyro-Roof, no less, a model that saw frequent use among delivery businesses. It came standard-equipped with a roof and three wheels for extra stability—perfect for pizza parlors and other outfits that transported small loads around in unpredictable weather conditions.

"Hey, Chiho, what's up with Maou?"

Rika couldn't help but ask. She had hoped Chiho's ice-cream bribe would be enough to restore his motivation, but ever since Suzuno returned from her errands, Maou had been acting unusually freaked out. Childish, even.

Chiho let out a distressed smile as she stood up to whisper into her ear. "Maou's failed the scooter driving test twice," she whispered. "He messed up the written exam the first time, and during the second time, he had to ditch the test center to help me out."

"...Oooh."

"I can't believe you're being so mean to me! That's the exact kinda bike I'd be using for MgRonald deliveries! What the hell is this if it's not a dis against me?!"

"How can I help it?" Suzuno countered, Maou's flailing panic not bothering her at all. "I could hardly return home on a scooter unless I had my license—thus, I had a need for a license." Her stern eyes settled upon him, seated next to Chiho. "Or...what, were you expecting to travel around Ente Isla without any sort of long-distance transport?"

"I… No, but…"

"Someone with your or my powers—our presence would be detected the moment we started flying through the air. We are fighting against at least two archangels and a high-ranking Malebranche, I remind you."

"Y-yeah, but I've got their positions nailed down…pretty much…"

"Perhaps, but be that as it may, we need a way to quickly hide ourselves if our Gate opening is detected. Otherwise, this mission will be over before it begins."

"Well, sure, okay, but a scooter in Ente Isla? Like, they don't even have engines in Ente Isla. If we wanna stay undercover, shouldn't we buy some horses or something once we show up?"

"Can you even ride a horse?"

Suzuno was clearly growing impatient at Maou's aimless whining. Her parting shot was enough to shut him up.

"We have no idea how long we may be forced to wander Ente Isla! We will need to bring ample supplies with us! I have no idea how accurate our Gate control will be yet, and speed is going to be everything with this effort! That is precisely why we must put our ducks in a row in Japan, ahead of time, as much as humanly possible! Or, what—were you intending to pedal a bicycle across the Eastern Island?! Could you even earn the money for a team of coach horses?!"

"…"

Maou sat down next to the window, sulking in silence. "Okay," he groaned. "No, I've never handled horses before. If we're talkin' wyverns, though, I'm the best damn expert in the land."

Even in a land as exotic and mysterious as Ente Isla, no human had ever attempted to tame a wyvern before. The sight of a man mounted on one would be even more conspicuous than any motorbike.

Suzuno sighed.

"…Listen, Devil King."

"What?"

"Look at that scooter. It seats one person."

"Yeah?"

"The laws of Japan will not apply to us over there, but I am not interested in you riding piggyback with me."

"Uh...no?"

"Th-that's a twenty-thousand-yen fine!" Chiho exclaimed, oddly sensitive to the mere suggestion.

"That's for a bicycle, Chiho," Rika butted in. "There are different fines and points and stuff once it's a driver license you're dealing with."

"Indeed. So..."

"So?" Maou asked.

Suzuno paused for a moment, then continued, her well-formed lips forming a sentence nobody expected to come out:

"I have purchased another scooter for you to ride. You will need no license for navigating Ente Isla."

"......Another?"

"Yes."

"A scooter?"

"Yes."

"...You bought it?"

"Who else would?" Suzuno fired back.

The room froze for a moment.

"No waaaaaaaaaaaaaaaaaaay!!"

"Dude...Maou, seriously—quiet down," came the protest from the closet.

"L-look, I was always kinda wondering about that, but... Geez, how much of a one-percenter are you, anyway?!"

"Yeah!" Even Chiho was shocked at this. "I don't really know or anything, but I don't think scooters are that inexpensive!"

"They are not, no. Used models, however, are reasonable enough. And Amane should be here soon with the second one. Together, the two of them cost, oh, I'd say around five hundred thousand yen. They come from a reputable dealer, and thankfully, they had some inventory ready at hand."

The six-figure sum tumbled all too easily from Suzuno's lips.

"Five... Five hun...hun...dred thousand..."

Maou's brain attempted to picture the amount of zeroes involved. It short-circuited. He promptly fainted, crumpling to the floor as though he had practiced the act several times before. Chiho and Rika immediately ran to him.

"M-Maou! Maou?! Maou, speak to me!"

"Is—is he all right? He looks pretty pale..."

Chiho peered into his face, white as a sheet and emitting an oily sort of sweat. Her view was then blocked by the back of Acieth's head.

"Okay! Mouth-to-mouth, mouth-to-mouth, okay!"

"He's breathing!! He doesn't need it!!" Chiho attempted to pry Acieth away from him, face locked in horror. "Just go back to your ice cream, Acieth!"

Rika, watching their struggle, cooled Maou's face with a nearby fan.

"...This sure ain't what I thought was gonna happen..."

Then, from afar, the sound of a small engine puttering along came into earshot. They could all hear it stopping in front of the apartment building, followed by the sound of someone climbing the stairs. The door to Devil's Castle opened, revealing Amane Ohguro, tanned skin and jet-black ponytail shining brightly from underneath her helmet.

"Hey, sorry, guys! I had another stop to make and I kinda got lost. Found some supercheap gas, though!"

Then she spotted the unconscious Maou and the half-wrestling Chiho and Acieth. Her eyes opened wide.

"...Uh, what's going on in here?"

Inside Devil's Castle—which, between Chiho and Suzuno and Rika and Amane and Acieth, was seeing far more of a female presence than usual—Maou was lying on the floor. He was awake, but still notably paler than before.

"Five hundred thousand for two, huh?" he murmured. "Like, I'm glad we're well-prepared...almost too prepared, even...but aren't you spending too much money for this? Do we really need to prep that much in advance?"

Suzuno rolled her eyes before turning to Acieth, who was currently gauging the scene from a corner as she licked at her ice pop.

"You do, indeed, possess overwhelming power right now," she said. "Considering what happened to Emilia after her, ah, merger with Alas Ramus, you might be able to defeat Gabriel and Camael in a simple battle of muscle, Devil King. But do not forget that Alciel, Emilia, and Alas Ramus are being held as de facto hostages at the moment. We may not be able to avoid a fight at the end of it all, but until that fateful instant strikes, we must take every pain to work quickly, work undercover, and engage the enemy as little as possible."

"They made my sis hostage... They suck! Give them electric chair!"

"Whoa, you're gonna drop your ice cream!"

Amane's warning fell on deaf ears. Acieth's second dessert of the day slipped through her hands and made a not-so-clean landing on the tatami mats.

"Aaah! My ice cream... The angels, they will be paying!"

"Oh, I'll wipe that up," Chiho said as she went to the sink and came back with a wet washcloth.

"Chiho! No throwing it away! It is the waste!"

"Oh, um...okay?"

She returned the ice pop to Acieth as she began wiping up what was left on the floor. Acieth promptly brought it right back into her mouth, not a care in the world.

"Hey, um..." Rika raised a hand in the air. "Can I ask a question?"

"Ah, yes," Suzuno replied. "My apologies for Sada...ah, for the Devil King's petulance. We had promised to explain matters to you."

Rika turned face-to-face with Suzuno.

All in all, the scene inside Devil's Castle didn't look too much out of the ordinary. The only real difference was the cast of characters—a tad different from the norm—and the fact that Suzuno was calling Maou "Devil King" in front of Rika.

"Okay, so... Um, I'm sorry to butt in on this when you're all busy with...other stuff, but... So what're y'all, anyway?"

Chiho felt an unexpected well of emotion inside her. It was the exact same question she had asked, not all that long ago.

Then Amane pointed at her. "Hey, we've got Chiho here and everything. Why don't we have her talk about it?"

"Huh?" Chiho blinked, washcloth still in hand.

"If we leave it to just Maou and Suzuno, I think Rika probably wouldn't know what to believe once they were all done. Chiho, on the other hand—she's involved with this the exact same way Rika is, so that kinda impartial viewpoint would be a lot more believable, no?"

"Indeed," Suzuno said with a nod. "That might be a good idea."

And even within his current befuddlement, Maou's thoughtful gaze at Chiho seemed to indicate that he agreed with it.

"W-well, if you think that'd be all right, then sure. Assuming you're okay with it, Suzuki?"

"Uhmm... If I could ask something before that, I guess you're pretty used to whatever wacky stuff's going on with Maou and Suzuno, right, Chiho? You aren't, like, some kinda comic-book superhero who flies around and fights bad guys and stuff, are you?"

"Pfft!"

Rika's reply was, in many ways, not quite what Chiho had expected.

"Well, um... I'm not sure, actually."

But she couldn't deny it out of hand. Even if it was only a single piece of holy magic from Ente Isla, she had a gift that no other human on Earth enjoyed.

"Chi's not like that, no," Maou answered in her place. "She wasn't involved with us at all at first—she was just a new hire I was training at MgRonald. Just another teen."

His wording hurt Chiho a bit, despite herself. She let it slide, knowing that Maou didn't quite mean it that way.

"But then she got involved with me and Emi's stuff, and she kind of found out. Just like you did. And she's had to deal with a lot more horrors than you have—or I'd say she has, anyway—but Chi told me that she didn't want to forget any of it. That's why she's still with us. With me and Emi and so on."

"Really?" Rika asked, turning to Chiho. She found it hard to gauge how serious she really was about this. Chiho pondered a bit before reacting.

"If you put it that way…more or less, yeah."

Not like Rika has it easy, she thought. It wasn't every day a squadron of armed attackers storms the building you're in.

"For me," Chiho said, "I guess the first time I saw how much power Maou and everyone had was when that highway overpass was about to collapse and crush all of us, so it was—"

"Uh?"

Rika's face tightened. Chiho made it sound as though she were talking about last night's dinner menu. It was a tad hard to swallow, but then Chiho kept on going—telling her about how she was taken to the roof of Tokyo's city hall; about how she was surrounded by the armed Heavenly Regiment; about how she witnessed all-out war between demon factions at close range; about how she was admitted to the hospital after being exposed to too much demonic force; about how she flew around Tokyo Tower and fought against her aggressors; and about how she had deliberately faced down gigantic demons on two separate occasions and never blinked.

"Looking back at it all," she concluded, "I guess it's pretty amazing that I'm alive and well, isn't it?"

Silence.

"…"

Chiho knew it wasn't her imagination—the blood had drained from Rika's face a bit. "Oh, but," Chiho hurriedly added, "but Maou and Yusa and Suzuno protected me every time, so I've never been really hurt or anything!"

"Y-yeah, but you keep getting into all this dangerous stuff, right? And you did get sent to the hospital…"

"Well, that, uh… That was kind of unavoidable. Or, really, more my fault than anything else. There wasn't any problem with me in the end, though, so they discharged me after two days, um…"

Chiho, realizing she had mostly succeeded in stoking Rika's fears, fell silent. Maou felt obliged to throw her a lifeline.

"The thing is, though, she's had the right to have her memories of all of us erased any time she wanted. You're free not to believe us if you think this is too loony to accept. But no matter what you decide, we'll fully respect it. And whether you decide to forget about us or not, I promise you we'll do everything we can to keep anything from happening to you."

"Ooh..."

"If you don't want to see any of us again, that's perfectly fine—but we'll never stop protecting you, if we need to. And if this is too much for you to deal with today, you're free to come back some other day, too. 'Course, I'm gonna be out for a little while, so you'll have to wait 'til I'm back, but..."

"Y-yeah, but if I leave here after all that, I'm just gonna get more curious... More scared. But...but if you go off to wherever you're going, that...that's gonna be pretty dangerous for you, isn't it?"

"Yeah," Maou admitted. "Could be."

"I doubt it would be as safe as your typical holiday in Japan," Suzuno added.

Rika sized both of them up. "So," she began, choosing her words carefully, "if Emi's really from this different world...something that isn't Japan...then, like, she's been gone from there a pretty long time, hasn't she? Is... Is she all right? It can't be all that safe for her there either, right?"

"""""...Ah."""""

Something about the question made Maou, Chiho, Suzuno, even Urushihara in the closet realize something all at once.

"Wh-what?"

"...Okay, so this might sound kinda cold, laying it out for you like this...but if you're asking whether Emi's hurt or her life's in danger or whatever, then, um, I don't think we need to worry about that, no."

"Huh?"

Maou found himself struggling to articulate his intentions.

"...So Emi... She's strong—like, really, really strong. I mean, beyond any scale built around the human race."

"Yeah," a crestfallen Chiho added. "She said she broke her leg when she saved me once, but looking back, it sure healed up pretty fast..."

"I suppose," Suzuno said, "we are all struggling to explain this, Rika, in a way you could swallow."

"Dude, it's easy," the voice in the closet countered. "If she's back in Ente Isla, you couldn't hurt Yusa with a knife, or a gun, or even if you shot her with a tank round at point-blank range."

"That's totally a comic-book superhero!" Rika exclaimed. She had to. But Maou coolly accepted it.

"Yeah, that's a pretty normal reaction. But look at it the opposite way: All that strength, and Emi still hasn't come back. That's a problem. If it's not something physical keeping her over there, then it could be something emotional, and that's what I'm more worried about."

"Huh?"

"Oh?"

"Mm?"

"Uh?"

Something about Maou's reply caught Chiho, Suzuno, and Urushihara off guard. Maou grunted in reply, surprised at this.

"Wh-what, guys? Did I say something weird?"

"...You haven't realized?"

"...Guess not, dude."

"Maou... You really are such a kind person, aren't you? I'm glad to see that."

"Wh-what? Come on, guys!"

"Um, hello...?"

Maou was honestly clueless. Rika, even more so.

""Oh, nothing,"" Urushihara and Suzuno said in unison.

"Eh-heh-heh," Chiho added as she gave Maou a doting look.

The halfhearted reaction unnerved Maou more than a little, but he kept his eyes on Rika.

"Uh, anyway, what I'm trying to say is that, sure, Emi can take a tank round and brush it off like it's nothing, but she's still human. If you can't overpower someone, you can take advantage of their feelings, or their connections, instead, right? If something's keeping Emi down, I think that might be it. And maybe you know this already, but due to assorted reasons, Alas Ramus is together with her right now. We gotta think about her safety, too. It might look to you like we're being pretty chill about all this, but we really need to take the time here to assess the situation and make the preparations we need."

"Oh." Rika brought a hand to her forehead. "Y'know, it's getting kinda hard for me to grasp the scale of all this..."

"So what's it gonna be? I guess we've already revealed a lot, but are you gonna cut yourself off from us, or...?"

"Like I said, I gotta hear the whole thing before I decide on that."

That reply, at least, came loud and clear.

"...You do?"

"That's what you did, didn't you, Chiho? Then I gotta do that much too, I think. I want to think about it once I've come to grips with all this...stuff about Emi."

"Aww, ain't that all sweet and innocent?"

"What's 'innocent,' Amane?"

"Oh, it's when she's so cute, you just wanna hug her. See? Like this—squeeeze!"

"Squeeze, squeeze, squeeze!"

Chiho, ignoring Amane and Acieth in the outfield, turned back to Rika.

"This might be unfair of me, telling you this before we talk about it..."

"Chiho?"

"I...I was thinking that I'd like Yusa to have another real friend. Someone besides me."

"..."

Rika fell silent for a moment. This caught her off guard. She took

a look around, sizing up Maou, then Suzuno, then the face of Urushihara, who had popped out through the door. She sighed, then
turned to Chiho.

"It's not like I couldn't lie about this...but I guess I'm not the only
one with stuff I can't talk about too easily here."

"Suzuki?"

"I promise I won't let my emotions overwhelm me, Chiho." Rika
was back to her normal self—her iron will clear in her eyes as she
looked at Chiho. "I won't let my emotions get to me, and I promise
that I'm willing to accept it all. So tell me. Tell me about Emi, tell me
about Maou and everyone, and don't hold anything back."

Chiho let out a soft smile.

"Okay. I guess I'll start by talking about how I met all these
people..."

Slowly, she began to talk about the truth behind Maou, behind
Emi, and behind the world of Ente Isla.

"Whewwwww..."

Once Chiho was done with everything, Rika let out a long sigh.

"Well, no wonder Emi had it in for Maou."

She gave Maou a look.

"You're willing to believe me?"

"Well, I've already seen Ashiya disappear, Suzuno and Urushihara
leap over tall buildings in a single bound, and Maou and Acieth fly.
It ain't that much of a mental leap."

That wasn't all. During the lecture, Suzuno had transformed her
hairpin into her war hammer for Rika's edification, Maou oblig-
ing with a few in-and-out Acieth fusions of his own. Rika had little
choice but to accept it.

Rika nodded tiredly at Chiho's question. A beat. Then:

"Aahhhhh, I can't stand this! This is so embarrassing!"

She grabbed her own head, reared back, and fell flat on the floor.

"S-Suzuki?!"

"Oh God, this is so embarrassing. I just want to crawl into a hole!"

"Wh-what's wrong?" Maou asked, surprised at this reaction. Rika sat back up, tears in her eyes, turned straight toward Suzuno, and reached out for her hand.

"R-Rika?"

"Suzuno, I am so, so sorry! Please, just forget all about that day for me! I know I was the only one who didn't know anything, but everything I did... Oh, I'm sooo sorry! I could just die right now!"

"Um, which day was this?" Suzuno asked, eyes turned wide at this unexpected confession.

"The day I first met you, Suzunoooo! Oh, God, I went on that crazy tangent and started going on about all sorts of crap. I had no idea I was... Oh, auuuugh!"

"Oh. That was it?"

This was enough to jog Suzuno's memory. The first time Rika had met Suzuno, she had fallen under the mistaken assumption that Suzuno was vying with Emi for Maou's love. That conviction caused her to meddle with the Devil's Castle neighbor in all manner of uninvited ways.

"Keep in mind, I all but guided you toward making that misunderstanding. And we resolved it right there and then, did we not? I hardly see any reason to dwell on it. You barely knew us anyway."

"That's not the thing, though! The thing is that maybe I didn't know, but I did all that in front of Ashiya, and... Daaaahhhh!"

"Um?"

This sounded odd to Suzuno, but she nonetheless rose up and gave the tearful Rika a reassuring hug, patting her on the back.

"Ahhhh, I feel like such an idiot!" Rika wailed, face flushed as Suzuno tried to soothe her.

"Um, are you all right, Suzuki?"

"I'd have to guess," Maou replied, "that she wasn't actually ready to accept all of this."

It was cause for concern, but given that she was more shocked about some social faux pas than about the truth behind Maou and Emi, Rika seemed to bear no ill will toward any of them, at least.

"Amazing how flexible young people are with their imaginations these days, hmmm?" Amane observed. This seemed to surprise even her a little.

"Well, great. So if Rika Suzuki's okay with all this..."

"I'm not okay with all this! How could I even look Emi and Ashiya in the eye when they get back...?"

"...Then we'd better start discussing our plans once we're in Ente Isla."

Whatever it was—Maou had no way of knowing—it seemed there was a landmine he had managed to step on between Rika, Suzuno, Emi, Ashiya, and himself. One with a pretty killer payload, by the looks of things. He couldn't afford the time needed to assuage her bruised ego, though, so he opted to ignore Rika and place a few sheets of paper on the table.

"This is a detailed map of the Eastern Island that Ashiya left for us. I guess he figured early on that if Emi ran into trouble, it was probably gonna be in Efzahan, on the Eastern Island."

"Wh-why is that?" Suzuno asked, arms still wrapped around Rika.

"I dunno, but I'd guess a lot of it's due to Olba convincing the Malebranche to build their base of operations there. Olba's like Chiho, in a way—just a regular guy who knows all about Emi's powers and history. And you see how Efzahan's been waging war on pretty much every front possible, right? It's, like, totally suspicious. And hey, uh, Urushihara?"

"...Yeah?"

An arm emerged from the closet. It held a wrinkled-up business card.

"What's that?" Chiho asked as she grabbed it. It had a cell-phone number written on it.

"For calling Gabriel."

"What?! Why do we have something like that?"

"Wh-why would an angel have a cell phone? The Devil King and the angels are calling each other now? Like some kind of nuclear hotline to Moscow?!"

Chiho's and Rika's reactions very succinctly summarized the differences in each of their recent life experiences.

"Yeah, so, that idiot left that here when he visited Urushihara ear-lier, and thanks to that, we know for sure that all of 'em—Ashiya, Emi, Alas Ramus, Emi's dad—they're all in Efzahan right now."

"You know for sure?" Chiho raised an eyebrow at Maou's convic-tion. "Why?"

"'Cause I called him up and he told me."

"...And you're sure we can believe him?"

Chiho, well familiar with Gabriel's penchant for being an unreli-able narrator, couldn't be blamed for doubting that information. He was weaselly that way, someone who could be relied upon only for being unreliable. Sometimes he openly attacked them; sometimes his actions came to benefit Maou. It was hard to see where his heart truly lay.

"I know what you mean," Maou said with a chuckle. "But with this, at least, there's no reason for Gabriel to lie right to our faces. Remember him and Emi? If he had kept quiet back then, we'd have no idea where to go."

"Dude, but what if he knows we're assuming that?" Urushihara sheepishly replied. "He could do the ol' bait and switch on us real easy."

Maou sagely nodded. "Yeah, that's why I'm tellin' you to stay in Japan, just in case."

"Sure thing, but at least save it for after I'm healed..."

When it came to discussion about work, Urushihara's voice usu-ally settled into a low groan of anguish. But this groan sounded even lower than usual.

"He's not coming along with you, Maou?" a curious Chiho asked. Suzuno was always a given for this voyage—as long as she had a worthy amplifier, she was the only one who could open a Gate for Maou. Chiho's Idea Link skills made her totally unique among the human race, but not even she was immature enough to want to join Maou on a planet far more dangerous than her own. Having some-one like her, far weaker than Suzuno, on the battlefield would be an unthinkable drag on Maou and his friends—something made all too clear in the battle against the Imperial Regiment at her high school three days ago.

But Urushihara, despite everything, was still a fully qualified Great Demon General. The power he wielded while saving Chiho from danger was real, and massive. On Ente Isla, he could provide just the firepower this little search party needed.

"Or, shall we say, we cannot take him along."

It was Suzuno, freeing herself from Rika's arms, who finally gave the answer.

"I conceived of several approaches, but considering we must make a return trip as well, myself and the Devil King are about the best I can manage. Besides..." She glanced at Acieth, standing by the window. "She is far heavier than I thought."

"Hey! I am not fat like that! So mean!"

"That," Suzuno said instead of engaging her, "and remember: Ideally, we are bringing Alciel and Emilia's father back with us. I imagine Emilia's force would be enough for me to formulate a suitable Gate for us all, but the more people I must bring through, the more difficult it becomes to keep it under control. It is best to avoid taxing our resources to the maximum."

"No telling what they might do here in our absence, either," Maou added. "I'd hate to have Chi and Rika become targets while I can't do anything about it. That's why I want him here. Just in case."

"Yeah. It'd sure be easier on me here, assumin' nothing happens... Dude, owww..."

Chiho had no doubts about Maou's or Urushihara's skills, but here in Japan, with Urushihara unable (if not unwilling) to unleash his full powers, it was hard to say how much of a defensive line he could put up.

Maou, sensing Chiho's concern, gave her a nod. "I wouldn't worry, though. If push comes to shove, there's always Amane."

"Oh, here we go. Saw that one comin' a mile away." Amane tossed her now-bare ice-cream stick into the trash bin and nodded, a little dejected. "That's not exactly what I intended when I came here, y'know."

"Would you mind telling us what you did come here for then, maybe?"

It was a valid question from Chiho. Amane had yet to reveal why she was currently in Sasazuka to anyone, but that didn't stop her from tossing her stuff into Suzuno's room. By what the Church cleric said, Amane's luggage was all perfectly normal—a suitcase full of clothes, her purse, some cosmetics, a phone charger—so she surmised it was nothing related to her supernatural occupation. Amane herself had been pleading the same story over the past three days: "I told you! You guys nearly ruined my family business. My dad came home, and he was so pissed off, he kicked me out of the place. Y'know, saying he wasn't gonna let me mooch off the family any longer? That's all there is to it!"

If Ashiya had been around to hear that, it would have provided all the inspiration he needed to boot Urushihara from the room.

"Look," Amane protested, cheeks puffed out a bit in childlike fashion, "I appreciate Suzuno letting me stay here and everything, but I had assumed one of the other apartments would've been unlocked when I showed up. My aunt Mikitty gave me the okay and everything, too. But…" She sighed. "All right. I owe you for the room and board, I guess, so…if something happens, I'll try to keep Chiho and Rika safe. That's kind of my duty here anyways."

The promise was a relief to Maou's ears, even if he didn't know what kind of "duty" she was talking about. Rika had mentioned earlier that Amane rescued her three days ago while simultaneously ignoring Ashiya and Nord's plight. That, he imagined, was because neither of those two were in immediate mortal danger. Rika, on the other hand, was.

"So," Suzuno bluntly stated, "what will it be, Rika Suzuki? Are we erasing your memory or not? Because, if I may be frank, that would absolutely be the safer option for you."

"I don't care about my memory, but I just wish I had that day to do over again…ugghh…" Rika shook her head a little, ignoring the easy out Suzuno had given her. Then she sighed and looked up. "Just listening to you right now," she clearly said, "honestly, I'm still pretty scared, and there's a ton I still don't understand about you all. But if I'm gonna have you do that, I want to see the real Emi again first and talk things over with her."

"Suzuki!" a happy-sounding Chiho exclaimed.

"That so?" Maou acknowledged with a light smile as he nodded. Suzuno and Amane having no further complaints about this, the group once again turned their eyes to the papers on the table.

"Right. So getting back on topic, the only thing Ashiya could tell us here was that he's somewhere in Efzahan. The question, though, is where—and I think I've got a pretty good idea."

"And what is your basis for this?" Suzuno prodded.

Maou pointed a finger at a map depicting Efzahan's major population centers. "So we know that the heavens and Olba and the Malebranche guys were all after Emi's sword, right? And judging by how Gabriel and Raguel have had Emi's mom and dad in their sights for a while now, I can understand why Nord was kidnapped. But why Ashiya? Why did they have to make off with Alciel, too?"

"Hmm?"

"Even Barbariccia knows by now that we ain't exactly down with the Malebranche tribe. And Olba must've known that Alciel could've regained his demon form the moment his body found itself in Ente Isla. He knew he'd put up a hell of a fight. I mean, Alciel was the only participant in the Tokyo Tower rumble who actually blocked one of Gabriel's attacks. But Gabriel kidnapped him anyway—even though he'd do nothing but get in the way over there. Which means that our little gang of conspirators in Efzahan sees some advantage to Alciel that outclasses all the many disadvantages."

"Yes, and what would that be, exactly?"

"Gabriel told me himself: 'Emilia's gonna be paying me a visit, too.' She's paying a visit—right to wherever Gabriel and Alciel are."

Maou glowered at a certain point on the map.

"And if they're gonna make the Hero Emilia and the Demon General Alciel do something in the same physical location—no matter what kind of stupid thing it is—I can think of just one place."

He pointed at the map.

"It'd be the first place me and Alciel ran into the Hero. The only place where the Hero failed to defeat my general in battle."

Suzuno, Urushihara, and Chiho—especially Chiho, given how this was news to her—stared at the point.

"Heavensky Keep. The capital of Efzahan and the Azure Emperor's seat of power."

THE HERO DISCOVERS SHE
CAN'T COME HOME AGAIN

"What are you planning to do?"

Emi growled at the items just delivered to her chamber.

"Isn't it obvious?" the man replied breezily as he spread them out on the tabletop, pointing out each one.

"Are you looking to die, Olba? You actually want to arm me?"

She was addressing Olba Meiyer, one of the Church's six great archbishops and her former traveling companion on the quest to rid the world of the Devil King Satan. Now, though, he was nothing more than an adversary. Which made it all the more confusing that her nemesis had just brought in a double-edged sword and a suit of armor, complete with full-face helm. The equipment was all obviously top-of-the-line, and judging by the workmanship on the armor, it was from Saint Aile on the Western Island not Efzahan, where Emi was.

"Oh, I have my reasons. We're moving you to the capital in Heavensky tomorrow."

Emi lowered her eyebrows. "You want me to speak to the Azure Emperor? I thought Efzahan was taking on the world in order to get a holy sword. You can't be planning to offer me and my Better Half up to him and sue for peace, are you?"

She had only met the emperor once during her duties as Hero. An old, decrepit man, as she recalled him—one who'd be lucky to see another week in life, much less another year.

Olba brought a hand to his chin at Emi's question. He smirked at her. "I could say that you're closer than you think."

"What?"

"But that is not the issue. You do remember, Emilia, that there's a fair distance between Heavensky and here in Phaigan, yes? And we certainly cannot risk using a Gate or other magical device to transport us there. If your holy-sword child will need anything, ask one of the maids for it before the day is through. We leave tomorrow morning."

With that, Olba showed his undefended back to Emi and left the room. Picturing herself plunging a dagger into his chest in her imagination, she waited for him to politely lock the door behind him.

"What was that about...?"

Gathering her thoughts, Emi walked up to the sword and armor Olba left behind.

"It's just normal battle gear, isn't it?"

She took care not to touch it—it could always be outfitted with traps—but after careful scrutiny from up close, it all appeared to be perfectly typical equipment. The gear of the commanding-officer class in the Saint Aile army, yes, and of rather high-end make at that...but that was it. Emi had worn similar armor as a member of the Church knight corps, before she gained her Better Half and Cloth of the Dispeller skills.

"The sword's sharp, too. It's no living-room piece. What is he even thinking?"

Considering her circumstances, being given this equipment could easily allow Emi to storm Phaigan's military port and singlehandedly lay waste to it. Olba must have known that. She cursed herself for being too weak-willed to go through with it, but regardless, here it was—and she would be wearing it on the way to Heavensky.

She recalled her previous quest to slay the Devil King. This very port was where she, Olba, Emeralda, and Albert established their first base of operations in Efzahan. The Eastern Island was under Alciel's full control by then—she recalled how it took them a full week of careful undercover travel to reach the capital from there, taking a long, looping detour around and behind Heavensky before storming it. It didn't quite erupt into full-scale combat against Alciel during that visit, but...

"Why do they need to take all this time to arm me and take me to Heavensky?"

Emi engaged in a staring contest with the helm for a few moments. Then, letting out a deep sigh, she flung herself onto the bed.

"If I knew this was gonna happen, I wouldn't have let Eme and Olba handle all the travel arrangements and strategic decisions for me during our quest. I knew I shoulda used my head a little more..."

It was a declaration of defeat, and it sounded just as pathetic as the words portrayed it. This sort of espionage wasn't beyond Emi's abilities, but when it came to political guile and negotiation skills, she could never keep up with Emeralda and Olba—two people who made such skills their career. This made them the brains of the expedition, which meant that Emi and Albert were the brawn, more often than not.

That had already been hurting her in Japan. She was fully aware of it now, but no matter what the topic, it always seemed like Maou had a deeper understanding of issues than she ever did.

"Heh. The Devil King's the company boss, after all. I was just a temp worker."

Then she remembered something else. Back before Suzuno was fully on her side. One time, Ashiya explained Emi and Maou's relationship to Rika by portraying them as business rivals.

"Wow, that seems like ages ago... I don't think Alas Ramus was around yet, even."

Emi lay on her back in bed, staring up at the ceiling.

"Wish I could go back to Japan..."

"Mommy...?" a worried Alas Ramus asked within her mind.

Emi smiled a little. "It's all right," she said, trying to calm her adoptive daughter. "It's all right now."

"*Yeh?*"

"Yeah. I'm with you, after all."

It wasn't really an answer, but it was enough for Emi. She sat up and looked at the water pitchers near the room's entrance. There were two of them for some reason. At the bottom of one, a large number of black granules had settled. Emi had deliberately avoided that pitcher over the past few days. It helped her maintain the rage in her heart—keeping it from turning into helpless timidity.

"That's all it took, though… To keep me from fighting. If Olba and his people are planning something…do I have what it takes to fight?"

The black mass at the bottom of the pitcher sent Emi's memories back to the first day she returned to Ente Isla.

✳

A light began to come into view at the other end of the rainbow-hued Gate. Emi could feel something powerful tugging at her hands. She was being pulled in—not by the friend ahead of her, but by the world waiting at the other side.

The next moment, the digital static that dominated the Gate's inner space disappeared. Her heartbeat started to ring in her ears.

"Uh… Whaaa?!"

Emi couldn't help but scream upon opening her eyes. She was someplace she was not at all expecting to be. She could feel the pull of gravity against her body. One second, two seconds, five, ten, twenty… Time wore on and on, and her body kept falling, irresistibly attracted to whatever lay below.

"Wh-why are we in the—*Gapff!*"

The thinness of the air around Emi made her involuntarily cough. There was hardly anything to breathe. She turned her eyes down, mind still adrift in chaos, only to find a level field of cloud cover below.

"We don't know who might see us, sooooo…!" shouted the easy-going friend who had just led her through the Gate.

"Okay, but isn't this too high?!"

It must have opened up well into the stratosphere. Emi let her body fall, observing the full table of stars spread out above the cloud field.

"Ah…"

Then she noticed two particularly large heavenly bodies, sparkling brighter than the rest as they looked down upon the two of them. A blue moon, and a red one. Two moons of mystery that were like nothing on Earth. It was the exact sky that Emi had spent the majority of her life looking up at.

"Emiliaaa! We're going in the cloooouds! Cover your eyes and eeeears!"

The warning snapped Emi out of her reverie. She looked back down.

"*Ngh!*"

Adjusting her position, the Hero closed her eyes and plunged into the carpet of white headfirst. The wind pounded against her ears—but only for an instant, compared to the cacophony inside the Gate. She was out of the clouds in the blink of an eye, something she could tell by the change in the soundscape around her.

Emi opened her eyes and took it all in.

"Ente Isla…"

The tears were rolling from the corners of her eyes, keeping them from drying out in the wind. That's what she told herself. But either way, there was no stopping them now. Her life hadn't changed a bit since the day she set off as the Hero of legend. If anything, it had only grown more complicated and chaotic. This was no safe haven for Emi. But to her, the vast landscape could have been nothing else.

"I'm…home…"

It was home, on a faraway world, something she dreamed about, something she even cried about as she searched within her dreams.

"Emiliaaa…"

The warmth of her friend wrapped around Emi's outstretched hand. She looked up at the smiling Emeralda Etuva, her irreplaceable friend, the one who had just guided her back home.

"Welcome baaack!"

"...Thanks!"

Emi used her free hand to wipe away the tears she could no longer make excuses for.

"Ah-ha-haaa! We'd better find some clothes for us firrrst..."

No matter how dry Emeralda's laughter was, it wouldn't be enough to wring out her and Emi's wet clothes. And they weren't just wet, either. They were covered in mud, from head to toe.

"Well, at least our luggage is safe..."

"I-I'm sorryyy! I didn't realize there was this huge maaarsh where we laaanded..."

Emeralda was being endlessly apologetic. She had set up the Gate to discharge them into the sky to keep the resulting gigantic energy discharge from being detected. Her Gate-opening skills had less to do with her conjuring ability and more to do with the angel-feather pen Emi's mother, Laila, had given to her—but either way, it still generated a large burst of holy energy.

That was why, even when they went into the ensuing free fall, Emeralda didn't cast any kind of flight spell on Emi until she was just about ready to pancake on the ground. They planned this drop at night to reduce the chance of eyewitnesses spotting them in the sky. Magic-driven flight would envelop the two of them in an eerie glow—something a nearby watchman or knight corps could easily spot and investigate.

Considering the current political headwinds in Ente Isla, they had to eliminate any potential trail. The Hero Emilia was one thing, but if Emeralda, a major Saint Aile authority figure, was caught smuggling her to safety, the fallout would be dramatic.

So she kept the two of them in free-fall right down to the surface before she deployed her magic. Everything worked well up to then—but considering all the holy energy flying around in the air uses, she had opted to glide themselves down to a safe landing instead. What she didn't notice until too late was the marshland within the forest she picked as her touchdown point. She and Emi wound up splashing down near the edge of it.

Emeralda had attempted to take off again once she realized her mistake, but the moment had already passed. The air from her gliding flight was already kicking up marsh water at them. It left her and Emi forced to stare at each other sheepishly, both of them smelling slightly like raw sewage.

"…Oh, it's fine. Maybe smelling like this will keep us safe from animal attack anyway. The bag's fine, at least. See? It'll take a lot more than this for Japanese flashlights to stop working."

Emi fumbled through the large knapsack she brought along for her trip home. She took out a headlamp and flicked it on.

"I'm sorryyy!"

Emeralda, head still bowed in apology, stood in the middle of the light beam. To say the least, she needed a change of clothes.

"It's all right, okay?" Emi said as she tightened the lamp around her forehead. "I'm more worried about you than me, Eme. That's a court robe, isn't it?"

"Ooh…I'll just say I tripped and fell while inspecting a pig styyy…"

It sounded like a pretty far-fetched excuse to Emi, but there was no point dwelling on it.

"Okay, so where are we?"

"Well, ummm… Ooh, all this mud…"

Emeralda took a map out from inside her robe, griping at the water already making its way into it here and there. It was a close-up map of the eastern section of Saint Aile, the empire that dominated the Western Island and that both Emi and Emeralda were native to. She pointed at it, drawing an imaginary line toward its southwest.

"Your home village of Sloane is over heeere, and I think we should be here, in this forrrest."

"If I follow that path, I should run into a few big towns and villages, right?"

"Indeeed," Emeralda said. "And few of them have retained the size they had before the warrr. Lucky for us, perhaaaps, but…"

Emi could guess what war she was talking about.

"So…"

"Yes. The walled ciiity of Cassius is being rebuilt muuuch more quickly—it has an official Church-run cathedral within its boooundaries, after all. The surrounding villages and towns… Well, they've hardly been touched, saaad to say."

"Hardly been touched? How is that possible?"

Emi blinked in surprise as she pointed out a dot nearby Sloane.

"I mean, this village was home to a stagecoach guild and a warhorse breeding farm. I thought it was flourishing."

Emeralda shook her head. "Well, based on our investigaaations…"

"Uh-huh?"

"This probably isn't what you want to hear, Emiiilia, but quite a number of the villagers here gave their liiives up against the Western Island invasion forces led by Luciferrr."

"I've come to terms with it, okay? Don't sugarcoat it for my sake. What happened after that?"

"Well, by the time Al and I met you in Japaaan, the cathedral in Cassius was buying up a lot of ownership and develllopment rights to this land."

"Buying it up? So the Church was running the rebuild work? How is that possible? Isn't that Saint Aile's job?"

The Church, centered at its headquarters on the far western edge of the Western Island, was the largest religion in Ente Isla. Its sphere of influence extended well beyond the Western Island itself, spilling out across a variety of regions worldwide, and it enjoyed the faith of several hundred million followers.

This meant that high-level Church clerics often wielded far more power than the kings and nobles of smaller, less influential nations. Saint Aile, however, was not one of them. It had the political force to take on the Church in its home turf, preventing it from fully dictating its terms on its home continent. The idea of the Church being the sole director of recovery work in and around a city as large as Cassius seemed unthinkable—unthinkable, at least, within the boundaries of Saint Aile.

"Oh, they were craaafty with it," Emeralda explained. The way she put it, not only had Lucifer's invasion force killed off the majority of landholders in the area, but once the demons' dirty work was done, it wasn't even clear where most property boundaries lay any longer. After Devil King Satan and his army were expelled in the climactic battle in the Central Continent, Saint Aile naturally solicited its citizens to settle back down in these lands, so they could get back to normal as quickly as possible. They also deployed merchants to ferry over the resources they needed, as well as knight corps to lead the rebuilding operations.

"The Churrrch started by bidding on rebuilding projects for Cassius, where their catheeedral is based. They gained the right to lead the recovery effort in all the lands around the ciiity."

And rebuild they did. Things proceeded at breakneck speed inside and outside the walls of Cassius—and while no one was looking, they had expanded the boundaries of the city's walls, calling it "repair work." This was followed by the Church offering the new immigrants to the surrounding villages the right to move to these new frontiers at low prices. Having this influx of new population within direct control of the local cathedral instead of spread out across the countryside provided assorted advantages for the Church at large.

So what happened to the villages these people abandoned? On paper, at least, a large number of Church-affiliated people had poured into them. But it was strictly on paper. On the ground, it was clear that recovery work had barely started at all, if any had been embarked on in the first place.

"Wh-whoa. Hang on a sec. What're the Saint Aile knight corps doing, then? They were stationed in Cassius and all the villages, weren't they? Even if the Church snapped up the land rights in the area, that doesn't mean they get to just take over everything, does it? They can talk about all the rights they have, but they're still bound by Saint Aile law!"

"Well," Emeralda rumbled, "hate to saaay it, but that piece of traaash Pippin and his gang seized controlll of the area."

"That piece of... Huh?" Emi was startled. It wasn't like Emeralda to use her prim voice to curse at someone like that. "Do you mean General Pippin of the Saint Aile Imperial Guard?"

"Oh, no need to call him generrral. Just call him Piece of Traaash Pippin, please."

"...So you don't, um, like him or something, Eme?"

Guard General Pippin Magnus was the head of Saint Aile's Imperial Guard—essentially, the top authority figure ruling over the empire's knight corps. Emi had met him during her attempt to rescue Saint Aile's emperor, but only casually. She couldn't quite picture what he even looked like any longer—but it was obvious that Emeralda, someone who hardly wore her emotions on her sleeve, detested his very existence.

"Oh, why couldn't Luciferrr just kill that little sewer raaaat of a general when he had the chaaance?"

"Um, Eme?"

"When the Church forces selected the kniiight corps leaders deployyyed for the recovery effort, they almost alllways chose that sewer rat Pippin's laaackeys, it pains me to say."

"Oh...really?"

"The Saint Aile corrrps director in Cassius was totally iiin on it, too. Not only did the Church briiibe him to the point where he rubber-staaamped any plan they wanted, but he also falsified the state of immigration into the nearby villages. That's how that dunnng beetle Pippin gets away with dancing to the tune of the Churrrch. He's sucking on their teeeat like the little rat he is."

"Hmm..."

"No doubt about it. The recovery effort's seeeriously behind schedule, and it's all thanks to that stiiinking old man's meddling."

"How much do you hate General Pippin, anyway?"

He couldn't have been a very upstanding citizen, given Emeralda's consistent appraisals of him, but Emi still couldn't help but feel bad for the Guard general currently being subjected to this onslaught of abuse—whether she could remember his face or not.

"He's a craaafty rat, never letting anyone catch him in his evil

deeds. And the worrrst part of it is, I don't even know why he's deliberately delaaaying the rebuilding work. I escaped the confines of the
court so I could 'inspect' the delaaays in the planning effort."

"...I see."

"So the biggest issue heeere... Well, it's that this rotten Pippin and
his men may have sunk their dirty claaaws into Sloane as well."

Emi let out a light gasp.

"Given that Sloane was your hooometown and all, they were
pretty caaautious with rebuilding it. They decided to delaaay work
on the village early on. So for Sloane, at least, the delay makes
sennnse, but..."

"But you think General Pippin and the Church people he's working for don't mind that one bit, either?"

"Mm-hmm. So do be careful, all riiight?"

Emeralda folded up the map.

"Now, then... I have your identificaaation here, Emilia..."

It was similarly waterlogged, but there it was nonetheless—a
wooden card with a symbol branded on it.

"Any card released under my authooority will have the mark of
the Holy Magic Administraaative Institute on it. General Fessster-
ing Mold and his men may not appreciate that too muuuch, but to
heck with them."

"Can you at least call him Pippin for me?" Emi chuckled. "It's too
confusing for me otherwise. I'm surprised you're calling him that,
even. Do you ever refer to him that way in front of other people?"

"He and I are eeeven by now. His men call me Lady Midget
Broccoliii."

Plainly they were born destined to clash against each other. That,
or the Imperial Guard and Emeralda's Holy Magic Administrative
Institute had had this sort of bureaucratic rivalry for generations
before.

"Why does someone like that get to throw his weight around,
though? What about General Rumack?"

"Of course!" Emeralda replied, leaping at Emi's question. "Wouldn't you thiiink she'd care at all? I don't think any of this would've happened if Rumack was in the couuuntry." Grief began to cross her voice. "But Rumack was volunteered as the Western Island represennntative in the Federated Order of the Five Continents, the group rebuilding the Central Connntinent. Ever since Efzahaaan declared war on the world, she's been traaaveling back and forth between there and Saint Aile. She's got no time to relax at all heeere."

If Pippin Magnus was Saint Aile's top general at home, Hazel Rumack was the nation's commanding officer on the front lines. Emi had collaborated with her multiple times—from the first raid on Lucifer's forces after her journey began, to the operation to take back the Northern Island, to the final push toward Devil's Castle. Their relationship had never grown that familiar, but she was the veteran of many a battlefront, and in Emi's eyes, she seemed like the ideal general—fair, talented, and aboveboard in all her actions.

"But on the othhher hand, someone as slooow and smelly as Pippin could never engage in the delllicate, high-level diplomatic negotiations Rumack can. A mixed blessing, if you will."

Emeralda seemed to have similarly lofty words for Rumack. But the only conclusion Emi could make from all this was that once she was away from Emeralda, it was easiest to picture everyone around her as an enemy.

"All right. Well, I think I get the picture. I'll use this ID if the times call for it. So…"

"…Yesss?"

"This 'Amy Yousser'… Is that supposed to be my alias?"

"Ooh, I thought it'd be easy to get uuused to…"

Easier than a wholly unfamiliar false name, she had to admit. But something about it still didn't sit right with her. It wasn't like "Emi Yusa" was her real name, either, although people tended to forget that lately. Then again, she recalled, she decided to go from "Emilia" to "Emi"—did she really have any right to accuse Emeralda of a lack of originality?

"That… Ah, whatever. It's fine. Thanks."

She carefully inserted the pass, emblazoned with the seal of Holy Magic Administrative Institute leader and court sorcerer Emeralda Etuva, into her bag.

"I'm prepared to camp out for a week with this stuff anyway. I'll find a clothing shop somewhere outside Cassius's walls without coming too close to them...and then I'll figure out the rest myself. I'll keep this ID hidden until I really, really need it."

"That would be smaaart, I think. Also, it won't repay your ruined clooothing, but here's a little money for traaavel expenses. This is mostly Airenia silver coin, so make sure to waaash it first."

Emeralda nodded to herself before meekly offering Emi a thoroughly soaked leather pouch. She took it, marveling at its weight.

"...Thanks a lot. I'll try to pay you back somehow."

"Huh? Oh, don't wooorry. I can scrape up thaaat much anytime I want."

"Yeah, but it's the thought that counts, okay?"

It couldn't be helped, but life on Earth had changed Emi to the point that she couldn't simply accept other people's money for nothing. And considering the weight of this bag, if it really was all Airenia silver, it didn't matter whether you converted it into Japanese yen or Ente Isla's going rates—it was a hell of a lot more than Emi could procure by herself.

Emi considered the literal and figurative weight of this money in her life as she wiped the mud off the pouch. "Merchants can only operate outside the castle walls in the daytime, right?" she said. "I can't help but think how nice it'd be if there was a Denim Mate 24 or a Donkey OK nearby. Guess that's proof Japan's slowly poisoning me, isn't it?"

"What're thooose?"

"Um, those are clothing stores and general stores in Japan. They're both open twenty-four hours."

"Whaaat?! That's increeedible, isn't it? Did you have much occaaasion to purchase clothing in the middle of the night in Japaaan?"

"Not me, no...but I guess someone does, if they're open that late."

"Those Japaneeese sure like working hard, don't they? My

goodness, a store open all day and niiight... I couldn't imagine how they keep it going! I can hardly belieeeve anybody works in the late hours, eeeven."

Emi had to chuckle. "Don't bother trying to copy them. It just somehow all...works in Japan, you know?"

Conventional wisdom in Ente Isla dictated that the only people walking around at night were watchmen and pickpockets, both who often caught eye of the drunkards. No matter how safe a given region was seen as being, a woman traveling by herself was nothing short of suicide—unless the woman in question was the Hero, basically. The system in Japan worked precisely because 99.9 percent of people there were born hard-wired not to rock the boat—to live out their lives crime-free and without bringing shame upon themselves and their families.

"It's really kind of a miracle," Emi said to admonish herself. "I'm gonna have to be a lot more careful walking around by myself here."

"The Hero's party never has it eeeasy, no..."

"Yeah, you said it." The statement sounded familiar to Emi's ears. She sighed. "But enough wallowing in memories. Thanks for taking me here, Eme. Where should we meet up for the return trip?"

"Well, about thaaat... Wouldn't it be better if you kept this, Emiiilia?"

Emi watched as Emeralda presented something to her. It was the angel-feather pen. A grand treasure, one that let anyone open a Gate whenever they wanted. Straight from the wings of her mother, Laila. It gave her mixed feelings.

"You can have it."

Without much hesitation, Emi pushed it back toward Emeralda. Among all the dirt and muck that covered them both, it still shone a pure, untarnished white. "Even if I don't want to, I might run into some kind of interference. There's maybe a one-in-a-million chance, but it's still there. So I want either you or Al to keep it. If it actually happens, it's better to keep our cards spread out."

"...All riiight!" After a moment's pause, Emeralda seemed convinced enough. She put the pen back in her pocket. "In that caaase, there's no need to tell you where to meet, Emiiilia. I'll travel to Sloane for youuu."

"Are you sure?" Emi replied, not expecting her to go that far for her.

"I want you to spend as much time as possible in your seeearch... and I'm meant to inspect the general aaarea regardless, so it'll be more naaatural this way."

"...All right. I promise I'll find something useful for us!"

Emi was astonished, deep down. At every occasion, no matter what, Emeralda was prepared for anything.

Her friend, perhaps sensing that Emilia was starting to get a little too ramped up for her journey, placed a finger to her lips, smiled at the world-leaping young Hero before her, and spoke in Ente Isla's language.

"<No need to work yourself up too muuuch. What do I always tell you? Stay calm, stay cool, stay relentless on the battlefield.>"

Emi gulped. The words were harmless enough, but she could sense the force Emeralda put behind them. There was no doubt Emi could destroy her in one-on-one battle, but Emeralda was the most powerful sorcerer in the human world, an equally shrewd and seasoned politician and courtier, and a clever fighter whose multilayered strategies could take down even the greatest of powers. Her words, coming from the lips of someone capable of surviving alongside Emi in battle, sunk deep.

"Yeah. You're right."

"Oh, I knooow! And it's no longer just you in your body, eiiither."

Emeralda smiled, the inscrutable edge now gone from her voice.

"I wish you wouldn't put it like that."

"Well, am I wrooong? Hmm, Alas Raaamus?"

"Ugh... Alas Ramus?"

With a sigh, Emi brought a hand forward and summoned the child.

"Yeh, Eme-sis?"

"Ooh, you're soooo cuuuuuuute!"

"Hoooh?!"

Emeralda's near-scream made Alas Ramus's body tense up in midair.

"Please don't make her cry again, Eme."

That was exactly what had happened when Emeralda had come to see Emi in Japan, screaming in delight at the child and freaking her out to the point of tears.

"Awww, I'm sorry. C'mon, Alas Ramus, can you look at me? I'm not scaaary."

"Oooh…"

Emeralda tried her best to comfort Alas Ramus. The child wasn't buying it.

"Alas Ramus, watch over Mommy for me, okaaay? Don't let her do anything too craaazy."

"Crayzee?"

"Oh, and be good, okaaay? Listen to what Mommy says."

"Yeh! Alas Ramus good!"

She nodded, both stubby arms in the air. It was enough to make Emeralda lose all self-control.

"Aaaaiiieeeee! So cuuuuuuuute!!"

"Ahhh, *waaaahh!*"

"Eme!"

She had Alas Ramus's rapt attention, and she just had to shout at her anyway. The tears were already forming.

"S-sorrrry!" Emeralda said, clearly not sorry at all as she stuck out her tongue. Then she pointed a small fist at Emi. Emi smiled in response, face stern, and reached out her own arm, crossing fists with hers.

"<Do not retain hope.>"

"<Proceed forward.>"

Then, together:

""<You must blaze your own trail to survive!>""

The motto had found its start among the human forces after the battle against Lucifer, the first victory for mankind in the Devil King's Army war. Even with Lucifer gone, the continued threat of the demons ruling in the central, northern, eastern, and southern lands remained fresh in every human being's mind. The Hero's appearance, and her wresting the Western Island back, gave hope to all of them, but even then the frontline soldiers couldn't find much in the future to be optimistic about.

The world had almost fallen to its knees in the face of the burning rage of the Devil King's Army. The rebound engineered by the Hero was nothing short of a miracle. They needed to save the world while this miracle was still fresh. If they had the time to retain hope in their hearts, they had time to fight, to push forward, to change the world. That was what the fighters of the Western Island learned, and that was what they constantly told themselves.

Remembering it reminded Emi and Emeralda once again that, heart and soul, they were embroiled in battle once more.

"Well, good-bye, Emilia. Take care over the next week."

"You too, Eme."

"Eme-sis is gone?"

"Uh-huh. I'll have to travel by myself… Well, with you, too, Alas Ramus."

"Okeh. I'll be a good girl!"

"Yeah, try to go easy on me. Come on back for a bit, okay?"

Emi wiped some of the mud off her hand before lightly tapping Alas Ramus's head, fusing the child back within her.

"…Might as well head for Cassius first. Gotta do something about these clothes."

The mud was one thing, but she had a bigger concern in mind. Her outfit was still from Japan. The only clothes she brought with her from Ente Isla to Japan were what she had on under her armor at the time. She thought about having Emeralda provide something, but Emeralda had balked. She needed to keep acting as natural as possible, or else there was no telling how General Pippin and her other rivals would react.

"Why do all these people find hurting others so much fun?"

She sighed again—for the nth time today, for reasons she couldn't articulate—and there, inside the dark forest, made her first muddy step back home.

＊

"Please… Just one convenience store…"

Day 2 of her return to Ente Isla. As weak-kneed as she knew it sounded, Emi was already starting to crack.

She was at an inn about a day's walk east of the Cassius city wall. It was a gathering point for the stagecoaches and merchant caravans that plied the lands of eastern Saint Aile, and despite its relatively small size, it was a remarkably lively place.

"Ngh…hnh…"

Alas Ramus was sleeping in bed, a pained expression on her face. She didn't have a cold or anything, but it appeared that her dinner hadn't settled well with her. Emi was taking her meals in her room to hide the presence of the child, but most of the food she could take up there wasn't anything someone her (external) age could eat.

It simply amazed her. Was the culinary scene in Saint Aile and the Western Island really so crude and unrefined? To her, it seemed like nothing but meat, meat, alcohol, meat, and the occasional veg-etable for variety. Trying to obtain prepared food rewarded her with incredibly salty meat that turned her stomach at first sight—and here were all these people chowing down on it in broad daylight, using it to sop up the booze. The village market she attended wasn't totally bereft of fruits or vegetables—but while they looked like what was available in Japan, they were completely different from the well-cultivated produce of her former home.

On the first day, she stopped at a small, inexpensive inn near Cassius, using its kitchen to prepare whatever she could find that looked close enough to Japanese stuff and feeding Alas Ramus with it. But it was strange—the child was never a picky eater over there, but just a single bite of carrot was enough to make her twist her face and spit it out.

Seeing that made Emi realize exactly how much she had gotten used to the food and water in Japan. Was the cuisine really that bad where she grew up? Whenever she picked up one of the ingredients in her pack, Emi felt more and more depressed.

The vegetables in Japan were so flavor-packed, so sweet, so soft—Emi had no idea why Japanese children were so finicky with them. That was thanks to the farmers and produce companies who constantly improved their crops to make them more palatable, perhaps, but sadly, the vegetables in the Saint Aile region of the Western Island simply weren't up to snuff. The carrots were bitter, earthy, and left stringy fibers that stuck in your teeth. The tomatoes were acidic, enough to almost stab at your tongue; the cucumbers more bitter than Emi thought natural plants could ever be; the corn drier than a TV dinner left in the freezer too long; and so on. Emi had grown up on this stuff, eating it on a daily basis until she came to Japan, and now she could barely stand to chew it.

She could have just stuck to fruit, of course. The problem with that, though, was the price. In a word, it was ridiculous. Emeralda had provided her with a more-than-ample travel budget, but if she wanted something at least as good as what got sold in cans at the supermarkets in Tokyo, she'd be giving up at least one silver piece a go.

Saint Aile's history as an avid producer of fermented beverages meant that most of the decent fruit grown across the empire was hoarded by distillers or the local nobility. The common folk would have to be satisfied with what apples or oranges they could find, and it was all low quality (by Japan standards, at least) and cost several times as much as the veggies.

Emi figured she could conceal the taste of all this stuff in a sandwich or something, at the very least. But the kind of white bread she could buy in Japan for 100 yen a loaf didn't even exist at the local bakery. Instead, it was nothing but wheat, wild oat, and rye bread, the kind of thing that went for a premium on Earth. There was no milk or sugar used in its production, no cultivated yeast to aid in the process, and it was all brick-like and sour-tasting without exception—nothing like what Alas Ramus had eaten before.

All this meant that, in order to keep her charge's stomach full, Emi found herself resorting to the ready-made food she had brought from Japan—strictly meant as emergency rations—on Day 1. She quickly had to revise her entire approach to keeping themselves fed for the next week. The clothing issue had worked itself out quickly, even for Alas Ramus's swaddling. But she had never expected something as basic as food to be such a major issue.

Still, she made it. And here they were. On Day 2.

It turned out there was another problem facing both of them—one that she was too tensed up on the first day to notice.

"I can't believe how…dirty that toilet was…"

Emi reflexively wrinkled her nose as she watched Alas Ramus struggle in bed.

The bathrooms here were simply a mess. She knew not to expect anything as advanced as a flush toilet or reliable indoor plumbing, but every latrine she had the misfortune to run into seemed to present a new case study in sheer nastiness.

And it wasn't just a matter of being disgusting. It was a matter of being disgusting and being charged for the privilege. Travelers had to pay up every single time they used a toilet. There was some old guy poised next to each one, taking tolls. Five copper coins were the going rate, and even that only got you a plain stall—if you were lucky—with a door.

There was, of course, no toilet paper. The lack of cleaning, regular or otherwise, made the stink overpowering. Emi could hold her nose well enough, but she couldn't stomach the idea of making Alas Ramus do her business in them. So she resolved, as annoying as it made her life, to stick to the diapers she brought along for the trip instead.

Thus Emi found herself suffering at the start of her grand adventure thanks to the food and the sanitation—two musts for any civilization that seemed to be so incredibly lacking in this one.

Tonight, at least, she had managed to cook the food well enough that Alas Ramus ate her entire dinner. She mashed up a few potatoes, seasoned them with salt and pepper, then further mixed them into hot water. Adding mushrooms, onions, and minced chicken breast, she boiled the whole mixture into a ready-to-eat soup. That, at long last, was enough to earn an "Mmmm" from her audience.

If she was traveling by herself, she wouldn't bother making these things that took up so much expensive water, fuel—all right, more like kindling—and kitchen usage fees. But that wouldn't pass muster with Alas Ramus.

"Ugh... A convenience store...a microwave...some heat-and-eat food...some vending machines...a curry joint..."

Emi could almost feel herself tearing up as she swore in her heart that, whenever she realized her life's goal and returned to her homeland in Ente Isla, she'd bring at least a microwave and fridge along with her. She knew she must have looked haggard and weak at the moment. At least she didn't have to feel discouraged over it every time she looked in the mirror. There'd never be a luxury item like that in a cheap inn like this.

Suddenly:

"Amy? Amy?"

A knock on the door. Emi stood up straight. It was the innkeeper.

"Y-yes?"

She stood to her feet, tied her hair back up, ran to the door, and warily opened it a sliver to keep the visitor from seeing inside.

"Ooh?"

It really was the innkeeper, that old man standing in the hallway. His face looked honestly surprised.

"What is it?"

"Oh, er, I wasn't expecting you to open up."

"Oh..."

Emi cursed her tactical error. This wasn't Japan. There was no guarantee the innkeeper was an honest person. If he weren't—if this was some highway bandit disguised as the innkeeper—he would've elbowed his way inside the moment the door was unlatched. It was standard manners in Saint Aile to keep the door locked after a knock until you were sure everything was safe on the other side.

Even here, her experiences in Japan were hatching potentially troubling results for her.

"Um, regarding what you asked about, it looks like we have a caravan 'ere that's slated to head through Valcroskh. I reckon they'd let you ride with 'em for the right compensation."

"Oh, was that it?"

Emi nodded. The village of Valcroskh was about half a day's walk from Sloane. When she paid for this room, she inquired about immigrants or caravans traveling not to Sloane, but to the assorted villages that surrounded it. It would be foolish to reveal her real destination to anyone at the moment. Both Sloane and Valcroskh were a long hike from here, but if she could grab a seat on a wagon caravan, that would cut down her travel time immensely.

"Thank you very much. If you could give them a deposit for me..."

Emi took out two silver coins she had ready in her pocket and handed them to the innkeeper. A cheap inn like this, with no security whatsoever, meant that Emi could never reveal how much money she was carrying—not even to the boss. She remembered that much, and yet she had just flung the door open in front of this guy. So stupid.

Two silver coins were pretty high for a "deposit," but Emi meant one of them as a tip for the innkeeper. Don't cheap out when the times call for it—that's what Albert had taught her.

"Hmm. Very well. Good evenin' to you, then."

The innkeeper gave a satisfied nod to Emi as he cupped the coins and left. She locked the door and breathed a sigh of relief.

"This is all so hard. It used to come so naturally to me, too..."

She undid her hair again, slowly sat on the bed, and gently caressed the hair of Alas Ramus, who looked like she was still suffering under a bad dream.

"Though, really... I've only been alone once in my life. That year or so in Japan before I met the Devil King. Other than that..."

Until she awakened to her Hero abilities and freed the Holy Empire of Saint Aile from Lucifer, Olba and the Church knight corps were her benevolent companions and guardians. Once she freed Saint Aile, she met Emeralda, who became her inseparable friend. Albert she'd first met on the ship to the Northern Island after she defeated Lucifer and freed the entire Western Island—and thanks to his knowledge and power, they'd managed to persevere through the northern and southern lands' harsh weather conditions.

Alciel's forces retreated from the Eastern Island before Emi and her comrades could test them in battle. So the four of them, buoyed by the will of the entire human race, smashed their way into Devil's Castle on the Central Continent—and then Emi drifted into a world where life-threatening danger almost never appeared.

"I acted all big and strong as the Hero, but in the end, I couldn't do anything by myself. And now I'm freaking out over all these things I'm running into during my trip... It's not even funny anymore."

"Mnh...mmm..."

"I'll try to whip up something nicer for you tomorrow, okay, Alas Ramus?"

Emi smiled a little, then climbed into bed—no changing her clothes, no taking off her boots, no waking up the child.

"Going to bed in my shoes... Talk about bad manners, huh?"

She recalled how she, Maou, and Alas Ramus went shopping together in Seiseki-Sakuragaoka for a child-sized futon. She had scolded her, hadn't she, for climbing up on the train seat in her shoes, yearning for a look out the window?

"Come on, Alas Ramus. Listen to your mommy."

"Ugh, she always listens to you..."

Emi groaned at the words.

If something about the food or the weather here put Alas Ramus in a bad state, she was sure that so-called "daddy" would give her a whole bunch of sarcastic lip back home. Like he always did. She wanted to avoid that, and another part of her couldn't believe she actually cared what he'd think. She sighed painfully.

"Daddy, huh...?"

It was hard for her to admit, but compared to before, the drive in her to hate the Devil King, to slay the Devil King, was falling out of sight. Learning that her own father was alive contributed to that, but really, it was Satan, the Devil King himself, who had triggered it. Sometimes, the Hero just couldn't understand him anymore.

There was that doubt in her mind again. The one percolating within her for the past several months they had spent together in Japan: Where did the personality, the character, the thoughts of "Sadao Maou" bubble up from? By this point, Emi was starting to wonder if Maou was really Satan at all. Her image of Sadao Maou, and her image of Devil King Satan, were no longer one and the same—to the point that she returned to Ente Isla without a single doubt that Maou, her sworn enemy, would do anything villainous in Japan while she was gone.

"Maybe being back home will kindle some of that old hatred again…"

Emi looked at the sleeping Alas Ramus as she pondered the idea.

No matter what kind of "person" Maou was now, Maou's presence behind the armies of Lucifer—which had destroyed her home—was the unmovable truth. Even the news that Nord was alive was given to her by an archangel, a completely unreliable source. There wasn't a shred of evidence to back it up.

Right now, Sadao Maou was still her enemy. The villain who irrefutably killed her father, destroyed her village, and ruined her young life.

She had told this to herself time and time again. And yet the completely outlandish idea that her father was alive had moved her heart so much in another direction. It made her feel pathetic.

"…What am I fighting for? Who am I even fighting…?"

The unanswerable questions melted into the darkness as Emi's consciousness faded away.

✳

"Ya sure this is good? 'Cause you're more'n paid up for at least two more stops. We could take ya all the way to the walled city if yer willin' it?"

There was, perhaps, a slight trace of concern visible underneath the caravan boss's craven capitalist spirit.

"'Cause, I mean, ye see how Valcroskh's shapin' up at the moment—no travelers' inns or the like. And y'know, nearby ya got Millady, ya got Gohve, ya got Sloane, an' the whole lot's two or three stragglers short of empty. If yer makin' a pilgrimage or whatnot, then godspeed with ya, but I ain't too sure anyone's left to pray to, ah?"

Emi helped herself off the wagon once it stopped at Valcroskh, on a side road off the main path to Cassius.

"It's fine, sir. Thanks for the ride."

The caravan ride had saved her a good day or so's worth of traveling. A grown woman could do the trip from here to Sloane on foot in half a day.

"And you could call it a pilgrimage of sorts, I suppose. I lost track of someone important to me when the Devil King's Army invaded here, and I'm traveling in order to track him down."

"...Ah, sorry if I'm pokin' around too much. It 'ad to be sommin' like that, mm? For a girl to be travelin' alone like ye is?"

The boss, still seated at the coachman's post, removed his wide-brimmed hat.

"'Ey, I'll give a prayer to the god of commerce for ya, ah? So's you can meet that whoever guy. Yer overpayin' for my services anyways. Little bonus for ya, 'n all that."

"I appreciate that, sir."

Emi smiled at the gesture.

"Hope to see ya again," the man said as he replaced his hat.

"Right..." Then, with a flick of the reins, the caravan was off again. The men who staffed the six wagons each waved at Emi as they passed by, shouting their farewells before disappearing down the road. Emi watched them until they did, then brought a hand to her chest.

"Letting something like that move me... I really have gone soft."

The boss's sincere prayer really had moved Emi's heart, a little.

"...Things have been so peaceful, I almost forgot. This is Ente Isla, isn't it?"

She took a deep breath, attempting to cool down her newly

warmed heart. She could feel the power coursing through her body. That was no illusion.

"Warmth creates power. Nobody can beat me now."

Her body was brimming with holy energy as she exultantly walked away from Valcroskh and took her first steps toward Sloane.

In her previous journeys, the only thing Emi could rely on, traveling through the night, was the light the moon and stars provided. Now, she had a headlamp over her forehead, the LED flashlight in her right hand—yet another triumph of Earth's civilization—bathing the path ahead in near-blinding light. She was planning to rely on both of these light sources on the way to Sloane.

The flashlight was solar-powered and theoretically never ran out of juice—and even if she used it too much at night, it came with a hand crank, too. If she had the right cord, she could charge a phone with the connector on the bottom, and the foldable side stand made it useful as a desk lamp as well. She could even adjust the light between two levels to save on power. And if any wolves or bears decided to peer at her through the darkness at a forest detour, the built-in emergency siren let her scare them off without a fight.

"If there was a lighter or a Swiss Army knife on the back, I could mass-manufacture these and change the way everyone on Ente Isla travels."

Emi realized she was starting to sound like an infomercial as she spotted something on the edge of the woods: a small, seemingly abandoned house, one she could have easily overlooked. Once she caught sight of it, she turned off the light, not wanting to reveal her presence just in case any rogue characters were lurking inside. Or worse. Considering what this house was, the sort of people Emeralda was concerned about might be guarding it right now.

Slowly, Emi scoped out the area for any other presence, moving at half the speed from before. Soon, she spotted another building in the moonlight ahead, just barely visible. She stopped and looked around once more.

"…Not like anyone would be here."

She sighed. Not that she let her guard down, but—thinking about it—over a year had passed since Emi disappeared from Ente Isla, and it'd been a good half-year since any of the angels, demons, or Church officials had confirmed her presence. None of those forces had the free personnel to station here for a Hero who might or might not ever show up.

Besides, before the Devil King invasion, this place was nothing more than a farming village. Nothing special at all about it.

As she came closer, she caught sight of a flat area along the path, one where humans plainly used to dwell. This was the land they used to cultivate. Emi crossed the path that went through it, taking step after careful step toward the dark ruins that spread out across the night ahead of her.

Soon, she was at the village's "main street," just barely wide enough for two wagons to pass each other.

"…I'm back."

There was not a single insect cry, not a single mouse scurrying around. It was as though time had stopped for this village. The only thing that listened to Emi's shaky voice was the fresh night breeze.

The village of Sloane was in a state of quiet decay, serving as its own gravestone.

"It's okeh to go in, Mommy?"

Emi had helped herself into the house nearest to the path, one that still retained most of its original form, and pitched her tent inside. That, she hoped, would keep anyone from noticing the smoke and flame from her cooking, as well as the light Alas Ramus emitted when she took her out.

"It's all right. This…belongs to someone Mommy knows."

Emi flashed a forlorn smile as she quickly prepared for dinner. The menu for tonight featured yesterday's potato soup (packed into a paste), along with some instant rice—good old Auntie Nan's from

Japan. It cooked just as well simmering in a hot pan as it did with two minutes in the microwave.

She filled her all-purpose pot with water, then used a smoke-free portable camping stove to bring it to boil. Adding a little water to the paste to bring it back to soup form, she used the remaining water to heat up the rice. A little jerky she packed for the trip, and she had at least the bare trappings of an evening meal.

"The perfect feast for my triumphant return, I suppose."

"Mommy! 'Tatoes!"

Alas Ramus, illuminated by the flashlight propped up on its side, prodded Emi for her apparent new favorite food. The darkness of the unfamiliar place didn't seem to faze her at all.

"Oh, what do you say before that?"

"Mmm... Oh! Uhh, fanks for the meal!"

"Very good. Make sure to blow on it a little before you eat it, okay?"

She had taken care not to make it too hot for Alas Ramus. She wanted to treat this as just another dinner, for her sake.

"Pff, ffffft... Om!"

"How is it?"

"Mmm, good."

The feast inside Emi's rotted-out homeland continued calmly. Once Alas Ramus had her fill of potato soup and rice, it was Emi's turn to tackle her own meal. As a grown-up, her dinner was a little more basic—oat-bran bread, beef jerky, and just a little of Alas Ramus's soup.

"Um, Mommy?"

"Mm? What is it?"

"Why isn't Mommy's friend here?"

"...Well."

She must have interpreted "someone Mommy knows" as "friend." Emi coughed.

"There used to be this man named Kopher who lived in here..."

It was the home of a couple, to be exact. A rather chatty pair, as she remembered them, maybe around ten years older than her father.

"How 'bout over there?"

Instead of waiting for Emi to finish, Alas Ramus pointed out the window, toward the abandoned ruin across the street.

"Oh, um… I think that was old lady Lireena's place. She was really good at knitting."

"How come she's not there?"

Emi paused. What was driving Alas Ramus? What part of her will drove her to ask? Was it just a child asking a simple question, or was that deeper intelligence she occasionally flashed asking Emi for the truth?

"Well, these scary demons came to attack the village, and they chased them all out."

The village fell victim to Lucifer's slavering fangs not long after the Church took Emi in. Considering the distance from Sankt Ignoreido, on the Western Island's eastern edge, Sloane existed for maybe a month after she left. Or maybe not. Maybe the village was already a thing of the past by the time she had arrived at her sanctuary in the Church. The hatred, the grief, her youth, and the crushing feeling of being lost in a great storm made her memories of the time indistinct. There was no way to find out the exact date now.

She was attempting to swallow down her dark recollections with a bite of bread when Alas Ramus asked another question.

"Mommy, is Garriel a demon?"

"Huh?"

"Scary, make everyone cry… Is that Garriel?"

"N-no…?"

Why did Gabriel's name come up at a time like this? She knew that Alas Ramus had been relentlessly hostile to him long before they had this current relationship, but it seemed awfully sudden to her.

"Are demons the angels?"

"Um, I'm sorry, Alas Ramus, I'm not exactly sure what you mean…"

This triggered something in Emi's mind. Alas Ramus seemed to understand what angels were from the moment she met her. But did she know what demons were at all? Through her role as the Better

Half, Alas Ramus had seen Maou and Ashiya in their full demon forms a couple of times—and that did nothing to change her affection for them.

"Mommy, what are demons?"

"That, um..."

Emi couldn't answer. Half a year ago, she could have talked at great length about these merciless, bloodthirsty monsters. Now, all she could come up with was the words Gabriel had for her: that angels were living things. Humans.

"What...do you think the 'demons' truly are?"

Suzuno's question seemed as fresh as before. Here was Satan, the Devil King, living out his life exactly like any other young Japanese man. *He's a living thing, too...and what does that mean?* Emi had no answer for that, and therefore no answer for Alas Ramus.

"...Mommy?"

And there was another reason for her silence. The "scary demon" that chased them all away from the village was none other than the "Daddy" Alas Ramus adored. As the Hero—as a human being—there was simply no way Emi could tell Alas Ramus that her daddy was an enemy, worthy of her scorn. It wouldn't help her in life, a part of her mind told her. And more than that, she had nowhere near the amount of resolve required to tell her that Alas Ramus's blade would need to cleave through Alas Ramus's daddy sooner or later. Not at this moment.

At this moment, with the possibility that her own father was still alive, she wasn't sure whether that fateful strike even needed to happen at all.

Either way, betraying her daughter's love in order to dispel her own hatred would be exactly the kind of "demonic" behavior Emi detested.

"...This is getting so irritating."

Recalling the dopey-looking image of Maou in her mind, all the way over here, made Emi experience a sudden feeling at the pit of his stomach. Not of hatred, not of resentment, but of a light, dry sense of irritation.

"I give him a little slack and he starts causing trouble for me all over the place. I'm sitting here, going through the motions, talking breathlessly about my great ambitions or whatever. It's ridiculous, isn't it?"

"Oo?"

"Listen, Alas Ramus: Demons are cowardly; they're cunning; and they're incredibly egotistical."

"Cow...egogo...?"

"What does Chiho even see in that guy, anyway? It makes no sense to me."

"Ooo, I don' get it."

She knew she was getting irritated over completely inconsequential matters. But then Emi remembered something. She smiled in the flashlight's illumination.

"I know, Alas Ramus. Once we return home...why don't you ask Daddy?"

"Daddy?"

"Yeah. Try asking Daddy what a demon is. He's really smart, so I'm sure he'll tell you all about them."

"Okeh!"

It was positively devious of her. But it didn't seem fair, either, that Emi had to be the only one preoccupied about the relationship between Maou and Alas Ramus. It was about time Maou gave a little thought to her future, too. Imagining him falling into a panic at Alas Ramus's innocent query made a smile naturally emerge on her face.

"I better give him an earful once I get back."

"When can I see Daddy again?"

"Oh, in a little while. We've got Chiho's birthday party coming up, so I'm sure Daddy'll be around for that."

He would be. Emi didn't mean anything deep by it. She was just laying out her plans for next week.

"Well, it's still a bit early, but we'd better clean this up and get to sleep. I'll have to be up early tomorrow."

Emi inserted all her possessions except for her sleeping bag and flashlight into her knapsack, took Alas Ramus into her arms, and unzipped the bag.

"Mmm, fluffy!" the child exclaimed as she patted at the thick down lining.

"Hey, stop playing with it!"

She pouted a bit at this admonishment, but within Emi's arms, she quickly began to prepare for a good night's sleep.

"Mommy, tell me a story!"

"A story? Hmm…"

It wasn't that Alas Ramus had never asked for a bedtime story before, but it was far from common. Emi thought up a few fairy tales and fables from Earth, but then shook her head and turned the flashlight down to its dimmest setting.

"Well, how about I tell you an old story from Ente Isla? It's about a young prince who came to rescue a princess after she was kidnapped by a scary demon…"

She placed a hand on Alas Ramus's stomach inside the sleeping bag, moving it up and down like she was beating out a rhythm. Slowly, the night shared between "mother" and "child" advanced, inside the dead village where no moonlight reached.

Emi's eyes were open before the sun rose. Alas Ramus's eyes weren't, but it didn't matter—she could always just bring her back into her own body. This she did, as the first rays of light began to dance upon the ruined village.

It was just as silent as before, without even a single forest creature nearby. The last time Emi was here, she had stopped by in the midst of her quest, ridding the grounds of the wilder and/or more magical beasts that had taken up residence inside. If anything, the place had weathered the time in between pretty well.

But it was weird—nothing was familiar about the sight of this destruction, but she still instinctively knew where everything was. The Justina residence was eastward, toward the sun that even now was starting to rise above a faraway mountain. As if attracted to it, Emi left the "main street" and traveled to a point some distance from the village center.

Then she stopped. Something was there that she hadn't anticipated. It was a familiar tree, at the far end of the village. She'd eaten lunch there most days with her father as he took a break from his fieldwork. Which meant the now-wild fields that spread out before her...

"This is...my father's wheat...?"

As if summoned by Emi's words, dawn extended out from the mountains, brightly spreading its shine upon the land. The tears came all too naturally from Emi's eyes. The land was covered in deep, lush greenery, gently rustling in the morning breeze.

"It's still around..."

The green plants extended out across the entire land. Wheat plants. She knew it was that—growing wild and out of control, but still the same plants. They were being choked out by long, tall weeds dotted here and there, and their stalks held little in the way of harvestable grain. Some of the plants, Emi could tell, would likely collapse under their own weight before autumn arrived. But the sight was still enough to make Emi shout to the sunlit heavens.

"It's still alive! My father's wheat is still alive!!"

After being trampled upon by demons, after losing their sole master, after all these years, the wheat was still strong enough to stay alive, ready to give way to the next generation.

"Are you really still alive, somewhere? Can we live here together again...?"

All the proof Emi needed was right in front of her. Something she thought was lost in terror and despair was here, before her eyes. She didn't want to taste that despair ever again. No matter what, she had to risk her life to protect this.

"Mmh... Mommy? What are you—waph!"

Emi's scream shook at her very heart. It was enough to make Alas Ramus blink into existence in an instant. She held her small form, forgetting to wipe her tears.

"Alas Ramus, I…I think I can still do this… I have to…!"

"Mommy? …*Affh*…"

She tightened her grasp on the still-not-quite-awake Alas Ramus once more, then hurriedly ran down the road she'd taken. Picking up her things from Kopher's house, she immediately headed for the house she had lived in with her father.

That would be the base she used to reach the goal she had traveled to Ente Isla to fulfill. She knew something had to be there, under the roof she called home. Some fragment of the truth she could use to unravel the mysteries that surrounded both Ente Isla and Earth. After the unexpected miracle she had just witnessed, Emi felt all but assured of it.

✳

"Ahhhh… There's nothing at all in here…"

Emi, her concentration now a thing of the past, flung herself down in the area that used to be the kitchen. It was the afternoon of the third day she had spent exploring her home.

The sight of her father's surviving wheat fields on the first day had moved her to tears. She took it as an omen that she was bound to find a hint that would reveal everything she needed to know about this world, so she had moved her base of operations to her former house. Now it was Day 3, and she had nothing at all to show for it.

The Justina residence was just a typical farmhouse—nothing overly large or grandiose about the building or the plot of land it was on. It bore the same signs of damage that every other house in the village did, but by and large it still looked roughly the way Emi remembered it: the kitchen, where she used to cook for her father; the dining room, where she used to eat with him; the living room, where she used to stare at the burning fireplace to lull herself to sleep.

The sight of the bed she slept in as a child made her tear up all over again, but there was no time to lose herself in memories. This was Emi and Nord's home, but it was also the home of Laila, her mother, the woman who seemed to lurk behind the scenes in every-thing that linked Earth with Ente Isla. There had to be something she didn't pick up on as a young girl, something they didn't let her touch, someplace she hadn't been allowed into before now. But for all the effort she made, the Hero's fervent searching pro-vided nothing but further confirmation that her father was a strong, sincere, and unaffecting man.

They hardly had much in the way of shelves or chests to hide things in, for one. The village could have been subject to bandit raids after it was abandoned, but she figured they'd aim for jewelry and gold, not entire pieces of furniture. So she began by searching the attic and basement for anything hidden, but all the attic held was some seasonal furniture, some empty barrels and jars, a few nails and screws, and other typical household goods. And there wasn't even a basement in the first place.

It'd be nice if there were a secret basement or something at a time like this, she thought. But there was no point griping about some-thing that didn't exist.

She continued her search into the tool shed, behind the fireplace, under and inside the cooking hearth, and countless other places she never haunted as a child. She was rewarded with a face full of soot and dust, as well as Alas Ramus asking why she looked so "mean" over dinner. It was, to say the least, a disappointment.

"I guess if you hid something in a chimney or whatever, you wouldn't be able to take it out again anyway, huh?"

So much for that. But if you wanted to hide a tree, the best place to do that would always be in the forest. So on the second day, Emi decided to go through the few remaining books and papers that were left on the home's shelves. Bound paper books still being a luxury item in Ente Isla, even important documents were still often writ-ten with block printing on parchment, papyrus, and other rough materials.

There wasn't a lot left in the house, so she figured reading through it all wouldn't take too much time. But:

"...All this detail..."

She had started reading in the morning. She was still at it by the time the sun began to set.

The familiar sight of her father's handwriting made the waterworks start up all over again at first. He had used a valuable bound accounting book to record a journal of his agricultural life that went into meticulous detail. Most of its content involved his wheat and other duties, and he covered his daily routine in such minute terms that she couldn't bear to skip any of it, fearing that some kind of deeper meaning might be locked inside of it all.

After she tired of reading this agricultural record, she decided to take a look at the parchment and woodblock-print material. It was largely things like tax payment receipts, records related to the small amount of livestock Nord kept as a side pursuit, request forms, and the like, extending over twenty years into the past.

"...Oh, the inspector's seal changed."

After two hours, the first major change Emi noticed was a different brand on a wooden receipt. She decided to take that cue to stop her research and get a meal going.

"Hey, Alas Ramus?"

"Yehh?" she replied as she dug into her reheated corn soup.

"Do you feel any Yesod fragments or anything like that nearby?"

"Nope!" came the immediate answer. Emi hung her shoulders. She had only half-jokingly asked the question, but it made the reality of the situation even more distressing. Of course she didn't. If she did, Alas Ramus would've raised a massive hue and cry about it the moment they entered the village.

In the end, despite there not being all that many records left unscathed, Emi still couldn't thumb through them all before the day was through. Day 3, she decided, would have to be split between cleaning up the place and wrapping up her research.

"Hmm... Nothing from here, maybe...?"

Emi sat down on a surviving creaky chair and moved on to a sheaf of documents related to land rights among Nord's business contacts.

"Or maybe Olba or Gabriel or someone thought the same thing and took anything incriminating out of here?"

She tossed an area map depicting farmland boundaries into the "done" pile and reached back for another bound volume.

"I can't believe this is the only diary he kept. It's weird."

This was Nord's personal diary, the only real fruit to stem from Emi's search so far. Compared to his farming journal, it was nowhere near as thickly written and impenetrable. He made sure to add an entry in that journal every day of his life, but with this diary, he kept a pace of once a week at best. It was more of a weekly summary of events than a diary.

While it did describe assorted events of daily life, including Emi's formative years, it didn't even mention Laila's name once. The final entry was dated several years before the Devil King's Army invaded.

"The exact era I didn't need to know about..."

A bit of a harsh assessment, she knew, given that she was reading someone's diary without permission, but it was the honest truth. She respected the memories of her father, of course, but there was nothing from this era of Emi's life that would help her right now.

"Well, two days until Eme stops by, I guess..."

Dark clouds of doubt began to gather over her search. She let out a weak sigh.

"Land-division maintenance certifications... This is a guide to field boundaries, this is a record of fields left fallow for tax-deduction purposes..."

Emi delved back into the "to do" pile, reading through the wood-board certifications and dividing them up by category.

"Payments for town-maintenance deposits... Oh? Wow, the village mayor's new-year greeting got stuck in here. And over in these parchments... These are all permits and titles, huh?"

She was getting used to this now, sorting through the documents like a seasoned secretary.

"Fixed-period lumber rights for the common wooded areas... An ax-possession permit? Wow, I had no idea you needed that. After that... Our baron's home-building permit, construction permits, expansion permits—this is all house stuff, I guess. Farming tool shed building permit... Here's a permit to clear out a new field... Hmm?"

Emi's hand stopped on a certain sheet of parchment.

"I thought all the land-related stuff was in this pile. Did this get misfiled?"

The field permit was filed at about the same time as the house Emi was in right now was built. Nord must not have been fully categorizing his business documents, yet perhaps it was forgotten about over time. Emi was just about to replace the field-building permit with the others when something caught her eye.

"...Wait, what?"

She gasped a little and peered at the lettering on the parchment.

"Where is this?"

The permit granted the cosigned the right to establish a new field for farming purposes, provided by the local baron and village chief based on previous tax revenues and harvesting figures. It was a cheap way for farmers to obtain more arable land, assuming they were willing to clear it out themselves, but it also increased their tax burden, whether the new land produced viable crops or not. It wasn't the kind of request a farmer would make unless they had the financial freedom to take the risk. Especially not this request.

"Why here, of all places? That's so far away."

The location described in the permit was within the mountains toward the east of the village, wholly separate from any of the other plots the Justina family tilled. Comparing the permit with the map Emeralda gave her, it would be a half-day's journey from here on foot.

"Hmmm?"

It thoroughly confused Emi. She rifled back through the pages she read before. There, among a sheaf of irrigation-facility titles, she discovered another permit mixed in—this one for a shed. It was located right where this new, unknown field was.

"I...I never once heard of this place."

As far as her childhood memories told her, all the Justina family's lands were within a fifteen-minute walk of this house—fifteen minutes for a child, even. As far as she knew, Nord was strictly a wheat farmer—that, plus a few chickens he raised in a nearby coop so he could sell the eggs. *So what's with this field located outside the village entirely? What did he have this shed built for?*

Emi leaped to her feet, grabbed the agricultural journal she had spent yesterday reading cover to cover, and flipped back to the dates written on the permits. Slowly, she pored through that time period again.

"He harvested nothing... He didn't even plant anything. But..."

On a page dated three days after the shed permit, she spotted something she had overlooked at first—something in tiny, tiny text.

"Nine... The number nine?"

She thought at first it was just a mistake or a quick memo jotted down. Now the full meaning of this number dawned on her. It couldn't have been a coincidence. The Yesod Sephirah, the core of Alas Ramus and the Better Half, was the ninth Sephirah that grew on the Tree of Life.

Emi touched her chest with her hand, unable to restrain her rapid pulse.

"Alas Ramus?"

"Mph..."

Alas Ramus was apparently taking an afternoon nap inside her. But she couldn't wait. She had to know what this meant now.

Suddenly, Emi turned toward the sky, even now streaked with the color of evening. She had two days until Emeralda would come calling. The field was half a day's journey away. If she'd have to engage in another wide-range search over there, she might not make it back in time for their rendezvous. But waiting for Emeralda and taking her along seemed out of the question—not with the cover story her friend was bound by.

"...Guess I'll have to fly over."

As long as she didn't go too quickly, she didn't think mere flight would arouse the attention of her "enemies."

"This isn't Japan, anyway. Here, holy magic's getting used all over the place."

It was used to power the lights at night in Saint Aile's cities, for one. It also saw use in a vast array of categories, from magic-driven weapon forging to the sanctified crops Suzuno brought into Devil's Castle in Sasazuka. The culture of magic was much more advanced on the Western Island than elsewhere, too—it consumed 30 percent more of it yearly than the rest of the islands combined.

Considering the time she'd be aloft and the position Emeralda was in, extending her stay here posed far more problems than quibbling over whether to use magic or not.

"…I kind of promised Chiho, too," Emi said to herself as she looked at the beloved Relax-a-Bear wristwatch on her left arm. She had left it on for the trip so she could compare the passage of time on Ente Isla with that on Earth.

It was a miracle, perhaps, but it seemed to her that the two planets operated roughly on the same day-night schedule, accounting for time-zone differences. And Chiho and Emi's birthday party was scheduled for September 12, Earth time.

"No point breaking that promise."

Emi tucked the two permits into her knapsack, then began packing up the rest of her open equipment.

"Hope I can stop by again real quick before I go," she said before stepping out the front door. She gave her home another look. By and large, it looked just as it did in more peaceful times. Her lips tensed up.

Maybe she could have Emeralda build the Gate back home in the sky above her house. They were due to meet up here anyway.

"I'll be back."

Her body slowly floated into the air, and soon she was off, flying toward a new destination far from her home village.

Judging by her map, the mystery area was located in a mountain glen covered in broad-leaf trees. She thought it was untouched by man at first, but apparently it served as a seasonal hunting ground as well. The remains of several settlements—inns and meat-processing houses, no doubt—could be seen at the base of the hill. They were abandoned and unmanned now, but she still managed to find a map in one of them that seemed to describe the path up the mountain.

She had pictured something of a secret forest sanctuary, but judging by the ledgers left in the abandoned inn she found, it actually played host to a fair number of hunters when the season rolled around. Perhaps her father was simply trying to enter the hunting-lease business when he wasn't busy with the harvest. Hopefully not just that, she thought—but given how many joint-controlled hunting cottages tended to dot land-leases like these, owning one of them could earn you some decent side income from the hunter's guilds.

"Maybe he was more of a businessman than I thought..."

These new insights, something she could only know about now that she was grown up, filled Emi with complex emotions.

"But he applied for a new field and a shed, didn't he? I don't see what that has to do with hunting..."

Regardless, it was the first real lead she had to go on. She had to go up and investigate for herself.

So she pushed her way into the mountain, only to find a narrow dirt trail that was a climbing path in name only. She wasn't expecting the kind of well-kept hiking paths you'd find in Japanese tourist sites, but it seemed to wind endlessly though the vast thickets that covered the mountain. Once the sun set, an amateur climber would have trouble figuring out whether he was going up or down, even. Even now, in the daylight, the trees in this primeval forest kept much light from getting through.

She could sense life all around her. No formal hunting had taken place since the Devil King's Army, so the path was blocked by foliage in many places. Large animals, the likes of which would never be spotted anywhere near Japan's public paths, often loomed ahead in the distance. It made the climbing effort seem to go on forever. Wild animals were nothing Emi couldn't easily handle, but she was the intruder here—she wanted to avoid hurting any innocent creatures she didn't have to.

"Maybe it'd be better if I scoped it out from above...or maybe not."

Emi wiped the sweat from her brow as she looked upward. The vibrant branches of all the deciduous trees surrounding her were what made this forest so dim. They would block any potential overhead view of the ground.

"I hope I can find this today," a nervous Emi told herself as she compared Emeralda's area map with the one she took from the inn.

The mountain was enormous, for one. For two, the permits described the plot of land in words only—and her current map offered no pertinent clues. Once the sun went down, she'd have to call off the search—and she couldn't camp out in this forest loaded with vicious beasts. She'd have to return to the base.

"The fifth checkpoint on the south face… That's still a lot of terrain to cover, and it's not like they maintained this path. There's no telling where that even is. I think I've gone up a fair distance, but…"

Emi had started her climb from the west, but it wasn't as though the cardinal directions were clearly marked on this mountain.

Then:

"Hmm? What is it? What's up all of a sudden? …Huh? You want to go out?"

Alas Ramus was calling for her in her mind.

"O-okay, okay, wait a minute… Oof!"

The act bewildered Emi, but she summoned Alas Ramus nonetheless. She tried to hang on to her, but the child was having nothing of it.

"This way, Mommy!" she said as she slipped out of Emi's hands and toddled forward.

"W-wait! Alas Ramus?!"

"Come on, Mommy! This way!"

The child almost sounded irritated as she turned back around, still proceeding down the narrow path. Emi didn't have to worry about losing her, at least, but it was still cause for surprise.

"Alas Ramus, wait a minute! Where're you going? Let me put some bug spray on you, at least…"

Emi had the children's insect repellent in hand as she hurried along the trail. She had the foresight to dress her in pants and a long-sleeved shirt, but there was no end of things to worry her. What if a mosquito found an open spot? What if all that running made her diaper fall out of position?

The only certain thing was that Alas Ramus was a girl on a mission. She seemed to know exactly where she was going, running through a forest that offered no notable landmarks to navigate by. It went on for what must have been fifteen minutes or so.

Finally, she stopped at the base of a large tree by the side of the trail.

"Wh-what was that about...?"

Emi managed to keep up with her well enough, giving her a chance to scope out the tree. It was large, certainly, but it was still just one out of the thousands of trees that enveloped this mountain. There was nothing special looking about it, no rare foliage or unusual size. There was only one difference from the others surrounding it.

"It's dead, huh?"

Looking up, Emi couldn't find a single leaf remaining on the branches that spread wide above. The moss and ivy growing around its trunk would never find purchase on a living tree.

"What's up with this tree, Alas Ramus?"

The little girl nodded at the question, looking up at the towering tree herself. "Here!" she said—and then she went inside the trunk.

"...Huh?"

It took a few moments for Emi to realize what had happened. With a faint light, Alas Ramus's tiny body was absorbed by the dead tree's trunk, like some kind of teleportation magic trick.

"A-Alas Ramus? H-hey, come back here!"

Emi tried to take the child back into her own body.

"...Alas Ramus? Hello...?"

But she didn't return. The Holy Silver that formed the sword within her showed no sign of coming back. Calling for her produced nothing but silence.

"Are... Are you kidding me? What's going on, Alas...?"

Just as Emi was about to go into full panic mode, she heard something.

"Mommy, you ready yet?"

Alas Ramus, looking completely unperturbed, stuck just her head out of the tree. A white, misty light formed the border between her body and the trunk of the tree, a little purple light coming out of her forehead.

"Alas Ramus!"

"Mommy, over here. You can go in. Hurry!"

Then she sunk her body back into the tree.

"What do you mean, I can go in...?"

The child was safe, but the flustered Emi didn't know what to do with her. Gingerly, she touched the tree's trunk.

"It's just a tree."

It felt exactly like a dead tree. Even when she applied a little force, there was no sign she could just waft through like Alas Ramus.

"A-Alas Ramus, come back! I can't go in there!"

This time, there was no response to her pleading.

"What are you...? What's even going on here...?"

Emi crouched down to examine the tree's base, where she last saw Alas Ramus. Touching it, it felt exactly the same as before. Then she realized something. The child's head glowed purple when she stuck her head out just now. That glow came from the Yesod fragment at her core.

"Is, is that what it is...?"

Alas Ramus and her Better Half sword were already inside the dead tree. That left two fragments for Emi to work with: the Cloth of the Dispeller and the one that used to be engraved on the sheath of the jeweled sword that belonged to Camio, the Devil Regent.

Emi took out a small bottle with the fragment inside, the keychain of sorts she had made with parts from Tokyu Hand not long ago. She instilled it with holy energy, not sure if it would work at all or not.

"Agh!"

She had only put in a little, fearful of angelic detection, but the fragment inside the bottle fired a beam of purple light straight into the middle of the tree trunk.

"Um, is this what you need?" Emi asked nervously as she placed a hand on the point it lit up. It went right through without any resistance.

"Ahhh...!"

At the same time, Emi felt a powerful force pulling her into the tree. In an instant, there was no more trace of her.

"Owww..."

Between the load on her back and the complete lack of resistance, Emi found herself tumbling to the ground in very un-Heroic fashion. The ground smelled earthen to her, wrinkling her face as she slowly rose.

The sight before her made Emi gasp. Beyond the light of the tree, there was a path. A rough one, trodden mostly by animals—but it was lined with well-kept trees at regular intervals, like a sidewalk in Tokyo. Nothing was natural about it.

"Hi, Mommy! Hurry!"

Alas Ramus was a little ways ahead, waving furiously at Emi. She was glad the child was safe, but her face hardened quickly afterward as she proceeded forward. Once she was sure Emi was on her way, Alas Ramus continued on.

This path had to be connected to her parents somehow. The mere fact that Alas Ramus and Emi's Yesod fragment sniffed it out was ample proof of that. Time seemed to pass here, just as it did outside the dead tree's light. Emi moved on, holding the Yesod fragment to her head like a flashlight in the darkness. It was a quiet trail—no birds, no insects, no other creatures—nothing to stay her pace for the next five or so minutes.

Once she did, she suddenly discovered an open space that housed a single small shed. The land next to it had been plowed—the remains of a field, perhaps. Several trees bearing edible fruit were planted in it, trees the likes of which Emi never spotted outside. Nobody was around, and it looked as though nobody had been for a fair while, but it still made Emi's heart race like it never had before during this trip.

The sun was already threatening to disappear entirely beneath the horizon. In its place, two moons and a fleet of bright stars were taking their places in the night sky, just as they would have outside. From their positions, Emi could tell she was on the mountain's south face, where her father's land was.

"Mommy?"

Alas Ramus was waiting at the shed door. Emi put the Yesod fragment in her pocket and walked up to her. "Alas Ramus," she found herself asking, "what is this?"

She had, after all, made a beeline for this shed from the outside—but the answer she had was beyond all expectation.

"It's not your house, Mommy?"

"…What made you think that?"

It sounded more like an accusation than a question. Emi hated herself for phrasing it that way.

This was something she constantly thought about—why Alas Ramus called her "Mommy" in the first place. She had likely been born in the Devil's Castle that Maou built in the Central Continent. The only link between her and Emi was the other Yesod fragment Emi happened to possess. And yet she was "Mommy."

She had no idea the answer to that concern would come at her so suddenly.

"It smells like you, Mommy."

The answer felt all too cruel to Emi.

"It…smells like me…?"

The sky seemed so high above, the view from this mountain face so wide and majestic. But it all made Emi's heart wither. Just as it had on the day she was separated from her dear, beloved father.

"…Um, Alas Ramus?"

"Yehh?"

"Could you tell me what…Mommy's name is?"

"Mommy's name?"

Alas Ramus gave Emi a quizzical look for a moment, then opened her mouth.

"Laila."

When Alas Ramus had dropped down on Villa Rosa Sasazuka, she immediately called Maou her "Daddy" on the spot. But when asked who "Mommy" was, all she did was point at Emi.

Emi recalled the scant few months she had spent with Alas Ramus. She had called her "Mommy," but not once had she ever called her by her given name.

There was, of course, no doubt that Emi was the "Mommy" that Alas Ramus loved with all her heart. But from the moment she came to Japan, "Laila" had been watching Emi from behind her back.

And if Satan, the Devil King, was "Daddy" to Alas Ramus... If Emi's mother Laila was "Mommy" to her...

"It was my mother...who saved him back then..."

It involved the past of Sadao Maou, the past he discussed with her on the Ferris wheel in Tokyo Big-Egg Town. She had already suspected it at that point, but having it thrust out like this made it a herculean effort to even remain upright. Her knees shook.

"That...stupid Devil King," came the shaky voice, pointed at a nonexistent Maou. "The hell do you mean, 'nobody you know'?"

That was the answer Maou had when Emi asked who saved his life in his early years: "Nobody you know." No, she didn't know her mother. She didn't even know Laila, this angel. The only thing she did know was that this Laila was the only mother she had.

"All this pain... It's like everyone's been seeing through me. Like they're trying to make it easier."

But no matter how much she moaned about it, everything Emi had seen up to this moment led her to a single truth: Her mother had saved the young Devil King Satan's life, Satan grew up and invaded Ente Isla, and so indirectly, she was responsible for ruining the happiness, the very lives, of Emi herself, her father, and countless others.

"I..."

Emi wasn't stupid enough to attempt to shoulder all the blame for everything her mother did, unbeknownst to her. Laila's motivations remained a question mark to her—and to Maou, back on Earth—but she couldn't have been operating without a script. So what purpose was there to rescuing a young Satan?

"..."

"Mommy, what is it?"

Emi turned her eyes down upon Alas Ramus—the child born from a Yesod fragment that Laila had given to Maou. Maybe she did that to ensure Alas Ramus was born in this world. But not only was Maou totally oblivious to Alas Ramus's existence until somewhat recently—he barely even recalled having the fragment.

"But..."

She recalled the day she, Emeralda, Albert, and Olba stormed Devil's Castle on the Central Continent.

The purple light her holy sword emitted was a guiding light, she thought, leading her directly to her ultimate destiny. The legend of this light had been passed down across generations in the Church, linked to the Holy Silver that formed her sword and Cloth. Now, she knew that the light was simply the pre–Alas Ramus Yesod fragment pulling Emi's own toward it.

"...Huh?"

Thinking things over this far, Emi stumbled upon another discovery. The "guiding light" of Church tradition was simply the side effect of two Yesod fragments attracting each other. What would have happened, then, if Emi had slain the Devil King back on that day?

"Would I ever have run into you?"

"Oo?"

Emi peered intently at Alas Ramus's forehead.

If she had killed Satan with her sword and that guiding light didn't meekly fade away afterward, it likely would've blown Emi's mind at the time. It would've turned everything she had been taught upside down—she would've kept following the light. And if she did, and tracked it down to Alas Ramus's fragment...

"Would we have...fused like this, then?"

The fusion between the Better Half and Alas Ramus was just a happy accident that took place during her battle against Gabriel on Earth—or so she had thought. But thinking about it—Alas Ramus had taken her sword, crumpled it up, and eaten it, all of her own volition. Two fragments attracting each other, just like Alas Ramus had attracted her sword and Cloth back there.

"My mother Laila...scattering all these broken fragments around... But is she trying to bring them back together over time?"

For what?

Come to think of it, Emi had no idea what the Yesod Sephirah even looked like—its size or its shape. There was no way to tell how many fragments there were. And if the Sephirah was torn apart by unknown means, there was no telling who could have done the task, and how. These were jewels fabled to form the cores of entire worlds—could you really make one shatter, like a porcelain coffee mug?

Not even Laila, Emi thought, was brash enough to do all of this by herself from the start. The presence of a single unclaimed fragment was enough to make the guardian angel Gabriel and archangel Sariel go into a frenzy to track it down. She had to have an accomplice—and if so, it had to be someone in heaven, someone close to her.

But who?

Based on the events Raguel triggered at Tokyo Tower, Laila was clearly no longer welcome in the heavenly realm. Unfortunately, though, the only similar case Emi could think of was the fallen angel Lucifer, better known these days as Hanzou Urushihara.

Hang on, though...

"...Nah. No way."

Emi felt safe dismissing the idea out of hand. Not because

Urushihara was so different from the other angels, nor because he lived like an unemployed college dropout. It was that, if he was aiding and abetting Laila's little Yesod game, he would've reacted a lot differently to Emi's sword and Alas Ramus.

She had fought Lucifer on the Western Island and in Sasazuka with the Better Half, and on both occasions, Lucifer didn't act like the Better Half was anything besides this really powerful weapon the humans had. When Alas Ramus showed up at the Devil's Castle in Sasazuka, it seemed as though he was just as harried by the group's new child-rearing responsibilities as Maou and Ashiya.

"So somebody I don't know...?"

Emi sighed. She was running out of threads to traverse. But this experience was still fruitful for her.

If Laila was the one who saved the young Satan—Maou—that meant she was active all the way over in the demon realms. There might be other fragments over there. And if her mission was to bring the fragments back together (Emi couldn't guess why yet), the Church tales surrounding the holy sword and Cloth of the Dispeller were lies, retellings of the truth packaged by Laila over her long life in a way humans could more easily digest.

And more than anything else:

"My father knew all of it."

The memories granted to Chiho. Of her father, and of a second holy sword.

When the Church arrived to take Emi away before her village was destroyed, Nord told her that her mother was still alive, somewhere. And even without that evidence, there was simply no way into this realm she was in now without a Yesod fragment. That alone proved Nord knew everything about Laila his whole life.

He must've applied for those permits simply as a pretense, so he'd have a provable motive for bringing the farming tools and construction equipment he needed into the mountain. Whether he actually intended to use this field and shed or not, the village and its governing baron didn't care. If he paid his taxes, all was well. They wouldn't bother sending an inspector to survey such a tiny strip of land yearly, either. Even if they did, all a normal person would find was uncleared forestland with a dead tree in it. They'd assume Nord failed to cultivate it, and that would be that.

"That…and now I know something else, too."

Emi reflected back on the single path she traced on her way to the dead tree.

"My mother was the one who really 'made' this place."

Her father was no master-level sorcerer—that much she was sure of. Even if he was, not even Emeralda could likely build a space locked away to everyone except Yesod fragment holders. So:

"I need to comb this place. There's got to be some secret behind my parents to find here."

She had discovered no answer, no shining path out of the complex maze of truths she was lost in. But she couldn't lie down and say uncle now. She had an enormous hint dangling in front of her.

"'Nobody I know,' huh…?"

Emi realized that, as she traversed that maze of thoughts, the shaking in her body had stopped.

"I haven't discovered anything yet… Not the truth, at least."

She didn't need to wallow in despair yet. Not until she found her answer.

"Well, better start by ransacking this shed, I guess!" she shouted, drumming herself forward in an attempt to brighten her mood. "Let's go, Alas… Um, Alas Ramus?"

She was out of sight again.

"Alas Ramus! Where are you?"

No answer.

"Oh no!"

This was steppe land poised on top of a steep mountainside. There were no fences keeping people from toppling over the far edge. Emi's face turned pale. Did she fall off while she wasn't paying attention? There was no concern about her wandering far away, and Alas Ramus could fly whenever she wanted to anyway, but could she exercise those powers when she needed to? That was hard to say. But if she hurt herself off the steppe…

Emi stepped behind the shed to kick off her search. It didn't take long.

"Oh, is that where you were?"

She spotted the girl from behind as she stood in place. It made her breathe a sigh of relief.

"Come on, Alas Ramus. Time to go back inside."

No response.

"Alas Ramus? What is it?"

Still no response. Emi walked up to her, only to discover what Alas Ramus was staring at.

"Did they plant something here?"

The passage of time had led to all manner of weeds covering it, but on the ground before Alas Ramus was a visible depression, as though someone had buried something large down below.

"...Aceth."

"Hmm? What is it?"

"...Aceth...Aceth!"

"Huh?"

"Mommy...where's Aceth?"

"Um, Aceth?"

"Aceth! Where's Aceth?" she shouted, staring right at the depression. "Mommy, Aceth! Here! Aceth was here! But she's gone! Why?!"

"H-hey, calm down a second, Alas Ramus! Who's Aceth...?"

Emi couldn't hide her concern for the child's sudden transformation. But she could tell something important was about to happen. Whenever Alas Ramus grew this talkative, whenever she started using this unfamiliar terminology, whenever she exhibited these sudden mood swings...

It always had to do with the Sephirah.

She tried her best to divine the proper name Alas Ramus was having trouble pronouncing correctly.

"Alas Ramus? When you say 'Aceth'... do you mean Acieth Alla?"

The term had appeared from her father's memories in the field, the ones replayed from Laila to Chiho and from Chiho to her. Nord said it himself. Acieth Alla. The "Bladed Wing," in the Centurient language. Emi had assumed it was the name of the "other holy sword" she had heard about.

But now Alas Ramus had just used it. Called it a "she." Said she was "here."

And Emi had already seen someone, or something, of the same nature as Alas Ramus before. It was Erone, a child born from the Sephirah known as Gevurah. So what was Acieth Alla, this presence with the same "wing" reference in her name as Alas Ramus?

"What's the name of the child born from the Yesod Sephirah?"

"Aceth! I came from it! Aceth! Where's Aceth?!"

Alas Ramus all but cried out for someone, or something, that wasn't there.

If Maou could be believed here, Alas Ramus would have been born from a Yesod fragment buried in soil. Emi could easily imagine the fragment that formed Acieth Alla being buried under this depression. And considering how much time had passed since anyone had been here:

"Alas Ramus… I'm sorry, but I don't think she's here anymore—"

"No! Mommy, find Aceth! I smell Aceth! She's here!"

"Please, Alas Ramus, calm down. I'm sure Acieth went off somewhere, just like Erone did."

Alas Ramus wasn't having any of it. She had demonstrated her own will before, deactivating the Better Half by herself against Emi's will during the encounter with Erone. But now, as she sought Acieth Alla's presence, she seemed even more severe with Emi.

"Mommy, please, Aceth…"

"Alas Ramus…"

She was no normal toddler, to be sure, but never before had Alas Ramus been so stubborn with Emi. She couldn't figure out what to do with her, so she reached out for her, attempting to pick her up and give her a reassuring hug.

"Mommy!"

For reasons only she knew, Alas Ramus used her tiny hands to grasp both of Emi's outstretched arms.

"Let's look together!"

"Huh? Together... Huh?! Wh-whoa, Alas...!"

Emi was in no position to stop her. Alas Ramus's forehead gradually glowed brighter and brighter, creating a purple moon in the air.

"Aceeeettthhh!!"

With that scream, Emi's vision was bathed in purple and white.

"Wh-why did this have to happen?!" Emi shouted as she tore down the mountain. She had to get out of there, as soon as possible. Her mind couldn't decide whether to abandon her belongings or not, but her body was frantically taking her downhill, her head warily watching the skies above.

Alas Ramus couldn't have been more reckless. Amid her screaming for Acieth Alla, she had manifested Emi's Better Half sword—at its final, most powerful level, now that Emi was back in Ente Isla. Holy magic, at a level she had never felt before, flowed out of it, and the circle of Yesod light that shot up from the spot could've easily been spotted from several dozen miles away.

Now was no time to worry about her knapsack. Or, really, about her regrouping with Emeralda. The Better Half, and Alas Ramus's outburst, emitted a shocking amount of energy—and Emi didn't like her chances that it would go undetected by anyone. So she ran. Without having a chance to explore either the shed or the flat space that surrounded it.

Everybody currently opposing her in the struggle over Yesod fragments now knew who she really was, and where she came from. There would be no going back to Sloane for her.

"...Not here. Aceth not here. Why...?"

Alas Ramus was bawling inside Emi's mind. Such a burst of holy energy, even in a land as vast as Ente Isla, would have picked up on other Yesod fragments—apparently she couldn't find any reaction from Acieth Alla's.

"Mommy, I'm sorry... I'm sorry."

Then the child must've grasped what she had just done. She apologized to Emi again and again, voice still strained from the tears.

"It's fine, all right? I'm not angry with you! It's not your fault, Alas Ramus!"

Emi blindly leaped from the smaller cliffs, letting the branches of passing trees slap her in the face and body, all but snapping them in half as she ran downward.

"Acieth Alla's just as important to you as Erone and Malchut, isn't she?"

"...Yeh."

"You've been aching to see her for ages, haven't you?! You've been alone all that time! Ever since you got separated from the tree of Sephirot!"

"...Yeh."

"...I'm with you, okay? Mommy's with you!"

"Mommy...too?"

"Yes! ...Ugh, screw this!"

Emi had had enough of her knapsack. It slowed her down too much. She tossed it, and everything inside, to the ground. Not having to carry around Alas Ramus's baby stuff, as well as the best camping gear and food modern Japan could offer, gave her an extra burst of speed as she continued downward. The only real "equipment" she had left was the smartphone in her pants pocket, meant for Idea Link communication with Suzuno and Chiho in Japan.

"I was alone all that time, too... I spent all that time searching. Because even if she's my enemy...even if I hate her enough to kill her...I still want to see her!!"

It was as though Emi's screaming was what allowed her to zoom down the mountain at superhuman speed. The trail began to widen for her, the slope growing easier to handle. Before long, they were back at the hunter's inn. There, making sure no one was near, she deployed Heavenly Fleet Feet and started to run. The skies, the land, it didn't matter. Any destination was fine, as long as it wasn't related to her past.

No more meeting up with Emeralda. No more keeping her promise to Chiho. No more returning to Japan, even. But Emi still couldn't chide Alas Ramus for what she had done. She didn't want to. Because there was someone she wanted to see. Someone she didn't have to hide her true nature from. Someone who knew the real her.

Outside of her involvement with the Tree of Sephirot, Alas Ramus acted like any other toddler would. There was no way to yell at her about it. Not when Emi considered how long she had been all alone in that Yesod fragment core—since back when Devil King Satan was barely a newborn.

Right now, she had to get away before the "enemy" found her. She could beat any enemy she ran into—but if Ente Isla was the battlefield, her foes would likely be much stronger than they were in Japan, just like how it worked with her. Depending on who showed up, she might not be able to go easy on them—and that would neatly broadcast to all of Ente Isla that the Hero Emilia was here. It would intensify the struggle over Emi and her Better Half, making it even more of a violent confrontation than before.

Emeralda and Albert would have to become involved. And the Church wouldn't be an idle spectator, either. Once their leaders knew Emilia was back, the fallout might prove to threaten Suzuno back on Earth. And if she was in danger, then Chiho, Rika, and everyone else in Japan were dramatically more so.

If she ran into the enemy right now, that was it. There would no longer be any safe space for Emi and Alas Ramus, either in Japan or in Ente Isla. There would be no discovering the truth, or attending birthday parties, after that.

For now, she had to hide. So she ran. Even if the "enemy" found her, she couldn't let the public discover her.

Then she stopped.

"What...?!"

It was just as she tried to cross the central plaza in front of the inn...

"Mommy...?"

Emi had no words for the nervous question.

The air was shimmering across the entirety of the inn's length, like a hole in the air or a crack in the ground. The very space was crumbling before her, like a dilapidated cityscape.

"A Gate…"

Emi gritted her teeth. She was out of time. The enemy had the slip on her. She had never expected they'd use a Gate and this massive array of fighters to pursue a simple Yesod fragment.

The first to emerge from the giant crack in the air was a group clad in the armor of Efzahan's knight corps from the Eastern Island. They all wore armbands of light green inside a white frame, identifying them as Knights of the Inlain Jade Scarves. They surrounded her from all sides like she was an escaped animal, keeping their distance as they pointed spears at her.

"Ngh…"

Emi raised her hands up, attempting to summon her Better Half even as Alas Ramus was still sobbing inside. She was stopped by a voice among the Jade legion:

"It'd be better for your health if you stopped, Emilia."

She stopped breathing.

"Yes, you could easy annihilate both myself and all the soldiers you see before you. But…"

"But somethin' tells me you'd regret it afterward, huh?"

Two men, looking markedly different from each other, stepped out from the squadron. One was an old man sporting a tonsure and a stiff, rigid robe. The other was a younger man wearing a leather jacket with English lettering and a hairstyle that could only be described as an Afro.

"Olba…" Emi begrudgingly groaned. "Raguel…!"

"Ahh, quit acting so scared, lady!" Raguel shrugged. "We can't really just stroll on over here unprepared after that light show you just busted out, y'know? Of course we're gonna open a Gate."

"Indeed. We wouldn't want to be…beaten to the punch."

Olba flashed an inscrutable smile—just as he had when he traveled alongside Emi; just as he had when he stood before her at Sasazuka as her enemy.

She glared at the tonsured head and the Afro.

"...So what's a traitorous archbishop and the angel of judgment doing here with all these Efzahan lackeys? That team-up makes absolutely no sense to me."

"What do you think, lady?" the wholly unaffected Raguel fired back, answering the question with another, more disparaging one.

"Well," Emi began, sizing up her foes, "if the Church and the heavens want me to join the struggle to free Efzahan from Barbariccia's control, I might be willing to listen to you."

Olba and Raguel paused, flashing surprised glances at each other.

"I would say," Olba intoned, "you're closer than you think."

"What do you mean?"

"Yeah," Raguel said, interrupting the current staredown, "well, we're not exactly here to strip your Yesod fragments from you, like I was in Japan. Assuming you're willing to cooperate, that is. The situation's changed a little bit, so... Emilia Justina, we need you to join us in Efzahan."

"No, thanks," Emi instantly replied.

Olba and Raguel, expecting this, didn't move an inch.

"Why not, if you don't mind me asking?"

"Ask your own heart. Try to recall what you guys did to Japan. You're willing to do all kinds of evil deeds for the sake of your mission, hurting untold numbers of people along the way. How could you guys ever dare to claim you're legitimate?"

"Mm," rumbled Olba. "I see. Stands to reason, I suppose."

"Yeah, can't really make excuses about that. But you're still gonna have to come with us, all right? We can't really take no for an answer."

"Say whatever you will. I'm already booked for the month. If you wanna keep having these stupid playground squabbles, go invite the Devil King to join you if you want."

Then Emi unleashed her Better Half, a physical personification of her iron will.

"You're right, Olba. If I truly wanted to, I could wipe all of you off the planet. I have no reason to hesitate doing that. Get out of my way. If you do..."

Emi was a hairsbreadth away from readying her sword for battle. She never made it.

"What's that...?"

Suddenly, the air around them began to vibrate. It was as though somebody had set off an explosion, far away—but they couldn't see any such destruction in the visible area. But Emi could feel it. It was far to the west, in the direction of her hometown of Sloane.

"Dark... Is that demonic energy?!"

It was nothing angelic, or human, in nature. Only a denizen of the demon realms could wield it. And the shock waves from the explosion made it all the way from Sloane's direction.

Raguel, realizing that Emi had sensed it, flashed a distressingly sinister smile—one no angel should ever show.

"You ever heard of Draghi...um, something? I can never remember the whole thing. You know...from the Malebranche?"

He made a great show out of turning his gaze toward Sloane.

"I told him that the Great Demon General Malacoda met his end around this area. He insisted on joining me. Kept going on about revenge, you know?"

"...No..."

The color drained from Emi's face.

"I told him not to get violent here. This is the Western Island, and I can't have him getting killed by the Saint Aile knight corps. They don't know anything about this, besides. But...you know, if you aren't willing to listen to us...I can't be so sure he'll listen to me, huh?"

It was such a childish threat to lob at the Hero Emilia and all her boundless strength. Naturally, Olba saw fit to expand upon it:

"The Malebranche are demons," he said. "They cannot hope to harness much dark force here on the Western Island, now that it has started to rebuild. But he certainly has enough strength to render a certain abandoned, forgotten village nonexistent."

It was doubtful Emi would ever forget the devil Olba exposed from his heart then, as he addressed her, even if it was hidden behind his expressionless face.

"Emilia. If I recall, your one dream in life was to restore your father's fields, was it not?"

"O...Olba, you...how could you be so...?!"

"I actually paid a visit over there just now. Your father must have been cultivating some very hardy strains, wasn't he?"

The tip of the holy sword shrank back, its power draining.

"Well?" Raguel asked. She couldn't answer. Her mind raced, but she just couldn't come up with anything. Even if she shook Raguel and Olba off and shot herself over to Sloane, destroying a field and a human dwelling would be about as challenging for them as flicking a speck of dust off Raguel's jacket.

Olba would have known Emi's residence. She had showed it to him when they stopped by Sloane on the way to defeating Satan. There was only a little wheat left then, and without her father around she assumed there was no hope, that the field would never grow back again. The ensuing dreams she had on Earth made her cry every time—the smell of the wheat, the golden hue, the calm, peaceful life she had with her father in her homeland.

A single tear fell from her eye.

"I, I..."

The name of the Hero was a symbol of hope for all mankind. The true mark of justice. That was what she was told, and it rewarded her with nothing but a bloodstained past. But her companions—Emeralda, Albert, and Olba—all realized that her true motivation for fighting the Devil King's Army was gaining revenge for her father.

Then, in the morning light, she saw the frozen moment of her childhood spring into action again. She gained hope that her father might be alive. Hope that the wheat she had raised with him might survive. Hope that she could move on from the tearful moment she was separated from him. Now, it was all falling apart.

Revenge would have been easy. Whether they torched the field or not, she could have flown into a rage of hatred and tore apart Olba, Raguel, the Jade Scarves, and the Malebranche undoubtedly stationed in Sloane. But that would be the end of it. There would be nothing else for her.

It was just some wheat in a field. But to Emi, it was a ray of hope, one that she had placed her dreams upon from a young age, hoping against hope that it could all come back.

It was all too easy to break Emi's heart.

"What...should I do?"

Was this the heart of the Hero who had saved the world from oblivion?

As if to symbolize the meltdown, the Better Half in her hand shrank down until it was smaller than even when she deployed it in Japan, before finally disappearing.

"We told you, lady! Just follow us, and it'll all be good."

"...If I follow you, will you leave my village alone?"

"Of course. And like I said before, we're not tryin' to hurt you or anything. I'm just sayin', if you do anything weird like resist us or run back to Japan or whatever, that might not be the case any—"

"...I'm not going to do that."

"Oh? Well, lovely." Raguel and Olba gave each other satisfied smiles and raised their arms in an at-ease signal to the squadron.

"You ready, then?"

Emi nodded, meekly walking toward the Gate. For just a moment, right at the lip of the portal, she glanced back at the mountain she had just run down.

"...I'm sorry," she whispered into the air, before following Raguel's lead into the light of the Gate.

THE DEVIL MAKES EVERY PREPARATION POSSIBLE

"I told you, I have no idea how many days this will take!"

"We have one week! I can't spend this much on stuff I'll only use for one week!"

"And how is that my fault? What are you intending to do if this takes more than one week, pray tell? We need to prepare for, and invest in, a potential long-term operation!"

"See, that's how you always are! Always thinking in worst-case scenarios! It's not about taking more than one week—it's the fact that we're gonna do this in one week in the first place! You gotta do the job in the time you're given!"

"What kind of sane person would schedule a time limit he has no chance of sticking to?! If bold words and idealism were enough to finish up your work, life would be far easier for all of us!"

"Look, I'm just saying you can't get everything that you want! There's only so much we can prep for! Maybe politicians can get away with padding their own budgets, but I can't!"

"If you start dictating what we can and can't have, you'll cut out everything we absolutely must have over there! If you're going to keep screaming 'streamline, streamline, streamline,' I can buy a parrot to do that for me, thank you!"

"What?!"

"What, 'what'?"

"Ughh! You're being too loud, you guys! Stop arguing so much!"

From Chiho's perspective, it sounded like the extension of some ongoing, meandering debate about consumerism and modern society. Which she didn't mind. Her issue was with their choice of forums—the camping-equipment section at the Donkey OK shop in Hounancho, about half an hour's walk from Sasazuka.

The spark that set off this latest argument was simplicity itself. If they wanted to travel through Efzahan while avoiding capture at the hands of forces from the Eight Scarves, Maou and his companion could never dare stay in a large town. They would likely be camping out most of the time, and they had come here to make the necessary preparations—but when it came to how they would camp out, Suzuno and Maou had some very apparent differences in opinion.

"Look, it'll just be three of us over there! It'd be easier for all of us if we just buy a single tent! The fewer things we have to abandon if we're attacked, the better!"

"Fah! Such nonsense! We require two tents and one sleeping bag for each of us! We have a need to keep our bodies in tip-top shape, and besides, Acieth and I are women! How could we possibly share a single cramped tent with the likes of you?!"

Between the amount of weight they'd be transporting on their scooters and the strict one-week time limit he had assigned to the mission, Maou firmly believed that one tent would be enough. Suzuno, on the other hand, was focused on bodily stress—and, for that matter, not having to share a roof with Maou.

"I-I think she's right!" interjected Chiho, just as eager to keep Maou from sharing sleeping space with the opposite sex. "It's not good to sleep with girls in the same bed like that, Maou!"

"Oh, you think I'm gonna choose this moment to molest you guys? Geez! I thought I was something more to you than that!"

"Y-yeah! He's right! Maou is a real gentleman!"

"Chiho, can you please pick a side and stick with it?"

"S-sorry," a carried-away Chiho replied.

"And it is not a matter of him being more to me, or less to me, than anything! We are talking about a man who works every day of his life yet still lacks the money to purchase so much as a simple canvas tent!"

"Hey, not everyone gets to live the rich Tokyo socialite lifestyle you got, all right? I got mouths to feed back home!"

"'Mouths to feed'? You actually consider people like Lucifer your family? Such a nasty man!"

"...Look, getting back to the point, one tent's really all we need for this. Once we regroup with Emi, we'll have to open up a Gate right on the spot and duck outta Ente Isla anyway! If we don't, we lose!"

"Have you lost your mind?! Operating a Gate is impossibly complex! You make it seem as arduous as hailing a taxi, but it is far more difficult! And what if Emilia and her charge are in no shape to move when we find them? There's no guarantee we will even be able to open a Gate on the spot. We may need to conceal ourselves, and for that, we will absolutely need multiple tents!!"

"I… Well, can we at least go with these summer sleeping bags, then? They're cheap, they're compact, they're perfect!"

"Ente Isla is entering the latter half of its autumn! The temperatures might flirt with freezing, or worse! Rescue will be the last thing on our minds if we catch a virus!"

Any further progress seemed unlikely to Chiho. She decided to guide them in another direction.

"Uh, uhhhhhmm," she began. "Uh, hey, so can we drop the tent debate for now and just focus on buying all the other stuff you need? Maybe we can figure out the tents once we know how much everything else weighs!"

"Devil King! I told you, we have strict limits on the load we bring along! What are you expecting to do with all of that mineral water? We need to bring our own gasoline along, I remind you!"

"Hey, I'm not who I used to be, okay? I'm human! What if the bugs in the water over there screw up my stomach real bad?"

"You pathetic excuse for a demon! The water in Efzahan is among the purest in the land, and the food there is equally abundant! There are thousands of rivers and natural springs we can rely on for water—this filter and storage tank will suit our needs perfectly!"

The water argument raged on. The topic of food was proving just as fruitless...

"Rice, okay?"

"No. Udon noodles."

"Udon over the campfire? Are you serious?"

"More serious than you know. An amateur like you would be hopeless, attempting to cook rice with camping tools. A supply of dried instant udon is easily prepared, takes little time to cook, and is lightweight to boot. Truly, the ideal for us."

"If you're gonna go to that extreme, why don't we just go with protein bars or army rations or whatever? We ain't gonna be there that long."

"Food lies at the core of any expedition. There is no need to go into survival mode with our meals from the beginning, unless it proves necessary to do so."

"Well, okay, but udon?"

...and although things were slightly rosier in the field of insect repellent...

"We will need some insect spray, Devil King."

"I hear you there. I'm sure there's a ton of bugs out there at night."

...they were slightly bumpier when it came to light sources:

"We must bring a fuel lantern!"

"No! I want an LED lantern!"

"There are oil-powered lanterns in Ente Isla as well. If we are forced to abandon our belongings, that will lower the chances of them tracking us down!"

"But it'll just make more stuff for us to carry around. We can turn a battery-powered one on and off with the flick of a switch! See? You charge 'em with this crank and it'll even charge your cell phone for you!"

"A fuel lantern or nothing! We can procure extra lantern oil in Ente Isla, and that will save us precious cargo weight! If you need to charge your phone that badly, bring along an external battery! And...and it hardly even matters anyway! Your phone can serve only as an Idea Link amplifier in Ente Isla, so it matters not a bit whether it is charged or not! Your obsession with battery power is utterly baffling to me!"

"There's nothing baffling about it! An LED lantern's a billion times more useful! Or don't tell me you're afraid of using an electronic device as simple as this one!"

"What?! How could you let science and civilization poison you so deeply?! And you dare to still call yourself Devil King?!"

"...Stop! Can you guys just stop already?!"

"Whoa!"

"Uhh!"

Despite it all, it was Chiho who finally lost her temper first.

"Guys, I think we've made one thing pretty clear here, okay? Neither of you have any camping experience, do you?"

"I, uh..."

Maou distractedly scratched at one of his cheeks.

"C-camping, well," Suzuno reluctantly added, "it was usually our monks-in-training who handled the particulars of our missionary caravans, so..."

"Well, if you don't know anything about camping, then you're just wasting your time without a concrete picture in your mind! It'd be a lot easier for all of us if we just asked the staff! That or go to a specialty camping store and have an expert make a plan for us!"

"...Okay," the crestfallen Maou and Suzuno replied in unison.

"Ooh, Chiho! Very strong!"

Suddenly, Maou's body began to glow a shade of purple—and at the next instant, there was a silver-and-purple-haired girl next to him, where there was empty space a moment ago.

"I notice now," she said, "but Maou, he is no match for the women, yes?"

"Aghh!"

Maou and Suzuno furtively looked around, spooked by Acieth's sudden entry into the scene. Nobody else was around them. That came as a relief—but Chiho's face was clearly strained as she looked at the ceiling.

"Ummm, guys! Guys! Let's get out of here right now!"

The other three followed Chiho out, question marks above each of their heads.

"You have to be more careful, okay?" Chiho spat out once they were outside. "There was a security camera focused right where we were."

Considering the extreme care Emi took whenever summoning Alas Ramus or putting her away, Maou was being completely irresponsible with his own charge.

"Y-yeah… Sorry. Hey, Acieth, I thought I told you that you can't go in and out by yourself…"

"I had not considered the presence of such cameras," Suzuno admitted. "Well spotted, Chiho. You are truly a member of the modern generation."

"Ooh! Chiho! So nice!"

"If Suzuki was around to see this, I think she'd start doubting whether you're really the Devil King or not…"

Chiho found herself sighing at the three astonished faces looking at her.

"Oh! Suzuno, did you ask Yusa what kind of preparations she made for her trip? We could use that as a guide once we start browsing around a real camping store."

"Hmm… Hard to say. Emilia had Emeralda making the arrangements. She was planning to travel alone once she arrived, however. I suppose it depends on her plans for Alas Ramus."

In other words, Suzuno didn't know.

"…Well, let's just go somewhere else," Chiho replied as she took the lead. "We could try Tokyu Hand, or I'm sure there's a camping equipment store somewhere downtown. I think we could use some expert guidance right about now. We're kinda short on time, too."

She took a glance at the three people meekly following her. It made a question pop up in her mind. Once Emi safely came back, what then? Rika was taking this calmly enough, or at least acting like she was, but would she forgive Emi for essentially lying to her face during their entire friendship? She had gone directly to work after their chat at Devil's Castle, claiming she was on the clock for that day. The conflicted look on her face as she left remained an unaddressed concern to Chiho.

Watching Maou and Suzuno continue their debate from Donkey OK behind her, she realized all over again what a unique position she was currently in.

"Juggling different cultures like this is so difficult...but even if Yusa and Ashiya come back..."

She spotted the sun getting blocked by the clouds above, symbolizing the current state of her heart.

"I wonder...how long we'll all get to stay together..."

Nobody in the world could hear the barely audible whisper.

✳

"Thank you for calling today!"

""""Thank you for calling today!!"""""

"Bringing orders to customers quickly and accurately!"

""""Bringing orders to customers quickly and accurately!!"""""

"MgRonald Delivery!"

""""MgRonald Delivery!!"""""

"...And those are the basic keywords, I suppose."

Kisaki's cold eyes scanned the papers in front of her.

The crew of MgRonald's Hatagaya station store—Maou and Chiho included—were reciting the lines in front of Kisaki in the staff room, faces taut as they awaited their boss's next command.

"Well, this won't be in operation for a while to come yet, but you guys are gonna be my main weapons for the time being, so I'm handing training manuals out to you all now. Brush up on what's written in there for me."

Maou gave the small stack of copied sheets handed to him an earnest look.

"You can also go to stores where it's in operation for training purposes; I can pay you all hourly helper compensation for that. Anyone interested, you can talk to me later. There's not much of an open period available, though, so the sooner, the better."

"Y-yes, ma'am!!"

"Oh, and I know I don't need to remind any of you about this…" Kisaki rapped a finger against her copy of the manual and shrugged. "But it's a given around here that everything we provide, we provide with sincerity. I believe that all of you here, in this room with me right now, aren't the type of greenhorns who think they have to recite this manual by memory in order to provide that sincerity. Let's make this day another well-fought battle, all right? Back to work!"

Maou stole another look at his copy of the manual as the team members shuffled away from the meeting. He would've killed for one of the on-site training sessions Kisaki mentioned, but—painfully, for him—he still had yet to obtain a motor-scooter license. It'd be hard to train very well without one…and aside from that, he wouldn't even be at work (or on the planet) during the available period.

After navigating a gauntlet of shift juggling and favor promising, he had finally managed to obtain the time he needed for his renewed conquest of Ente Isla. He'd owe nearly every crewmember at the Hatagaya store for it once he returned, but it spoke volumes about his job dedication and his close relationships with his coworkers that so many of them agreed to take on shifts for him, albeit very grudgingly at times. It was nothing he could've engineered by going it alone this whole time.

"Maou…are you sure you'll be all right?" asked Chiho, perhaps concerned over Maou's conflicted staredown of the manual.

"Yeah, I'm sure. Kinda sucks that I can't attend any training, though. Like, no way I'd fail that exam again, but I'll pretty much be going by the seat of my pants once delivery starts."

"Oh? ...Oh." Chiho blinked, not quite expecting this response, then emitted a smile of relief. "Well, I'm glad you're still the same old you, at least."

"Huh?"

"I thought you'd be a lot more nervous about tonight."

"...Oh. Right." Maou smiled with Chiho. He knew what she meant.

Once he was off duty tonight, he would be making his way to Ueno—in other words, he'd be departing for Ente Isla. It would have to be late night, since this was the one shift he simply couldn't weasel out of, no matter how hard he tried. He had to pick up that manual, at the very least.

"I mean," he continued, "once we're over there, it's gonna be a pretty simple job. We go over, we pick up Emi and everyone, we go back. If we get any interference, we'll just have to send 'em running."

His face sagged a bit.

"Over here, though, it ain't gonna be so easy with this delivery stuff. I'm not really handy with the maps we'll need to use yet. We have to get the food delivered before it turns cold, but there's all kinds of traffic rules we'll have to stick to, too. Red lights, speed limits, hook turns..."

"Guess it's a lot of rules for someone like you, huh, Maou?"

Only in Japan would the Devil King, capable of free flight for the past several centuries, need to worry about how to handle right turns in a legal manner. Chiho smiled at how silly it all seemed.

"Plus, dealing with customers over the phone... You see how much it takes out of Emi, even, y'know? It's not like I relish dealing with the weirder characters we get in here. And I guess there's some kind of freaky meter or monitor attached to the scooters the company's giving us. Like, what if it spots that I got lost somewhere and docks me points for that on some evaluation system? I'd be so scared of that, I wouldn't know what to do. Geez, I wish I could attend the training!"

"Ah-ha-ha..."

Even with all her concern, not being able to join him in Ente Isla, she couldn't help but laugh at him.

"Hey, it's not that funny! I tell you, it's a hell of a lot easier if you're allowed to do whatever you want when you're dealing with people. Human society puts up all these barriers to that. It's a huge pain."

"So once you rule over Japan as Devil King, are you gonna get rid of all that?"

"...You're doing that on purpose, aren't you, Chi?"

"Yes."

Maou sighed at her shameless poke.

"It just kinda sucks that I have these things I'm worried about, and I can't deal with them before I have to go, y'know? Have a little sympathy."

"Well," the undeterred Chiho replied, "keep in mind that this time, I'm just gonna be standing here waiting."

"Hmm?"

"That's why just seeing the regular ol' Maou here makes me really happy, you see?"

"Ermm..."

"So maybe you could try to put my mind at ease a little?" Chiho sharpened her lips in a show of dissatisfaction. "Like, maybe 'I'll totally be back here soon' or 'I'm gonna bring Yusa and Ashiya back safe'? Something I could rely on a little would be nice."

Maou understood what she was getting at. It didn't make him act any less pained over it.

"If I did that, that'd all but ensure I died in the third act of the movie, wouldn't it? I heard something like that from Urushihara once."

"Died... Oh, Maou!" Chiho protested. It sounded like an inappropriate joke to him, but Maou refused to budge.

"Like, if this were a movie and I said something like that to my heroine, then it's a given that I'll either die or, you know, things won't go the way I'm planning them, right? If I go around making these huge promises to people I care about, that'll get me all psyched up and make me lose my head out there. So during big moments like these, I'd like to… Chi?"

Maou intended to give a serious response. Now, though, there was a carefree smile on Chiho's face.

"All right! I hear you loud and clear! That's more than enough for me!"

Maou raised an eyebrow at Chiho's apparent rapid mood swings. Hearing him use the term "heroine" raised her flagging spirits, no doubt. And there was certainly no denying that Maou was the hero of the adventure film running in her mind.

"Oh, right! Do you have that thing in hand yet, Maou?"

"Mmm? What thing? We're pretty much all set with our Ente Isla gear."

"Not that! I mean a present! For Emi!"

"A present? For Emi? …Oh! Ohhhh!"

It took a concerted search of his memory banks for Maou to remember.

"I totally forgot."

"Awww…"

If Emi had actually returned home when she promised to, the entire gang would've held a tandem birthday party for her and Chiho. Realizing that, Maou simultaneously realized that he had given exactly the wrong response.

"But I, uh, I still have yours, Chi, to…uh, I mean, I was thinking about it!"

Another misstep. Given that it was a tandem birthday party, if Maou forgot about Emi's present, it was a given he forgot about Chiho's as well. But Chiho didn't seem to mind. In fact:

"Oh, that's fine. I've already received it from you."

The response she gave made no sense at all.

Maou glanced aside. Something told him it wasn't the first time Chiho had said something like that to him. But at least Chiho wasn't hurt by his rudeness, and that was what chiefly mattered.

"Y'know, though, even if I had something for Emi, I sorta doubt she'd accept it."

"Oh, that's all right! Maybe she wouldn't, no, but the fact that you get something for her at all is the important thing. I certainly don't think it'd turn Yusa off, at least."

Maou saw little point in spending money on a present the receiver would never accept. It all seemed odd to him. Why was she so intent on improving Emi's impression of him at this point?

"That," Chiho continued, eyes fixed upon Maou, "and something tells me that Yusa's going through a lot of stress right now. Maybe her returning to Japan isn't going to be this magical solution to everything, but... I mean, if we want her to feel better once she's back, even just a little, I think you should really get her a present, Maou!"

She sounded serious about it. Maou remained dubious.

"So you're agreeing with me that if I go through with that uninvited offer, she'll yell at me and shout 'I'll never take a gift from the Devil King!' and stuff?"

"Oh, Maou! There's no way Yusa would...... All right, maybe there's some way she would, but... Oh, you know..."

Chiho fell silent. She was a lot more confident of her assertion at the start of the sentence, but by the end, it was clear Maou's scenario was a lot more probable.

Maou sighed. "Look, I know what you're trying to say. Once Emi's back, you want to do whatever you can to get her back to her loud-mouthed old self, right?"

"R-right! Yeah, exactly!"

Chiho leaned forward a bit, fist in the air to prove her point.

"Okay, so...what? What'd you get for her, Chi? I'd like something to work with."

"Me?" Chiho flashed an invincible smile of confidence. "I went with—"

"What are the two of you doing? Would you get back to work already?"

Their boss, exasperated that she was still missing two people up front, stomped up to them from the back room.

"I-I'm sorry, Ms. Kisaki!"

"Y-yes, ma'am!"

Both of them instinctively jumped away from the back room. Only then did they realize how long they had been talking.

In recent weeks, whenever Maou and Chiho shared a shift, they tended to staff the MgCafé space on the second floor. Their twin MgRonald Barista certifications were paying off for them, in other words. But as they found themselves chased up the stairs by Kisaki:

"...Pfft!"

Maou and Chiho each did a spit-take at the faces waiting at the other end.

"What's with you guys?" Kisaki asked.

"Er, no, um..."

"It, it's nothing..."

It couldn't have not been nothing. Because there, seated around a table at the far end, were Suzuno, Amane, Acieth, Rika—even Urushihara, who wasn't even supposed to be fully recovered yet.

"I told these freaks to wait in the apartment," Maou muttered to himself as Kisaki shooed him behind the bar counter, Chiho choosing to focus on the disinfected duster in hand as she cleaned the tables.

Once this shift ended, Maou and Suzuno were due to visit the National Museum of Western Art in the Ueno district. It would be their connecting hub to Ente Isla. And Maou knew that Rika asked if she could see them off, but it wasn't even dinnertime yet. They wouldn't be leaving until late night—how long did they plan to loiter in here, anyway?

Part of it could be explained, perhaps, by how Acieth couldn't physically go too far away from Maou, like with Emi and Alas Ramus. But they had already tested it out, and the distance between Villa Rosa Sasazuka and the MgRonald at Hatagaya wasn't a problem at all. Besides, he had to focus on his work shift. If she was here, that wasn't going to happen.

"So, are those your friends at the table over there?"

And Kisaki just had to say that first thing, before Maou could sweep them all out of here.

"I see Ms. Kamazuki and...um, Urushihara? Your roommate, right? That girl with the pretty hair; she's related to you, right?"

"Uh? Why..."

Maou stopped himself before he finished the sentence.

"Well, I mean, she's a dead ringer for that young girl Chi and Ms. Kamazuki brought in here before. She's your relative, too, isn't she?"

That was right. Suzuno and Chiho had brought her in once, when they figured seeing Maou at work would calm Alas Ramus's frayed nerves. From the eyes of Kisaki, who didn't realize that the toddler and Acieth were sisters, the conclusion to make was rather obvious. The fact that Alas Ramus was the older sister was a point Maou reasoned was better left unexplained.

"Um... Yeah, that kind of thing."

"You seem awful indecisive about it. And I don't know those other two, but..."

It was Amane's first time here. And Kisaki hadn't been around at Rika's last visit, either.

"By the way, Marko..."

"Yes?"

"Are you going on a long trip or something?"

"Huh?!"

"I don't see what there is to be surprised about. I mean, you taking time off out of nowhere is a surprise in itself, but you're gonna be trading off a heck of a lot of shifts. Something's got Chi all hot and bothered, too, I think."

"...What's Chi got to do with it?"

"Well, if it doesn't, then you really are a fool."

It had not been Maou's intention to hide it in particular, but having it laid out for him in black and white like this still made it feel tremendously awkward for him.

Kisaki looked at Chiho's back as she fervently dusted a table. "It'd be pretty damaging for my location," she observed, "if I had to lose two of my most vital weapons at the same time."

"...I'll see what I can do."

"Hey, um, Suzuno?"

"What?"

"I got her beat when it comes to womanly charm, don't I? Huh? Don't I?"

"...I couldn't say," Suzuno replied to Amane's furtive query.

"I don't think she even realizes she's supposed to be competing with you, dude."

"H-hey..." Rika turned to Urushihara. "Is that manager, like, some kind of superwoman, too?"

"Uh? What makes you say that?"

"I mean, the Devil King's practically her lapdog, right? Like, he's supposed to be this grand pooh-bah of the devil world, isn't he? Like some kind of god?"

"Kisaki's just a regular Japanese woman," Chiho interjected. "Just like you and me."

"Ooooh! Chiho!"

Acieth quietly squealed with delight as Chiho, duster in hand, came closer to them.

"She is, huh? But...you call him Devil King, and I've seen him make Acieth appear and disappear and stuff, so I'm just wondering, like, why is Maou spending his time working some Joe Schmoe job like this?"

"It is something"—here, Suzuno took a sip of coffee for dramatic pause—"that baffles me to this day, yes."

She was being honest with Rika. Maou tended to whine a lot about his lack of demonic force, but he still had at least a bare minimum stored inside him. Suzuno could tell. And she knew it would be more than enough to let Maou obtain all the money he wanted via illegal means—or mind-control Kisaki into giving him an hourly raise, for that matter. Whether it'd be worth expending magical force to do that was a question Suzuno chose not to ponder.

"I had thought," Chiho suddenly said, "that it's because Maou's such a nice and serious-minded person..."

She turned to the register counter, finding Kisaki lecturing Maou on the seven habits of highly effective coffee pourers. Both he and Chiho had passed the required certification exam, but there was still a whole other dimension between that and earning Kisaki's god-like coffee-making skills. Thus, ever since advancing into MgCafé, Maou had continued taking every chance to hone his bean-grinding techniques during slow times at work.

"If I had to guess," Chiho continued, "he had all that power at his fingertips back during his king days, so...probably, he's come to realize as a human that there's not a lot he can do by himself."

"Oh?" Suzuno prodded.

"I know this might put you and Yusa off a little, but something tells me that once Maou took over Ente Isla, he was intending to treat humans and demons as equals, at the end of it."

The Suzuno of a while ago would have immediately fired back and shouted Chiho down before the argument went any further. Instead, she remained frozen, waiting for her to continue.

"Why d'you think that?" Urushihara asked instead.

"Because I met Camio."

"Camio?" he shot back. It wasn't a name he expected to come up. The jet-black avian warrior and current Devil Regent, Camio had appeared on the Choshi beach while the demons were working at Amane's shop. Currently he was ruling over the demon realms in Maou's stead—and given the unblemished politeness he showed Chiho, he must have been shrewd at it.

"And... I mean, you and Maou and Ashiya all look a lot different in demon form, but Camio was way more different. Wasn't he? And Farfarello and Libicocco all looked so much different from you guys, too. It just made me wonder, do you demons have a lot of... I dunno if I should call them 'races' or whatever, but that kind of thing?"

Chiho looked down, realizing she was now clutching the duster with both hands.

"I guess Maou had to bring all these different ethnic groups under his control to take the throne, didn't he? So I just thought maybe he'd try to win the human race over that way, too."

"Ooh, I dunno," Urushihara said in a chiding tone. "All I can say is, he sure didn't give any orders like that."

"He didn't? Because I think he did." This visibly riled Urushihara a little. Chiho kept her face stony. "Or maybe, Urushihara, you executed those orders without realizing it?"

"Pfft! No way! And I know Ashiya'd tell you the same thing, dude. We wanted to rule over the human world, so we—"

"See? That's it right there."

"Huh?"

"When you say you want to 'rule over' us, you mean that you want to incorporate our society into your own, don't you?"

Urushihara and Suzuno, subjugator and subjugated, gave Chiho blank looks.

"I'm not saying that Ente Isla was better off ruled by the Devil King's Army or anything. But I don't think Maou ever intended to... like, wipe mankind from the face of the Earth, is all. Otherwise, why would he treat all us humans with so much respect and kindness once he joined our ranks?"

"That's a very astute observation, Chiho," said an admiring Amane.

"Yeah. I mean, demons can take people's sadness—their anger, their fear—and transform it into power. If he really couldn't stand the sight of mankind, he could've been a lot crueler with them than he was. He could've made them extinct, easy. But instead, he had four different Demon Generals 'rule over' the land. And that's what made me think—the Devil King's really that. A king. Not some kind of tyrant. A king can't rule if he doesn't respect the power of every single person in his realm."

"A king?"

Suzuno looked down at the reflection in her cup of coffee. She recalled what Maou himself had told her, on that bench in the Shinjuku electronics store: *"As long as we're dealing with other people in this world, it'd be a lot more fun to focus on the good stuff that comes out of it. Plus, I'm a king. I have a duty to live that way for my followers."* She didn't treat any of that seriously at the time—she wouldn't have wanted to anyway—but the way Chiho put it, she had to admit that the girl had a point.

"Well," Chiho continued, "still, this is all just supposition on my part. It's probably rude of me to guess at what he's thinking anyway, so..."

"What do you say, Chiho? The words, I don't understand at all!"

Acieth took just a few moments from the slice of cheesecake she was currently devouring alone to look Chiho in the eye and give her an incongruous thumbs-up. It made her laugh a little.

"What I mean," she offered, "is that you can have a lot of different thoughts in your mind at the same time, right? Even if they contradict each other. So maybe he's just the kind of guy who grabs out at whatever has his attention at the moment, instead of thinking about stuff too deeply. You know?"

"You mean Maou is not thinking of anything?"

Chiho paused. Acieth had a knack for interpreting things exactly the way the other party didn't want them to be.

"Well," Amane summarized as Acieth and Urushihara gave her confused and miffed looks, respectively, "I suppose it comes down to this. There are too many people in world history who you could say were born in the wrong place at the wrong time. But what you're thinking isn't as complex as all that, is it?"

She turned to Suzuno.

"Are you ready to go now, by the way?"

"Rika took us to a camping store in the city. We should have most of what we need. Oh, but you should have seen the stupor that spread over his face when I told him I would pay for everything..."

"Oh, yeah," Rika said with a nod. "And, y'know, something about that made me think, wow, maybe he really is the Devil King."

After their failure to communicate at Donkey OK, Maou and

Suzuno headed downtown at Chiho's suggestion—even though Chiho herself didn't have much of an idea where a good outdoor shop might be. So, figuring they had nothing to lose, they called Rika just as she got out of work—and of course she had a laundry list of suggestions. When asked why she knew so many spots despite not being an apparent outdoors enthusiast, she simply replied, "Oh, there was this time when, like, every fashion mag in the world was doing special features on 'glamping' this and 'mountain-chic' that, so I just kinda picked up on that stuff."

So they finally found a decent store, but of course Maou had to start grumbling about paying actual money for this trip again, so the increasingly impatient Suzuno bluntly stated that, all right, she'd pay for the tents, the sleeping bags, the food and fuel, and everything else they needed to be fully prepared.

Hearing that, for some reason, made Maou more panicked than anything else. He accused her of making him her "plaything." So they compromised by going one level cheaper on everything than the stuff Suzuno wanted to buy. It made Suzuno and Rika snicker more than anything—him putting on this blustery war of words over some simple tents and such.

"How long does the Devil King's shift continue for, Chiho?"

"Oh, until ten, just like me. I guess Ms. Kisaki was kind enough to put us together, and, ooh, I better get going for now, so…"

Realizing she was standing in one place for too long, Chiho gave the group a light nod and returned to the counter.

Suzuno placed her empty cup on the table, keeping a careful eye on Chiho's back. She was talking with Maou and Kisaki about something, giving their table the occasional quick glance. Her face was bright enough, so apparently Kisaki wasn't yelling at her about chatting with customers, at least.

"Wussup, Bell?"

Urushihara caught Suzuno blankly staring at the three of them.

"No, it is just… It feels so oddly funny to me. The fate of Ente Isla rides on the next few days, and it is all taking place not even a hairs-breadth away from the manager of this MgRonald."

"Heh, yeah..." He nodded his agreement. "She's the last to know, huh? And given how both Maou and Emilia look up to her, I guess that kinda makes her the strongest gal in the world, huh?"

"Ooh! Yes, yes! All time, Maou bows to her! I know Kisaki is strong!"

"Whoa there, Acieth! I used to be Maou's boss, too, remember!"

"Amane? Oh, Amane, who cares?"

"Well, thank you very much!"

Ignoring Amane and her odd rivalry with Kisaki, Acieth sat up, resting on her knees in the seat she was on, to gain a better look at the scene behind the counter.

"Hmm?"

Then she noticed someone coming up the stairs to the MgCafé space.

"What is it, Acieth?" Rika asked, following her gaze. She shouldn't have bothered asking.

"Yes! It is I! I have come to see you once more tonight!"

The voice battered against all of their eardrums.

"Pffth!"

"Oof."

"Hmm?"

"Is that...?"

The voice, which thundered upward even before the figure it belonged to was visible, made Suzuno laugh, Urushihara groan, Amane lower her eyebrows, and Rika search her memory.

"Who...?" Acieth began.

It was a man, about as small as Urushihara. Small, but blessed with a handsome face—even if his uniform told everyone in the room that he was currently skipping work.

"My goddess—Oop! Pardon me! Ms. Ki-Sa-Ki! Ms. Kisaki!! I have come for you! I, Sarue, am back for you tonight!!"

It was Mitsuki Sarue, better known to certain people seated at the table as the archangel Sariel, former nemesis to Maou and Emi and current manager at the Sentucky Fried Chicken across the street from this MgRonald. His lethal weakness against feminine beauty led him to fall into a deep love for Mayumi Kisaki upon first sight of her on Earth—enough so that he abandoned the heavens, and his heavenly post, to live in Hatagaya permanently. He had been banned from the location once thanks to a litany of inappropriate actions against MgRonald staff, but now he was back—with less fervor than before, but his once-every-other-day pace was still doing great things for MgRonald's sales figures.

Chiho's face stiffened behind the counter. Maou, on the other hand, already looked resigned to his fate. Only Kisaki, a relatively friendly businesswoman's smile on her face, was ready for him at the counter, as far as Suzuno could tell.

"Hmm? This man... I have seen...?"

Only Acieth continued to conspicuously stare at Sariel as he turned to the side, still unable to shake her initial surprise.

After he completed his order and Kisaki turned her back to him to prepare the coffee, Sariel casually turned around to size up the gang at the table. Then time stopped.

"Kaaaahhh!!"

Neither Suzuno, nor Amane nor Urushihara, and certainly not Rika, were able to stop her. Acieth had a good look at Sariel's face now, and faster than anyone could act, she shot to her feet and made a flying leap for Sariel. She raised a fist—the fist that had broken right through the archangel Camael's armor not long ago.

The look on Sariel's face was one of abject shock. Acieth had completed the entire motion in a single instant—faster than Kisaki or any of Acieth's boothmates could've seen—and the pure vengeance oozing out of every pore was palpable.

"Acieth!!"

No one was able to react except Maou, who flung his right hand toward the thin arm that even now was making its way toward Sariel's body.

"Maou...!!!"

With a scream of protest, Acieth disappeared in a puff of purple light, just like Emi dematerializing her holy sword.

"Mm? What was that?"

Kisaki had just turned around, totally oblivious to the tense half-second that just passed as she placed a coffee cup on the counter. "Um, Sarue? Marko? C'mon, Chi, what is it?"

To her, all three of them, along with the gang at the table, seemed to all be carefully studying the ceiling, pained smiles on their faces. The sheer force of hatred behind Acieth's actions was purely overwhelming. Chiho was used to stuff like this, but it still cowed her into submission, just as it did Maou and Sariel.

Sariel found his voice first.

"Er, no, um…"

He looked at Maou, then Chiho, then the table with Suzuno and the rest.

"I…apologize, Ms. Kisaki. Could I make that whole order to go, actually?"

"Sure, but…what's up? That's unusual for you."

Sarue's normal practice was to sit down, then come back for a few additional orders before he was done. The surprise on Kisaki's face at this request was obvious to everyone else. But the customer was always right. She took out the relevant bags and containers.

"Indeed, um," Sariel said in a near-whisper, "I just remembered that I have some work I still need to tackle after this, so…" For a moment, he gave Suzuno and Urushihara a look. "…I'll be on my way, then."

"What's with him?" the astonished Kisaki said as he left without another word. "Did he eat something rotten, or what?"

Maou and Suzuno had no response to this. All they could do was watch him carefully make his way downstairs.

"Well!" Suzuno near-shouted. "We'd best be on our way as well." She rose to her feet, Urushihara, Rika, and Amane joining her as they stacked their trays above the trash can.

Each one gave their farewells to Kisaki as they filed away.

"My apologies for the extended stay," Suzuno said.

"Thank you very much!" Rika said.

"Yeah, uh…thanks," Urushihara grumbled.

"I'll beat you someday," Amane mouthed.

"Thank you all very—huh?"

Kisaki stopped herself as she saw them off—and not simply because that last farewell didn't sound much like a farewell to her.

"Wasn't there one more of them…?"

"Oh, um, I think she went to the bathroom ahead of the others!"

"Oh? Huh. Must've missed it."

Whether Kisaki bought Chiho's hurried explanation or not, the manager shook her head. As weird customers went, she was still on the harmless side, as far as she was concerned. Then something else came to mind.

"Oh, hey, I'm going downstairs for a second, guys."

"Huh? Oh, sure."

"What for?"

"I'm gonna check our surveillance cameras down there. Something's bothering me about how Sarue just left outta nowhere like that."

"Oh…okay?"

Sariel may have been allowed back on MgRonald premises again, but that didn't mean Kisaki had so much as a shred of trust in his behavior. She must have feared that he was picking up chicks downstairs instead of dealing with her tonight—and when she finally, blessedly left the MgCafé, Maou and Chiho breathed a long-yearned-for sigh of relief.

"Wh-what was that? Acieth just, out of nowhere…"

"I dunno, but I'd have to guess it was because she saw Sariel's face… Hey, will you shut up already?"

Acieth must have been raising a royal hue and cry inside Maou's head. But Maou had to stop her, or else that fist that smashed through Camael's thick armor like so much papier-mâché would have struck the completely unprotected Sariel. The two of them shuddered. They didn't care that much about Sariel's safety, but the sheer force of the blow could've caused untold damage to the building itself.

"Guess Acieth's just like Alas Ramus, huh? They both have it in for the angels in the worst way possible. It's just that Acieth likes taking matters into her own hands a lot more, I suppose..."

"Erone seemed pretty chill, though."

"Yeah, well, let's just hope Suzuno and the gang can get the whole story outta Sariel... For chrissake, just zip it!"

Maou looked exhausted. The screaming in his head showed no sign of abating, and covering his ears did nothing for it. Now he understood completely what drove Emi to seek permission for Alas Ramus to visit Devil's Castle. The crying at night must have been traumatic.

Suzuno and her companions walked through the front door to find Sariel standing there, takeout bag still hanging from one hand, a weirdly humbled look on his face. He did not greet them.

"..."

"Rather calm, are you not?" Suzuno began. "I thought that experience would have shaken you a little."

"No," he sniffed. "I am surprised, yes, but not shaken." He turned to Urushihara. "Was that the child again? The one who fused with Emilia...?"

"They're kinda alike, yeah, but it doesn't look like it. Two peas in a pod, though, it seems."

"Mm? Is it because she's one of those, then? Another shard?"

"You know more about that than I do, dude." Urushihara shook his head. "I don't know jack about how to handle Sephirot. I skipped out of heaven a zillion years before you started messin' with that crap."

"Oh...did you?"

"Hey, um, Suzuno?" Rika prodded Suzuno as the two men continued talking, both stern-faced as could be. "That's the guy from Sentucky, isn't it?"

"Ah...yes, you have seen him before, have you not? That is precisely the man. In Japan he is Mitsuki Sarue, manager at the

Sentucky Fried Chicken...but in the heavens above Ente Isla, he was known as Lord Sariel, the archangel."

"Man, what is up with this neighborhood? Why're all these Biblical figures so obsessed with fast food?"

Rika looked exasperated. Suzuno took that as a good sign. Slowly but surely, she was starting to accept all of this.

"But... Hmm," Sariel mused. "Indeed. I think I know why Gabriel came here on the day of that big storm now."

"""""?!"""""

This stopped the other three onlookers in their tracks.

"So he's an archangel, though?" Rika asked. "Like, the same as Gabriel?"

"Hmm? Ah. You were with Emilia before, weren't you? When you visited my store?"

"Oh, God, don't remind me about that day again!"

Rika and Sariel had met only once, briefly, several months ago. On a day that, now that she knew the truth about Ente Isla, provided nothing but major trauma to Rika's mind at this point.

"I will admit to being out of the loop, but have you become aware of our...circumstances?" Sariel asked. "Like Chiho Sasaki?"

"I... Well, it's not like I wanted to! It's just that your friend or whatever went and—"

"Gabriel? What did he do to you?"

"You are not aware, my lord?" Suzuno inquired.

Sariel shook his head. "Nope. He had a team along with him to attempt my repatriation, so I, well, resisted a bit. Just a bit, mind you. But thanks to that, our sales for the day went down the toilet."

He stepped back and looked forlornly at the SFC he managed.

"I mean, heavens, they smashed all the windows, broke all the tables... All that grief he put my customers through! I really had to give him an honest piece of my mind for a change, if you follow me. Whether archangel or not, my Evil Eye, and my transdimensional barrier, are hardly things he can afford to sniff at. All it took were a few carefully worded threats to send him packing. I tell you, modifying the memories of every man, woman, and child in the store after that was such a pain."

"Er, yes..."

"Dude, why are you sounding so much like Maou now?"

Neither Suzuno nor Urushihara could believe how much Sariel, their former enemy, cared about his apparent new career in the world of quick-service chicken. When he first arrived in Japan, he couldn't have seen the franchise as anything more than a front to hide his true intentions with.

"Actually, can I ask you a question, Lucifer?"

"What?"

"Why did you leave heaven?"

"Because I was bored. That's all. I think I was just asked that a bit ago, too..."

"I think I am starting to understand your feelings a little, then."

"What do you mean?"

Before he could answer, the previously silent Amane stepped toward Sariel, a grim look on her face. He eyed this unfamiliar woman carefully but continued speaking.

"The thought never even occurred to me when I was still in heaven, but once I started working in this city, and once I encountered my goddess, Mayumi Kisaki... For the first time in my existence, I started to expend labor for something besides myself. And the strangest thing was...it didn't feel bad."

"Ooh, that's a little bit different from my ex—*mph*..."

Suzuno stopped Urushihara mid-sentence.

"I expended labor for the sake of someone else...and they were thankful for it. I had never experienced such a thing in my existence before. I suppose it comes as a shock to you in particular, Bell, but..."

"No. I...have long passed that point in time."

Only a truly devout follower of the Church of Ente Isla would understand the portent behind Sariel's words. They meant that this race, these angels, never gave a second thought about contributing to the world of humanity. That the prayers offered to the Church and its holy scriptures never had a remote chance of reaching the ears of divinity.

"I have no desire to return to that world. That world obsessed with protecting itself, where keeping the order of things takes precedent over everything else. And you can forget about my becoming involved in any sort of conflict. For now, my sole interest lies in how I can have Mayumi Kisaki recognize me for who I am, how I can walk hand in hand with her in my life. Did you see her now? The smile has returned to her face, every time I haunt her doorstep. If I had followed Gabriel back at this point, it would have been all for naught."

Kisaki was currently looking over the camera footage to check if Sariel had done anything illegal on the first floor before leaving. Everyone on hand silently agreed that what he didn't know wouldn't hurt him.

"So no matter what you do, know this: I have no intention of helping you, nor of getting in your way. My sole path in life involves me, and Mayumi Kisaki, and the future we are destined to share forever."

"That is so lame."

Amane's harsh judgment had no chance of reaching the completely self-infatuated Sariel's ears.

"Thus I care not whether Lucifer is in cahoots with Bell or not. And while I do have my concerns for the two beautiful women who have been opened to the world of Ente Isla, I will not allow myself to worry over them."

"You have concerns about them, dude?"

"It would be impossible for me to ignore such ravishing symbols of beauty. Now, this leaves the other girl, the Yesod fragment, and... well, considering what we've done in the past, it is not difficult for me to understand why she took such action upon first sight of me."

"Yeah! That! Let's talk about that!"

"Hmm? About what, Lucifer?"

"That's the part I don't get, dude. What the hell did you guys do up there? Alas Ramus and that girl couldn't even stand the sight of

Gabriel. Or, really, of any angel, pretty much. What'd you do to the Sephirot tree after I was gone?"

Urushihara's question struck at the root of Alas Ramus's, Acieth Alla's, and even Erone's existence. These shards—which bore no ill will toward people, demons, even the fallen angel Urushihara—possessed murderous hostility for all archangels.

"Well," Sariel said, "I wasn't the Sephirot's guardian angel. I was in no position to do anything, if you will, to the Tree of Life. Not directly, that is. But I can, at least, tell you what the angels' motivation was for reaching out to it."

Sariel leaned his body against a nearby tree on the sidewalk, as if this conversation was starting to tire him. He looked up at the sky, face serene.

"We were trying to interfere with the birth of a god in Ente Isla. A real one. That was the ultimate aim."

This was not enough to make Urushihara, Suzuno, and certainly Rika understand what he meant. Only Amane seemed to.

"...Well, that was a pretty stupid idea," she said listlessly, a trace of pity to her voice. "I don't know where you guys came from, but do you think any mortal being has a chance against the full fury of nature?"

"...?"

Sariel gave Amane a quizzical look; Suzuno and Urushihara seemed just as lost. It should have been clear to Amane that Sariel was from Ente Isla—from the heavens above that planet, at least...

"Because you must have thought you did, didn't you?" she continued. "That's why you tried doing something like that—because you thought you could. The Sephirot over in your world... It's created some serious karma at this point, after all."

"Who...are you...?"

"Oh, like that even matters. Lemme just warn you, though: This Ente Isla or whatever it is...it's gonna have it pretty rough now, going forward. You prodded the hornet's nest, and now it's gonna sting back atcha. Exactly how, I couldn't tell you, but it will, and bad."

"So be it," Sariel intoned heavily as he pulled away from the tree. "Let it happen. I have no intention of returning."

"Lord Sariel!"

Suzuno called for him as he turned around and began to walk off. His only response was a hand raised to the air. "I told you," he said. "I'm in no position to support you right now, but I'm not actively opposing you, either. I have no intention of telling you anything, and I have no intention of helping you. That training session before was the exception that proves the rule, all right?"

"That training session" must have meant his helping Chiho learn how to handle holy magic earlier. They offered to help mend fences with Kisaki in exchange, and he leaped at it greedily like a penguin chick greeting the arrival of summer. To Suzuno, he was in no position to act all prissy about it now.

"...But," he suddenly continued, "if Mayumi Kisaki were ever to fall into danger, I am prepared to toss my very life on the line. So no matter what you intend to do from now on, tell the Devil King this one thing for me: Tell him that no matter what happens, I will always step up to protect my goddess, Mayumi Kisaki; the MgRonald Hatagaya location and the crew that she loves with all her heart; and this shopping arcade that it is kind enough to call home."

"So," Amane said as they watched Sariel walk back to his job. "How's that grab ya, Rika?"

"Kind of hard to tell. We've only talked once. But something tells me he could do a lot better than this, y'know?"

"You're damn right, Rika Suzuki," Urushihara confirmed. "I think we can believe him, though. He's, like, pretty crazy for Kisaki, and besides, there ain't an angel or human who could beat 'im. Even with the demons, the only ones who'd try hittin' Earth right now are the Malebranche, and ain't no way they could take him on."

"Indeed," Suzuno added. "I am concerned with how much holy

force Lord Sariel has left to wield, but…this is perhaps an unexpected, and very welcome, boon for us."

Sariel had just declared that he would step up to protect the staff of the MgRonald in front of Hatagaya Station. Which meant that as long as they were on duty, Kisaki and Chiho were completely safe—especially with Amane on the scene, too. And no one was happier about that than Urushihara, given that it meant even the most dreadful of disasters wouldn't require him to leave his computer any longer.

"Okay, so…uh, I guess we kinda stormed outta the restaurant, but what'll we do now?"

Rika's question made Suzuno turn back toward MgRonald. "I had thought we would wait until the end of their shift," she said, "but perhaps we should return home and travel to Ueno later to prepare. My apologies, Amane, but would you mind driving the Devil King's scooter again for me? To Ueno, this time."

"No problem, but what for?"

"What other reason could there be?" a somewhat irritated Suzuno spat out as she glared at the second floor. "That idiot Devil King never acquired his license. If I let him drive it there and a police officer stopped him, he would be summarily arrested for driving without a license. As it stands, he would never agree to drive one right now. He would gripe endlessly about how he'd lose his job if he was found out, or how Alciel would scream to high heaven at him."

"Hey, I know I'm late asking this, but…he is the Devil King, right? Like, the king of an entire demon kingdom and everything?"

Rika remained not wholly convinced. This was a Devil King afraid of traffic citations, and a so-called Church cleric showing genuine concern about what should have been the personification of evil in her religion.

"…He is," a deflated Suzuno replied. "This man who upholds the law, respects mankind, loves his career, and shows concern for the woman who wanted him dead is the King of All Demons and invader of Ente Isla. And that is exactly why Emilia and I have so much trouble with him."

The emotions behind that statement were so deep, dark, and conflicting that Rika never would've had any chance at fully comprehending them.

✳

It was one in the morning at Ueno-Onshi Park, in a corner of Tokyo's Taito ward. Admittance into National Museum of Western Art grounds would normally be forbidden at this hour, but there were two people there, walking along a tiled path in the front lawn, watching carefully for guards or cameras as they pushed along a pair of roofed motor scooters packed with camping equipment.

"Hey, you sure we're good? No one's gonna see us?"

"...Look, are you sure you're a Devil King?"

Rika had already asked Maou that what seemed like a billion times. It didn't exactly put Maou's mind at ease.

"I'm just sayin', this is totally trespassing, what we're doing right now. Even this late at night, there's gotta be someone here in this park..."

"Indeed. There are quite a few drinking establishments in the area. Many of the clubs around here remain open until dawn, in fact. Indeed, indeed..."

"Look, Suzuno, can we just do this and get outta here already?! What if someone spots Chi and starts askin' questions or whatever?"

"Hey, um, Maou?"

It was Amane who finally voiced her complaints over Maou's excessive paranoia.

"This is supposed to be the Devil King's triumphant return to his homeland, ain't it? Aren't you supposed to act a lot more stately about it or whatever?"

"Acting 'stately' isn't gonna help me if I get arrested doing it! Ugh,

I so wish I had gotten my license before this. I know it's Ente Isla we're going to, but..."

"You're so anal about the smallest things, seriously," she continued. "Look, if something happens, I'll fix it for you all, all right? So snap out of it! D'you think Chiho wants to put up with all this?"

"Oh, no, um... I don't really mind, or..."

"Dude, I'm about to fall asleep. I can't stay up all night like this while I'm still hurt, okay? So can we get movin' with this, Bell?"

"Honestly, you people..."

For the grand departure that it was, it was sorely lacking in tension—something that drained the strength from Suzuno's face, even though she needed all the strength she could muster right now.

"Right," she began. "I need all of you to be quiet. Gate magic requires intense concentration." Then, without hesitation, she walked past a placard reading "SEISMIC ISOLATION PLATFORM—DO NOT STAND ON BASE" and stepped up to the platform their "gate" was situated on.

Suzuno, by and large, had one worry at the moment. *The Gates of Hell* was a sculpture of great portent, to be sure—vast history was chiseled into it, the story of Earth, mankind in all its permutations, writ large upon its surface. Whether that meant it'd serve as an amplifier powerful enough to open a Gate with was another matter entirely. The Gate's potential was strictly guesswork on Maou and Ashiya's part.

"..."

The bronze doors that formed Auguste Rodin's masterpiece loomed above her now. Flanked on both sides by statues of Adam and Eve, it was meant to depict the entrance of hell from Canto III of "The Inferno" from the *Divine Comedy*, which described a certain famous inscription written on its arch: "Abandon all hope, ye who enter here."

"'Abandon all hope,' is it?"

"What was that, Suzuno?" Chiho asked.

Suzuno smiled. "Oh, just recalling the past. Never in my dreams did I expect to savor those words shoulder to shoulder with the Devil King. I've a feeling we might just be able to do this."

She took a bottle of 5-Holy Energy β out from her sleeve and gulped it down in one shot.

"We never had any hope to begin with."

Slowly, Suzuno walked up to the gate, eyes fixated above. At the very top was a seated man looking down upon her. It was *The Thinker*, Rodin's other masterpiece, and it formed both the keystone for the gate's door frame and the artwork's representation of Dante Alighieri, author of the *Divine Comedy*. Suzuno gave it a sincere nod, took a deep breath, and extended both hands toward the door. The next words out of her mouth were none of earthly origin.

"<Holy soul, connecting life and time, divine our transient world from the yawning heavens!>"

As she pronounced each syllable, particles of light began streaming from Suzuno's fingertips to *The Gates of Hell*.

"Wh-whoa…"

Chiho couldn't help but gasp in awe. Her own magical training enabled her to understand just how much energy was coursing through Suzuno's body right now. She couldn't even fathom the sheer quantity of force this stroke of magic required. Not even a hundred Chihos could've been enough.

"Wow, this…this really looks like magic… This ain't CGI or anything?"

Despite having seen the Light of Iron and Acieth's disappearing act for herself, Rika, eyes darting between Suzuno and the gate, couldn't be blamed for blinking more than a few times at the display.

The light particles grew thicker, soon forming two bands of light that enveloped Suzuno's body and began to waver in the air. And amid the sound of her flapping kimono and the trees rustling in the wind, the sound of Amane muttering, "Huh. Weird," went unnoticed by everyone. All eyes were on Suzuno, of course, so they couldn't have noticed the fog that was billowing up from her feet and surrounding the entirety of the *Gates*.

As the show continued, the bands of light around Suzuno began to emit what looked like lettering in the air.

"<*Nnn...gh...* Almost...>"

The moment the letters appeared, Suzuno's expression clearly grew more pained. Chiho was struck with an impulse to lend a hand, but if she distracted her now, the entire spell would disappear in a wisp. It was absolutely massive, nothing on the level of an Idea Link.

"It, it's opening!" Maou shouted.

The *Gates*, being a sculpture, weren't literally opening for them—but now they could see the light dancing across its borders, and the air within was warping within itself.

"We, we okay?" Urushihara shouted. He sounded anxious. The wrinkle in space was forming, but it showed no sign of opening for them. As if something was snagged on it, it began to close just as it seemed ready to burst open.

"<If...if I open it...that'll stabilize it... *Ngh*...>"

Suzuno's face was in anguish until she looked up. The man at the top of the gate looked blankly down at the cleric from another world. Was this cleric incapable of opening *The Gates of Hell*? No. This was Crestia Bell, the Scythe of Death herself. What would be a more suitable fate for her than hell itself?

She took a deep breath, then another step forward.

"<Do not retain hope... Proceed... Forward!>"

The call to arms that sent mankind forward against its most formidable of foes.

"<You must blaze your own trail to survive!!>"

As her voice rang out, the light bands swirling around Suzuno's body whirlpooled down to a single point, flung themselves from her small hands, and smashed against the warped space in front of her.

"<It...it's open! It's open! The Gate is open!!>"

Her sweaty face told her audience exactly how grand and sublime a feat the opening was. Despite her inability to speak the local language any longer, she still had enough of her wits to raise a fist in the air and shout triumphantly.

"<Let's go, Devil King! It's stable now, but it will not be for long! Acieth had better be fused with you!>"

"S-sure!"

In a rush, Suzuno climbed on her bike, Maou following suit. Once the helmet was strapped on, she gripped the brakes and turned on the engine.

"Maou! Suzuno! Acieth!" Chiho called for her friends, just as they were about to depart. "We'll take care of things over here! Be careful!"

"Okay!"

"We'll be back!"

Neither Suzuno nor Maou nor the invisible Acieth needed much in the way of words right now. Everyone knew by this point that, no matter where they went, they'd be right back in that cramped wooden apartment in Sasazuka—in Japan—before too long.

The two scooter engines revved up, plunging Maou and Suzuno straight into the swirling light that spun in front of them. Then:

"...They're gone..."

That was all a dumbfounded Rika could say. Like the end of a grandiose magic trick, Maou and Suzuno disappeared with neither a sound nor a trace the moment they touched that crack that opened in front of the *Gates*. All that remained was a small rift, an eerie light emanating out from it.

"...Be careful," Chiho whispered once more. The ring she was clutching, the one with the Yesod fragment inside it, glowed softly.

"Okay, so...now what?" Rika asked, still clearly bewildered as her head bobbed between the Gate and Chiho.

"We wait. That's all we really need to do. Just wait for Maou and Suzuno to get Yusa and Alas Ramus and Ashiya back."

Unlike Rika's wavering voice, Chiho's was fully resolute. It was so sure about what the future held for them all that Rika was taken aback by it.

"B-but..."

"Well, okay, I don't mean juuust wait. I need to go to Ms. Kisaki during my next shift and ask her which location I can start my delivery training at."

"Huh?" Rika moaned, confused at the ever-so-slight difference in weight between what just happened and what Chiho had just told her. "Wh-why're you bringing that up?"

"Because Maou said he wanted to do it," she cheerfully replied. "I want to tell him everything I learned during my training session once he gets back. That'll take some of the burden off him once he starts his new position."

"I don't think I've ever seen such a helpful spouse before in my life," Amane ironically exclaimed. "Well, perfect! That's what teamwork's all about, anyways. Doing what you can for your friends."

"I..."

Rika still didn't know how to parse Chiho. So much younger than her, yet so much more...put together. Brave, even.

"Ah, you're still just a beginner at this, Rika," Amane advised. "Just try to picture Yusa back here safe and sound, all right? Try to mentally prepare for that and stuff."

"Prepare for it...?"

"...'Kay, I'm outta here," Urushihara characteristically muttered.

"Uh, but what about that rift?"

Just as Rika pointed at the Gate hole Suzuno had opened up, it gradually shrank into a single dot in the air before disappearing completely. Beyond it, *The Gates of Hell* loomed, just as it did during opening hours. Nothing had changed to it; the only evidence Maou and Suzuno had been there at all were the fresh tire tracks they had left on the tile as they peeled off.

"Well, shall we, then?" Amane suggested as the fog spouting from under her feet began to dissipate, returning Ueno-Onshi Park to its quiet late-night atmosphere. "While nobody's spotted us, at least?"

Urushihara took the chance to look at the park's clock tower. It was half past one—late enough that even a grown-up wandering park grounds might attract police attention.

"Hey, you sure it's okay for you to be walking around this late, Chiho Sasaki?"

"Oh, it's fine with my parents. I'm going to be staying at Suzuno's place tonight."

"Huh?" Urushihara's eyebrows rose. "You're comin' with me? I thought Amane was shackin' up in there already."

Chiho, in response, sized Amane up with her eyes. "Oh, you'll be fine in your room, Urushihara. No need to worry about us."

"...Dude, I don't really like how you're assuming I'm just gonna sit in the closet this whole time."

"That's not really what I meant," Chiho countered, "but this... Well, I can't even tell Maou about this, sadly. It's not really something we could do if he or Yusa or Suzuno were here, and really, if you wouldn't mind holing up in your closet... Okay, the room is fine, too, but if you could chill inside for a few days, that'd really help us out."

"Geez, dude," Urushihara replied, unable to pick up on what Chiho was saying between the words. "So now you're commanding me to be an outcast to society?"

Chiho, ignoring him, turned to Amane.

"Amane?"

"Hmm? Why're you lookin' so serious?"

"You said you couldn't tell Maou and the other demons about anything their landlord hasn't already said to them, right?"

Amane's face, a good length taller than Chiho's as she looked down upon her, suddenly brightened a little. She flashed a defiant smile.

"So what about me by myself?"

"...Well, that depends on what you're asking, I s'pose. But why do you think you deserve to know more than them?"

That was the only "examination" Amane saw fit to give her. And Chiho, without a moment's hesitation, passed with flying colors.

"Because I'm from this planet."

"...Yeah, you got me there." Amane scratched her head, eyebrows furrowed. "You're a lot more than just a faithful spouse after all, huh? Eesh, and I thought you were just an average girl with a little more nerve than most your age. Guess not, huh?"

Her words were ambivalent, but her expression was one of sheer joy.

"Hell, you're such a real monster, Maou and Yusa couldn't take you in a million years."

The only other witnesses to this human exchange between worlds were the two Dantes—one above the gate door, the other perched quietly across from *The Gates of Hell*.

THE DEVIL,
ONCE UPON
A TIME

Emi was having a dream.

She'd woken up in a panic and turned her eyes to her desk clock. Eight in the morning. She'd completely overslept.

She flung herself out of bed to prepare for work but wound up kicking the clock off the desk instead. A dull, stubbing pain danced across her toes.

"What's up with you, Emi?"

She looked up, only to find Rika sitting next to her, peering at her cube. Now Emi was in her uniform, crouched under the desk, blushing and trying to laugh it off.

"Uh, my pen got stuck between the partition and the floor, so I'm having trouble getting it out..."

"Ohhh. Oh, hey, speaking of which, I found this ramen joint that's supposed to be pretty good. Wanna hit it up for lunch?"

"Sure. I haven't had ramen in a while anyways... Oh, hang on, I got a call. Hello?"

"Good afternoon, Yusa!"

The voice was Chiho's. Emi, in her everyday sweats, sat down on her sofa at home to focus on the conversation. Chiho called her a few times a week at this point, reporting on Maou at work and chatting about this and that. Emi knew that the girl's adoration was causing her to filter a lot of the juicier details out, but she was nonetheless saving Emi a lot of stake-out time around the MgRonald. This was fully understood on Chiho's part. They were good friends by now, anyway.

"Listen, I'm sorry I'm late on this, but there's this club meeting I can't get out of, so I'm gonna have to skip dinner at Maou's tonight."

"Oh, no? Well, that's too bad, but school's school. You can always stop by after that, though, if your mom says it's okay... Sure. Lemme know if you can. Okay... Hey, Bell? Chiho said she might not be able to make it today."

When she hung up, Emi was in Room 202 of Villa Rosa Sasazuka, talking to Suzuno as her friend busily attended to kitchen duties.

"Oh? A pity. I was hoping she would try the rice omelet she taught me how to make..." Suzuno opened the refrigerator door. "...Hmm."

"What?"

"Heavens... Look at me, I've gone and forgotten to purchase any ketchup."

"Oh, I could run out and get some for you if you want. Um, ketchup, ketchup..."

Emi turned around, peering at the signs down each aisle of the Safepath supermarket off Sasazuka rail station. Walking down one of them, she ran smack-dab into Ashiya and Urushihara.

"...Alciel? Lucifer? What're you doing with all those eggs?"

"I was thinking I would try to make a...a 'quiche,' was it? Ms. Sasaki gave me a recipe."

"Dude, why'd you drag me here just because they were on sale? Mannn, I wanna go home. What're you doing here?"

"Just picking up something for Bell. Oh, by the way, Chiho might have to miss dinner today."

"Is that true? Ugh... Who am I going to have judge this quiche for me, then?"

"Aw man, so no fried chicken? Mehhh..."

Emi was taken aback a little. She wasn't expecting Chiho to have such a huge impact on the night's dinner. It was shaping up to be a rather eggy one.

Soon, the three found themselves wandering around the supermarket together. "It oughta be fine, though," Emi advised. "Alas Ramus likes eggs. Don't you, Alas Ramus?"

"Mommy," Alas Ramus exclaimed as she toddled along next to her, "I wanna see Daddy!"

"In a little while, okay?"

Now the stairway in front of Villa Rosa Sasazuka was right in front of them, Alas Ramus in her arms. Even after the renovations, climbing these stairs was still a dicey prospect, so she watched her step as she ascended and opened the door to Devil's Castle up top. The letters "MAOU" written in Sharpie on the bare wooden nameplate had faded a fair amount by now; Emi wondered why he had never bothered changing it out.

"You in there, Devil King? I'm coming in."

She pushed the chime button (like she always did) and was just about to push the door open without waiting for a response (like she always did) when:

"Huh?"

Nobody was inside. In fact, all the appliances, and furniture, and everything else were gone. There was no evidence that anyone lived there at all.

"Alciel? Lucifer? Where are you, Devil King...? Alciel?"

The two demons were with her all the way home, but now they were missing. Maybe they got split up on the way. Flustered, Emi knocked on the next adjacent door.

"Bell? Hey, Bell? The Devil King isn't in there. Do you know where he..."

But Room 202, where Suzuno was briskly cooking up dinner not a moment ago, was just as bare.

"Wha...? Uh... What's...?"

Emi fumbled for her cell phone and made a call to Chiho. She should've been free from school by now. But:

"We're sorry. The number you have dialed is out of service. Please check the number and..."

It didn't work. She had Chiho's number on her phone, but it didn't work. Disconnected. She called Rika; she called Suzuno; she called Urushihara's PC account—none of them worked.

A tidal wave of anxiety crashed over her. She decided to go back to Devil's Castle—but it didn't work. The door wouldn't budge. It had been unlocked two seconds ago, but now, push and pull as she did, Room 201 was tightly shut away.

"Devil King!" Emi screamed as she knocked on the door. "I know you're in there! Open up!" Nothing happened. "What're you doing in there?! Give it up and open the door! Did something happen to you? Are you all right?!"

The anxiety inside her grew, whether she wanted it to or not. What could have happened? Chiho, Rika, Suzuno, Ashiya, Urushihara... What could have happened to them?

"They're all gone! Do you know what happened to them? This is serious, Devil King! Listen to me!"

Suddenly, the doorknob turned. The door rotated inward, sending Emi tumbling inside.

"?!" She looked up, then gasped.

There, she found Devil's Castle—the one on Ente Isla's Central Continent. The final redoubt of the demons, the site of the fateful battle that Emi failed to consummate by a mere hairsbreadth.

A large, indistinct black shade loomed in the background. It wielded a sword shaped exactly like the one Emi had, and it was floating toward her. Reflexively, Emi readied her blade—or tried to. But, for some reason, Alas Ramus, in her arms the entire time over at Villa Rosa, was gone. The Better Half refused to materialize.

An empty dread fell upon Emi. No doubt about it: This was the Devil King. The Devil King she had to kill. And yet—somehow, at the very pit of her stomach, the sight came as a relief to her.

"Oh, thank heavens... There you are. You could've at least said something."

The dark shade loomed like the ominous dawn of death. Emi continued addressing it anyway. "I can't get Chiho on the phone," she reported. "Or Bell. She sent me out to pick up some ketchup for her, and then she just left. And I was with Alciel and Lucifer on the way home, too, and they just vanished… Don't you think that's so rude?"

The shade did not reply, sword still at the ready as it came closer to Emi.

"And, and I let Alas Ramus out of sight for just a moment, and she went away, too… And if you were gone, too…I, I don't know what I'd do with myself. What were you doing, anyway?"

Emi lowered her face, staring at the ground as the dark shadow shimmered in front of her.

"Look, I…I know Chiho called and said she couldn't make it over, but…Bell and Alciel, they were really working hard on dinner, it looked like. Couldn't we wait Chiho out a little bit, together? I… Not that I mind either way, but I think that'd make Alas Ramus happier, so…"

The shade lifted its sword into the air. The blade, purple light trailing behind it as it whirled, reflected the red light coming in from the windows, making the shadow's face seem to rise above the darkness.

"So…"

The face of Sadao Maou that floated into sight was, for reasons only he could understand, exhibiting a gentle smile.

"So…let's eat together again…"

"—!!"

The sound of her own voice awakened Emi, making her practically fly out of bed. Her entire body was covered in sweat, but before she did anything else, she brought a hand to her chest.

"What…was that…?"

Her pulse refused to slow, her breathing ragged. She had woken up right when the purple-glowing holy sword, wielded by the shadow with Maou's face, plunged right through her chest. It was a raw dream, one that filled her with fear and the kind of painful exhaustion only a nightmare could produce.

They had all showed up in it—her, and Rika, and Chiho, and

Suzuno, and Ashiya, and Urushihara, and Alas Ramus, and at the end… They were all yelling at each other, sweating it out with each other, annoying each other—and yet, just a few weeks ago, this was Emi's everyday life, one that long ago made her dismantle the armor covering her heart. That was the dream.

"How," she glibly whispered to herself, "could I be so stupid this whole time? So oblivious?"

She dreamed of Ente Isla and her father all the time back in Japan—but, looking back, she realized she had been visiting Japan every night for the past few days during her sleep.

"I've just got to have my cake and eat it, too, huh…?"

Now, Emi's reality involved the sound of the waves pushing against the port of Phaigan, the sword and armor laid by her betrayer in a corner of her room, and herself, bound by invisible ropes around the heart.

"Pphhh…phhh…"

Next to her, Emi caressed Alas Ramus as she babbled in her sleep, before she herself lay down once more. Another listless day in captivity awaited her tomorrow. Now was no time to let her distracting dreams keep her from a good night's sleep.

Somehow, though, Emi couldn't bring herself to wipe away the tracks of the tears that had run down her cheeks before she'd woken up. The tears of relief she'd shed upon discovering the shade of the Devil King.

The next morning, Emi's mind was filled more with suspicion than hatred.

"…What in the world is he doing?"

Olba had brought into her room a gaggle of commissioned officers, the leaders who guided the entire body of Efzahan's Knights of the Eight Scarves. Their legions were led by the Regal Azure Scarves, responsible for protecting Heavensky and the Azure Emperor who called it home; they were joined by armies known respectively as the Inlain Azure Scarves, Regal Jade Scarves, Inlain Jade Scarves, Regal

Citral Scarves, Inlain Citral Scarves, Regal Crimson Scarves, and Inlain Crimson Scarves. Each squadron had its own governmental duties, region of activity, and armaments.

Not everyone affiliated with these diverse forces were fighting men; some served as police officers or civil servants. But the people inside the room now were all high-ranking officials—deputy generals, regional commanders: the kind of lineup that would regularly greet noble visitors from foreign and exotic lands.

"Did you find fault with the armor?"

Emi didn't answer Olba's question. She stared at the armor and sword, still resting where they had been placed.

"I have the Cloth of the Dispeller," she replied. "Thanks for the fancy-looking outfit you gave me, but I'm not stupid enough to just put on something without knowing what's been done to it."

"Ah, was that it?" Olba smiled, not giving much apparent thought to the response. "I must apologize, Emilia, but I truly don't want you to exhaust yourself here quite yet. Would you be willing to put it on, for your own sake?"

"..." Emi paused, lips twisting into a scowl. She gritted her teeth at her helplessness. She had, in other words, no right of denial, and she had no idea what Olba's motives were. Olba wasn't going to reveal them, either.

After a moment, Olba nodded, content that Emi had acquiesced. "Right, then, could we have the maids come in and equip her? Once Emilia is ready, I and and my handpicked group of elite Eight Scarves officers will travel eastward to Heavensky from here. Let's go, Emilia. Do you have the...?"

He paused for a moment, taking his eyes off Emi and scanning the room before giving a satisfied nod.

"...Ah, good, the holy sword is safe. Perfect."

"Ugh..."

The lack of Alas Ramus in the room meant that she was fused into Emi's body. Again, no right of refusal. She glared at Olba's back even as she marched out of the room, urged by the Eight Scarves officials to change.

"Mommy…"

Her anxious voice echoed in Emi's head.

"It's all right. It's all right," she whispered, as empty as it sounded to her.

Ten minutes later, she was clad in a shining set of gold armor with a sword to match, feeling the weight of the heavy helm in her arms. It made her blush as she advanced down a corridor of the Phaigan naval base, surrounded by Olba and his Eight Scarves knights. This shouldn't have been a weight that would give her any trouble, and yet it felt like twice as much had been laden upon her heart.

"Hm?"

Then she realized something felt off to her.

"Is this…?"

She could feel a power inside her—a small one, but one that was threatening to overflow. After spending several weeks in Ente Isla, her holy force was pretty well topped off by this point—but there was something else, something warm flowing into her, bringing it a level higher than that.

"Wh-what is this?"

"You noticed?" Olba asked, not bothering to turn around as he walked ahead. "Can you hear them? Those voices, filled with hope?"

"…?"

Ahead lay a gate separating the base's front yard with the rest of the city. Olba was taking the group that way.

"We're going into the city?"

"We are."

"I hear them…"

She could hear the murmur of a large crowd. Emi's face twisted again. This was repulsive to her.

At the front yard, she found a legion of fully armored Eight Scarves soldiers waiting for her, accompanied by wagons filled to the brim with assorted supplies. Among the throng was a noble, refined white mare, patiently awaiting her master.

"That's your mount, Emilia. You haven't lost your riding skills, I wager?"

She was clearly a fine, well-trained steed. The mount of a general, to be certain, not some rank-and-file pikeman. Emi had never ridden one nearly as exquisite during her quest to slay the Devil King.

"Keep your helm under your arm," Olba commanded her as he climbed his own horse, a chestnut almost, but not quite, as fine as Emi's. "Show your face to the world!" Then, after two or three words to the Eight Scarves legion, with a grin he said:

"Are you ready? It is time for the Hero Emilia to take back Heavensky once more."

"T-take back...?!"

Before she could gain an explanation, the front gate of the base was whirled open. With it came the unmistakable cheer of an enthusiastic throng of onlookers.

"What...what is all this?!"

The high-street road that pierced through town from the gate was completely filled in on both sides with people, each one of them bearing eyes full of furtive hope. The calvaryman at the lead made a signal, and with that, the march began, greeted by another rush of jubilant applause.

"There she is! The Hero of the Holy Sword!"

"The stories were true! She was alive all along!"

"'Tis truly her! Just as I saw her when last she was in Phaigan!"

Emi's pulse raced. The people of Phaigan knew who they had before them. They knew, and they were placing some kind of unknown hope at her feet.

"Truly, the heavens haven't abandoned us after all!"

"So the Hero steps up again! To save Efzahan, and to save the Eastern Island!!"

Then Emi noticed something that almost made her laugh.

The last time she spoke with Emeralda, she mentioned that— whether Efzahan was a willing participant or not—Barbariccia and his horde now held power over this empire, and they had declared war against the other four islands in hopes of obtaining the Better Half. She didn't know how large the demon forces were, but unless it was likely about ten or so times larger than the platoon Ciriatto brought with him to Choshi, it wouldn't be able to function as an army on the ground.

Phaigan boasted one of the largest naval ports in all of Efzahan. It was a city of strategic importance, one lined with diplomatic offices and trading firms. And yet, from the moment she was brought here, she had neither caught sight of a Malebranche nor sniffed out any demonic force in the city.

"Olba…can I ask you something?"

"What is it?"

"Efzahan… It's joined hands with Barbariccia and his Malebranche forces, right? For whatever reason. And it declared war on the rest of the world, no?"

"…"

"You're the one who guided them to do that, aren't you? So are Barbariccia and the Malebranche aware of…of all this? What's the point of it all?"

Olba Meiyer, formerly one of the six archbishops who served as the most powerful clerics of the land, shook his head, smiling like a father whose daughter had just asked where babies came from.

"Emilia."

Among all the voices of joy and laughter that lined both sides of the procession…

"History is going to repeat itself."

…his was the blackest in the entire city.

"That was quite the nice little refrain, wasn't it? Do not retain hope; proceed forward; blaze your own trail to survive. Well, now look at them. These people of Phaigan, capable of nothing but clinging to whatever hope they can scrape together. Why, it is like…"

Olba looked to the sky. It was a pale shade of blue, the red moon just barely visible at this afternoon hour.

"It is like the Malebranche, back on that very day. Those foolish Malebranche leaders, who believed every word of it when I told them they could gain revenge against the foe who slew the Devil King and his generals."

"…!"

"I know you can hear them, Emilia. The rapt joy in their cheering. The cheering of these sad, sad people who have pinned their hopes upon you in an attempt at salvation—without raising a finger themselves."

"Olba...you...!"

The anger, sadness, and hate welling up from Emi's heart made her voice harden. She was afraid for a moment that her welling emotions would reach out to Alas Ramus, too, inside her.

"And now that you've exposed your face to the people like this, all their hopes are upon your shoulders. There is only one road left for you to take. You, the Hero Emilia, are the icon we will reach out to as we save the empire of Efzahan from the Devil King's Army that has taken it over. Don't worry, you won't have to do anything that goes counter to your nature. From here on in, you and I..."

The desperation and emptiness behind the words' meaning made them dark in her mind, just as his words felt on that day back in the village.

"We are going out to hunt the horrible demons that have eaten their way into the core of Efzahan."

✳

"Uh, Suzuno?" Maou asked, eyes wide open in disbelief.

"What?"

"You don't see anything...wrong with how you look right now?"

"Wrong how?"

"...Forget it. Just try not to move around when you're in eyeshot of me, all right?"

"Rather rude of you. What is so unacceptable about this?"

"It's not about being 'acceptable' or not, it's just... Ahh, never mind."

Maou sat down on the meadow and sighed.

It was their first camp on Efzahan, in the Eastern Island—the land in which all three of them, counting Acieth, found themselves upon reaching the other side of the Gate. Judging by the geography around them, as well as the positions of the sun and two moons above, they were in the forested areas north of Heavensky, along a mighty river that ran from the capital to the bordering ocean to the north. That was a tremendous stroke of luck—no lack of drinkable water, and no concerns about ever becoming too lost. The river would also be lined with villages, allowing them to gain useful intelligence along the way when needed.

As Suzuno put it, she was not quite able to pinpoint their destination through the Gate—not when using *The Gates of Hell* as an amplifier, something it wasn't built for. The fact they wound up in an uninhabited area was "complete happenstance," she admitted.

Thanks to the time-zone difference—whether Earth's or Ente Isla's, Maou couldn't say—they had left the museum late at night and reached Ente Isla in the early evening. Suzuno waited until the stars came out to calculate their position more exactly, and so, about six or so miles south of where the Gate had plopped them, they had set up shop for the night.

Not that Maou enjoyed every aspect of it.

"Hey, do you really think it's too early to be going around like that?"

He had dropped the subject once, but as he watched Suzuno hammer the pegs of her domed touring tent into the ground, he couldn't help but bring it up again.

"It is hardly any of your business, is it?" Suzuno countered. "I need to grow used to this clothing while we are still safe. This is practice."

"Wellll…yeah, but…"

"Ooh! Maou! Look, look!"

"Hmm? What is it, Aci—*pppft!*"

Maou took a moment from griping to look over toward Acieth. It took the words out of his mouth.

"See? Now I am like Suzuno!"

"I… C'mon, guys…"

Maou held his head in his hands.

Both she and Suzuno were walking around in their sleeping bags. These were so-called "mummy" bags, the type that covered your

body all the way up to the top of your head to keep you warm. They did the job well, to be sure, but one other unique trait of theirs was that you could undo the zippers along the sides and bottom to free your hands and feet while still "wearing" the bag. This let you do things like read or operate a lantern inside your tent without having to zip all the way out, or unzip your legs so you could run from bears or other campsite intruders.

Maou was aware of all the uses this sleeping-bag structure allowed them. But did they really have to go around in them when they were just setting up tents and stuff? It made them look like a pair of large, colorful butterfly larvae as they wriggled around by the river. The sight creeped him out, especially considering how otherwise attractive Suzuno's and Acieth's faces were. Besides, he himself had set up his own tent long ago; to him, the only reason they were taking longer was because they were cosplaying as gigantic maggots.

"You guys... You just wanted to try those things out, didn't you?"

"Ooh, yes!"

"Wh-what?! Nonsense! I would never dream of such a thing!"

At least Acieth was being honest with herself.

"Geez..."

"N-no! I-I-I fully intend to change clothes after this! I simply wanted to wear this because I could hardly bear the idea of you peeking upon me yet again... Ah!"

It was a painfully bad excuse, one accentuated by Suzuno flapping her arms wildly out through her arm holes. The physical activity made her accidentally kick one of the tent's binding pegs out of place.

"Ooh, all fall down!"

"Oh, no... Devil King! This is your fault!!"

She must not have hammered the other pegs in place all that well. Once one of them came off, the others joined them, making the entire tent tilt to the side.

"Look, I'll do it for you, okay?" Maou said as he snatched a peg from Suzuno's hand. "If you're gonna change, do it right now while I'm not looking."

"*Nnnnhh!!*"

The giant larva shooed him away, but soon it wriggled its way down to a hedge by the riverside, carrying along a cloth wrapping with what Maou imagined was her clothing.

"And don't forget the bug spray!"

"Silence! I know!" the irritated Suzuno shouted, hackles raised (not that it showed through the round sleeping bag) as she hid herself.

"Can you push that peg back in for me, Acieth?"

"Okaaay!"

The other larva shimmied its way up to Maou's right side.

"By the way, Acieth..."

"Oh?" Acieth replied, fumbling with the peg before finally driving it into the earth.

"When did you and Nord wind up in Japan, anyway...or on Earth, I mean?"

"When? Uhh... Pretty long back, I think."

"Pretty long? Like, about half a year?"

That was just about when Maou ran into Emi and Urushihara again—when his life started getting all screwy.

"Haffa year? Uhh, six of the months?"

Maou gave her a look.

"I was born, um, just one year. So before that, I don't know."

"Seriously?" Maou exclaimed as the larval Acieth laced a tent line through the peg.

"Ooh, yes. When I was born, I already live with Father. So before that, I don't know, really."

This was an unexpected pearl of wisdom for Maou. If Acieth could be believed, she was Alas Ramus's "younger" sister—but considering the difference in growth, Maou assumed Acieth had attained human form long before her sibling did. Being "born," to these things, must mean transforming from a seed or a Yesod fragment or whatever to what they were now.

Alas Ramus was "born" less than three months ago. There was less than a year's difference between the two of them taking human shape—but just look at the difference in growth rates.

"But how come you're the younger sister, even though you became human first? How's all of that work?"

"Um?"

"No, I mean... Let's pick up that topic once we have Alas Ramus back. So I guess that means Nord was in Japan a lot quicker than I thought, then."

"Ooh, yes, I think."

That was probably why less-than-native Japanese was the only language Acieth was capable of speaking.

"Man, what a pain."

"What is the pain?"

"Mmm..." Maou nodded, approving of the job they had done getting the tent back in shape. "Once this is all over, I think we're all gonna have to sit down and have one heck of a family conference."

"Family what?"

"I'll explain once we get to it. What's taking Suzuno so long? Did a bear swipe at her or..."

"No bear can defeat me!"

"Whoa!" Maou jumped in the air, shocked at the voice from behind. "Wh-what the heck? If you were back, say so, man!"

"It is your fault for leaving your back unprotected. I have often felt that you are greatly underestimating my powers, Devil— What is it?"

Maou had fallen silent, mesmerized by Suzuno's peevish state. It put her further off.

"Do you have some issue with my clothing again?"

"N-no, of course not..."

Maou frantically shook his head.

"It's just that...that's how you look here, huh?"

"What?"

Maou's surprise was, perhaps, justifiable. After completing her metamorphosis from her larval form, Suzuno had returned in an outfit quite unlike her usual kimono. She wore leather sandals, Church vestments that came down to her ankles, and a dark-red hooded overcoat. The clasp that kept the overcoat on her around the shoulders bore a jeweled motif—a holy-force amplifier, perhaps.

Clad in this, Suzuno was no longer the loudmouthed, nagging neighbor in the apartment next door. She was Crestia Bell, leader of the Church's Reconciliation Panel, and the majesty and mystery she now projected lived up to her title in every way.

"This is the garb of the Church's diplomatic and missionary arm. We have many monks and proselytizers working the lands of Efzahan, and the nature of my previous work means that few people would know my face. With this outfit, we would never arouse suspicion in any of the villages we— Why are you looking at me like that?"

It was perhaps unfair to say, but while this holy garb would go perfect with a holy scripture or the like in her hands, pairing it with the deflated mummy-bag shell draped across her arms largely ruined the effect.

"Did you just, like, molt or something?"

"Maou, what is 'molt'?"

"Devil King... You dare compare me to a snake, or some lowly shellfish...?"

"N-no, no! Stop picturing creepy animals like that! You're a girl, aren't you? You could've said 'butterfly' or something!"

Suzuno gave him a blank, confused glare.

"...Butterfly?"

Then, as she digested what he meant, surprise spread across her countenance.

"Y-you call me a butterfly? Well, of all the things a Devil King could ever..."

"Um, Maou, what is 'molt'?" Acieth interjected, still in larval form, before the flustered Suzuno could ask what he really meant.

"Oh, um... So 'molting' is when a snake or a crab or something sheds the skin or shell it was living in and grows bigger. That, and butterflies and cicadas make what's called a 'cocoon' that they grow inside of. By the time they come out of it, they've transformed into something completely different. That kind of thing."

"...Enough of this."

Suzuno sounded hurt, strangely enough, at Maou's biology lecture. She began to roll up the sleeping bag in her hands.

"Ooh, a butterfly? Boy! Suzuno is the beautiful molting!"

"Mm? Mm. Well, perhaps, yes."

"Suzunooo!" Acieth raced up to her. "Maou said you are beautiful!"

"Ah, did he? A pitiful joke of a Devil King, indeed," Suzuno replied, taking a neutral, philosophical approach to it all.

"Whoa, whoa, what's that supposed to mean?" Maou said, feigning shock. "I'm being totally serious here. Like, didn't Emi and Chi say as much to you at first? Your kimonos and stuff are fine and all, but you should try putting on something more modern. I think those robes look good on you."

"What...did you...?"

Suzuno's eyes opened wide, unprepared for this sudden bout of serious talk.

"No, I mean, I just never see you in anything except kimonos, so it's kind of fresh to me, is all. Regular clothing's a lot easier to put on, though. Cheaper, too. I think it'd work on you."

"You, you, y-you think so...?" Suzuno stammered.

"Huh?" A concerned Acieth turned to her. "What is wrong, Suzuno?"

"To, to be honest, I was... I was at my clerical post for so long, I had grown rather used to these long, heavy robes. The shorter, more revealing articles of clothing Emilia and Chiho wear... I had my qualms about them, one could say. Even after I realized it was no longer the norm, I liked kimono because they resembled my vestments in all of the...dimensions, perhaps...but..."

"Hmm?" Maou lent Suzuno an ear, as she nervously rolled up and unfurled the sleeping bag in her hands.

"You think it..."

"I think it...?"

"Suzunooo! Your face is red—*mng!*"

Suzuno shot a hand up to push the jaw of the intruding Acieth back into the shut position. She reflexively grabbed at the hem of her robe with the other one.

"You think," she softly warbled, "it would look...good...on me?"

"Is that what you're so worked up about?"

Maou doubted it was Suzuno's aversion to Western shirts and pants that made her act like this. He began to sweat a little, concerned he was overstepping his bounds.

"No! Not that! I just... No one has...has ever said such a thing... before..."

Her firm, resolved eyes, in a wholly unfamiliar show of weakness, began to waver.

"Well, I think everyone got used to regular clothes pretty quick over there, but...yeah, I think they'd look good on you."

"De...Devil King, what is this nonsense you spout, out of nowhere...? Do not expect any rewards for your petty compliments..."

"*Mmph fpph rrrrrpmmpphhh!!*"

Unbeknownst to Maou, Suzuno had gradually been applying more and more force to Acieth's jaw. It was wholly instinctive on her part, but enough to make Acieth voice her discomfort.

"Well, it's still the truth. Plus, Ashiya told me that as opposed to a kimono, you can just toss regular clothes into the washer as-is and it's no problem."

"...Mmm?"

"And, I mean, I buy a lot of stuff at UniClo, but you can find discount clothing stores in most shopping centers. And if you like something, you can buy a ton of it in the same pattern or size or whatever."

"...Mmmmmm?"

"*Pnngnngngnnh!*"

"I've never tried on a Japanese outfit before, but for someone living in our wage bracket, there's no way we could keep ourselves going without the more modern stuff."

"..."

"Plus, isn't the thing with kimonos—like, you're only allowed to wear certain kinds on certain seasons or occasions? You never have to worry about that with Western clothes, as long as you got the right type on. It couldn't be easier. Try it."

"...Mm. Yes. Indeed."

"Hmm? What?"

"…Nothing. Perhaps I caught a wild hair up my nose for a moment there. I think I shall meditate for a bit to expel these distractions from my mind."

"*Pngh!*"

The ashen-faced Suzuno finally released her grip on Acieth.

"Oh? Um, did I say something bad?"

"You did," she boomed as she made for her tent. "You misled my heart and nearly led me over the cliff. Truly, the whisperings of the devil."

It took this long for Maou to realize that he had offended Suzuno, somehow or another. "Oh," he attempted. "But, um, hey, I do mean it when I said, y'know, it might look good, okay?"

"…" Suzuno stopped, like the words had bolted her to the ground. "I…I refuse to be deceived!!" she shouted, turning her reddened face toward him for only a moment as she burrowed into the tent Maou put up for her. (They had previously decided, after a long struggle, to divide the tents by gender.)

"Huh. Guess I did say something bad."

It looked to Maou like Suzuno was flailing around inside her tent. He brought a hand to his head.

"Oooh, thag hurrgh," the teary-eyed Acieth groaned as she rubbed her own reddened cheeks. "Suzunooo! What do you doing?!" Then, still in larval form, she squirmed her way into the maelstrom going on inside the tent, the very picture of foolish bravery.

"…Great. Well, guess I'll get things ready for bed, too."

They were planning to discuss how they would trade watch duties after dinner, but levelheaded conversation was no longer on the menu for tonight.

"This sure doesn't bode well," Maou sighed, scoping out the stars that lit up the Ente Islan sky.

✳

"We went through a lot more gas than I thought… Think we can reach Heavensky like this?"

It was mid-afternoon on the third day of their jaunt through

Efzahan, and at a village tavern they had stopped by, Maou was sizing up Suzuno on the other side of the table.

"Our detour this morning cost us dearly, indeed. I was not expecting to all but run into a Regal Crimson patrol. We were going fast, and the roads were poor."

The fuel gauges on both of their scooters were one tick away from the "E" mark. They had extra gasoline with them, but considering the lack of flat, well-maintained asphalt roads in Ente Isla, they didn't have much wiggle room to work with. Food and water were not an issue, as long as they had access to the village they were currently in, but there was no hope of finding a gas station on this planet. That was the bottleneck.

"We will need to pick our roads a tad more carefully."

Suzuno spread Ashiya's hand-drawn map of Efzahan out on the table.

"However, it is also true that we are approaching Heavensky far more quickly than scheduled. If possible…I would like to reach this village by sundown. We are more likely to encounter Eight Scarves men the closer we come to the palace, but I would like to stay on our scooters for as close as we can bear to reach."

"Yeah."

For once, they agreed on something. As long as they had gas to feed them, they wanted to hang on to their scooters.

"…Not that I should talk, by the way, but things seem pretty peaceful around here. Looks like they've rebuilt a ton of stuff already. I thought it'd be a little rougher around the edges, still."

"No, you should not talk, indeed. But I had noticed that myself. Let me ask you, Devil King: How strong a force is this Malebranche within the demon realms?"

"How strong a force? Well, they certainly numbered a lot, is about all I can tell you. When I sent my army to invade the islands, the forces to the north, east, and west were a pretty even mix of races, but I'd say about eighty percent of the force Malacoda led to the Southern Island were Malebranche. Emi and the humans killed most of 'em, I assume, but…"

"Hmm. So rather few of them remain under the rule of Camio?"

"I can't give you concrete numbers. It's not like we had a census bureau."

Suzuno nodded as though Maoh's words were backed up by some theory in her head. "Actually," she said, "I was of the same mind as you. This land is peaceful—recovering. By which, I do not mean to say that your army's carnage has been wiped away by time. I mean to say that, considering the Malebranche have infiltrated the imperial government and declared war on the entire world, it hardly seems like a nation in wartime. I sense nothing in the way of demons near us, despite the fact our map puts us squarely within jurisdiction of the Efzahan capital."

"...That's a good point," Maou realized out loud. "Considering all the BS Ciriatto and Farfarello and Libicocco gave us, you'd think the demons would be throwing their weight around a little more."

"Indeed. And I do not like it. Especially now that I have seen what the angels are for myself—Gabriel, in particular. It sticks in my craw."

"...You said it."

It struck Maou as odd, too. If it weren't for Gabriel whisking Ashiya and Nord away, their understanding of Emi's disappearance and the political situation on Ente Isla would have remained rudimentary at best. As far as they knew, Olba had convinced Barbariccia and his second Devil King's Army to turn Efzahan into a puppet regime so they could declare war on the world—a second ploy by the demons to conquer the human world anew. But now, several angels had become involved—and both they and the demons had used Efzahan's military to take Ashiya and Nord away. Maou began to suspect that little was as it seemed around here.

"We had best examine the people of this land a tad more," Suzuno suggested, "if we wish to come closer to the truth."

"Yeah. It's not exactly bustling around here, but it's not like we're being subject to invasion or anything."

The two of them looked out a nearby window to the village's main street.

According to Ashiya's map, the village they arrived at after cam-
ouflaging their scooters in some high brush was named Honpha. It
seemed fairly humble at first sight but enjoyed a decently sized population nonetheless. Its security was handled by the Knights of the
Inlain Crimson Scarves, each one of their ranks bearing a red wrist-
band bordered in white. They spied a few of them here and there on
the streets.

"Maou, can I have more? This is yummy!"

"...I'm glad you're enjoying this."

As he and Suzuno assessed the situation, Acieth had been silently
nibbling away at his side. Before he knew it, she had scarfed down a
sizable basketful of bread. There was an empty bowl and plate in her
hand—they formerly held some chicken-and-vegetable soup and
freshwater fish done up in a pie with breadcrumbs, apparently a local
favorite—and she was already showing them to the nearby tavern
keeper. The Eastern Island enjoyed a surplus of water, much of it as pure
as one would find in Japan; maybe that was why they were all enjoying
the local food scene so much after spending so long over on Earth.

"You okay with seconds for her, Suzuno?"

He didn't have the authority to allow it by himself. Suzuno, after
all, was Maou and Acieth's sole source of economic support here on
Ente Isla. She had yet to bandy around words like "debt" and "interest," the kind of thing that struck fear in the Devil King's very heart,
but treating Suzuno like an ATM was bound to have consequences
later. In fact, to Maou, who had to keep a whole family (of sorts) fed
on his own salary, being wholly dependent like this made him feel
miserable. Like a plaything, as he put it.

"That is fine. Would you like another one of those fish pies? I
was just thinking I would like to try a bit more of those udon-like
noodles they had. <Madam! One more of those freshwater-fish pies,
and another bowl of stew for the girl, please. Myself, I'd like to have
some more of that rice-noodle soup, and if you have a recommenda-
tion for a nice after-meal liquor, I'd love to see it.>"

Suzuno's gifts in Yahwan, the official language of Efzahan, were
commendable. Her missionary experience preceded her.

"<My, I'm glad you're enjoying it,>" beamed the tavern keeper, a burly-looking middle-aged woman. "<Fair to say I wouldn't have the sort o' hooch a Church minister would favor much, though.>"

"Wait, did you just order liquor, Suzuno? You could get probation for DUI, man!"

Having personally dominated the lives of its native speakers in the past, Maou had at least a passing knowledge of Yahwan.

"Oh, shut up," Suzuno replied, expecting this. "I am not looking to drink it."

"<We'll be bakin' up a new pie for you right shortly. Want somethin' to drink in the meantime? This is about all we got, I'm afraid.>"

The woman came back with two bottles of fruit-flavored distilled liquor of some sort. Suzuno checked the labels, then nodded.

"<I see your distribution channels are healthy as always.>"

"<Beg pardon?>"

"<You brought those out because you knew I was a Western Islander, no? Both of those hail from there.>"

Suzuno looked up at the quizzical tavern keeper.

"<If I could ask you a question… Is it true, the rumors I have heard about Heavensky? That it has fallen under demon rule again?>"

The tavern keeper's face tightened a bit, conflicted. "<Well,>" she offered, "<if it's a yes-or-no question, then 'yes' wins the day, it does.>"

It was odd, though. To Suzuno's ears, it sounded as though the keeper wasn't afraid of this terrifying development so much as she was doubtful of it.

"<'Course, if you're askin' whether anything much has changed as a result, then it sure hasn't, no. We were all runnin' around like chickens with their heads cut off at first, mind ya. Thought it'd be the Great Demon General Alciel all over again.>"

The keeper took a look around, ensuring she had no waiting customers, then brought her face closer to Suzuno's.

"<And, you know, I'll be happy to tell a Westie like you, but to simple folk like us, whether it's Alciel or the Azure Emperor…why, it hardly makes a lick of difference to most of us.>"

"<I see.>"

"Is this talk about hard things? I want fish pie!"

"It'll be here soon," Maou barked at Acieth. "Be quiet for a sec."

"<Not to spit on the graves of all the knights who died under Alciel's boot, mind. But eastern Efzahan was in a state of civil war long before he showed up. And every few years, the Emperor would draft us common folk to build these high-and-mighty public works projects to make Heavensky a more majestic city or whatnot. Those things are death traps for too many of those unlucky saps, they are.>"

"<…Is that what happened?>"

"<Now, with a human ruler, at least we speak the same language. I wouldn't mind those ugly demons out of here tomorrow, if I could make it happen…but after Emilia the Hero drove Alciel out of here, it kinda made it all the more obvious to us. Whether it's Alciel or the Azure Emperor, we're gonna get exploited one way or the other. All there is to it. Oh, but look at me, talking about all these dreary matters…>"

"<No, no. I was the one who brought it up. I apologize.>"

"<Oh, not at all. It's all true, though. You've traveled a long way, Minister—you deserve to know what's goin' on. Why, once those demon armies marched into Heavensky, there's really only one thing that's changed, and that's how much the Eight Scarves have grown in size. That and the war talk, I s'pose.>"

"Maooouuu, come onnnnn… Where is steewwwww…?"

"…I'll give you mine, too, okay? Just shut up."

"<They've expanded the knight corps?>"

"<Oh, have they! Funny thing, no? The Eight Scarves was the first thing Alciel targeted for cuts, in fact. Now, this is just a rumor, but some folks're even saying that the Emperor forged a voluntary pact with the demons, just so he could satisfy his urge to conquer more land for 'imself. Alciel did a lot to weaken us, but with these demons, we've seen more money spent on distribution, on production, on armaments… You can see why a lot of us are a bit dubious about it all, eh?>"

Suzuno, face tensed, looked down at Ashiya's map. "<I see what

you mean… Thank you for the valuable lesson. Could I ask one more thing of you?>"

"<What's that?>"

Suzuno turned the full strength of her eyes upon the tavern keeper. "<Have you heard anything about angels appearing in Heavensky?>"

The keeper gave her an incredulous look. "<Angels? You mean the ones your scripture talks all about?>" She let out a nervous chuckle. "<Well, I s'pose there must be angels out there if there're demons, but I sure haven't heard talk of that!>"

"<…Ah. Certainly.>"

Maou and Suzuno gave each other troubled looks. The populace might be aware of the demons' presence, but the angels' behind-the-scenes machinations were still far from common knowledge.

"<Well, that little girl looks like she can't hardly wait any longer for some grub, eh? That pie should be done by now. Did you have anything else you wanted to ask?>"

"<Um, no, that is all. Thank you. I appreciate it.>"

"<Ah, it's fine, it's fine… Well, also…>"

The keeper fell uncharacteristically silent, wavering over whether to continue. Suzuno nodded at her. "<It is fine,>" she said. "<By my honor, I promise I will not tell anyone else about what you told us, good tavern keeper.>"

"<I would certainly appreciate that, yes,>" the woman replied. She seemed a mite relieved, but then she anxiously looked at Maou.

"<Do not fret. This is my attendant, a devout follower of the Church faith. He fully understands the sanctity of a confessional.>"

"…Dude."

Maou had no intention of interfering with their chat, but he still used his wide-open eyes to semi-voice his discomfort at this hasty excuse.

"Who's an attendant of whom, huh?"

Maou was still protesting the afternoon's events inside forested land seven or eight miles from Honpha, nearby a marsh.

"You took that seriously?" Suzuno coolly replied. "I would think you would understand how that smoothed over the conversation for both sides. I will remind you that I am bankrolling nearly this entire expedition. Allow me to say what I like, at least."

"Gehh..."

Maou had no response to that. Suzuno smiled at him as he silently squirmed.

"I do not intend to joke about this, though. If Alciel's map is correct, we will no longer be able to avoid settled lands before reaching Heavensky. If we started to be examined more closely by the authorities, it would be easiest for all of us if you and Acieth pose as the hired attendants of a missionary cleric."

"Yeah... The question is whether she'll hold up her end of the bargain. Better roll her back inside if she starts actin' up. Don't wanna treat her like I own her or anything, but..."

Maou looked over to the larva sleeping soundly in her bag by the campfire, stomach full after purchasing several more freshwater-fish pies to go from the tavern keeper.

"We can consider the matter after half a day's drive tomorrow," Suzuno replied, looking at Ashiya's map. "I would like to bring our scooters as close to Heavensky as possible, but if worse comes to worst, we may need to abandon them somewhere."

Maou flew to his feet. "What? No!"

"What do you want from me? The closer we travel to the capital, the more likely we are to be exposed. We have to avoid being conspicuous..."

"But I was just getting used to driving my Mobile Dullahan III! I can't just abandon my mount after that!"

"...What is the meaning of that 'mobile' whatnot?"

Suzuno knew Maou well enough. She all but expected that he would give his scooter a nonsensical name sooner or later.

"It is fine and well that you have an affection for it, but that could inadvertently put Emilia's life on the line. I have full ownership over both scooters, and I make the final call on what we do with them."

"Nnnnngh..."

"By the way, I was wondering... Why do you name whatever you are riding at the moment 'Dullahan'?"

"Huh?"

"The dullahan is a creature that appears in Earth's mythology, is it not? A headless horse pulling a chariot with a headless warrior on it?"

"Oh, you know that?"

"Indeed. And I have never heard of such a presence among the demons who invaded Ente Isla. Perhaps I am simply not aware of it, but..."

"Nah. There's nothing like what gets called 'dullahan' on Earth in my realms. It'd be kinda weird if someone could carry his head around under one arm and still stay, like, living, y'know?"

"Like you are one to... Ah, but enough of that. Why Dullahan?"

"Well, there's nothin' deep to it..." Maou shrugged. "I mean, before I made it to MgRonald, me and Ashiya kinda got fired from a couple of part-time jobs."

"Did you now!" Suzuno exclaimed. By the time she had arrived on Earth, he and all his demon compatriots, along with Emi, were indistinguishable from any other Japanese person on the street. She had assumed they were comfortable from the very beginning.

"Yeah, uh, sometimes companies would go outta business on us, so it wasn't entirely our fault. But before me and Ashiya divvied up our duties between work, chores, and research, I can think of at least two I got booted out of."

He made it sound as though he was reciting bitter memories of harrowing times. For a native Ente Islan, the idea that being laid off was the worst thing to ever happen to the Devil King's life was rather hard to swallow.

"So I started working at MgRonald after that, and once Chi signed on, she told me about someplace that sold bicycles for cheap. So I bought one of those and a coupla other big things. That wound up whittling our savings down to practically nothing. Man, Ashiya was pissed."

Suzuno wasn't around to witness it. But she could easily picture it.

"But that would really suck, wouldn't it? Like, if I bought too much and got fired without any savings to fall back on?"

"Certainly, but… Wait! No!"

Suzuno gasped, conjecturing the worst.

"So I kinda put a prayer on the bike," Maou continued, flashing an embarrassed smile. "So I wouldn't get fired again. The dullahan's got his head cut off, right? I didn't want to lose my head at the workplace any longer, so that's how the name stuck."

Suzuno, unable to look at him any longer, cradled her head with one hand.

"…Just awful."

"Oh, come on! You're the one who asked! What're you laughing about?"

She was. Her face was still covered in her hand, but softly, deep down in her throat, she was giggling.

"…Hee-hee-hee… You could have at least lied and said you named it 'Dullahan' because it sounded nice and demonic to you… Ha-ha-ha-ha!"

"That would just make me look like some preteen fantasy nerd!"

"…Ahhh, what a laugh. I do look forward to telling Emilia and Chiho about this shortly."

"Hey, no! Don't, man! Chi's one thing, but Emi's gonna torment me for the rest of my life if you tell her!"

"And how dearly I would love seeing that in person! The Hero, berating the Devil King for giving prayers to household objects!"

"Oh, goddammit!"

Maou turned his back to her, face flushed. It made him miss what Suzuno whispered next.

"Indeed…I would love to be there for it. To see it happen, on and on."

"Huh? What was that?"

"Nothing. There is nothing to be so worked up about. It just seems so…human of you. Laughably so."

"Will you shut up already?! Stop making fun of me!"

Now Maou was fully angry. His back was completely to the fire now as he tossed the stick he was using to prod the embers deep into the darkness. Suzuno found something oddly lovable about the sight. Then she picked up Ashiya's sheaf of papers again.

"Devil King."

"Whaaat?!"

"...Why did you come to Ente Isla?"

"Huhh?"

Maou's face, on the dark side of their little campfire circle, twisted a bit. Suzuno could see it.

"I am not talking about now. Before you drifted to Japan. When you, Alciel, and Lucifer attempted to conquer the five islands of Ente Isla."

"Oh, back to that right now? I thought I told you long ago. I wanted to rule over Ente—"

"That is why I am asking." Suzuno played back in her head the conversation with Chiho. "Why did you want to rule over it? Because I had thought you wanted to annihilate the human race...but ruling over something and annihilating it are two very different things. It is clear to me that Alciel ruled over Efzahan with an even, educated hand—that much I can tell from the way he practically memorized this nation's geography and its norms. But why?"

"..."

"You yourself asked me once—if I truly cared for Chiho's safety, why wouldn't I immediately erase her memory? Well, allow me to return the question to you: Why do you insist upon having Chiho by your side?"

"You're making it sound like I'm some bad guy stalking her or something."

"You never respond to Chiho's boundless courage. She fully accepts you, warts and all, and you string her along, and along, and along, never providing an answer. The very epitome of a 'bad guy'!"

"I...I'm not trying to do that, but..."

Maou let out an anguished groan. It was all Suzuno's fault, of course. She just had to be there when Chiho decided to reveal her feelings to him.

"The way you have been acting as of late is a complete mystery to me. And by 'you,' I do not mean Sadao Maou. I mean Satan, the Devil King."

Suzuno sighed softly, staring into the campfire.

"At first, I was all but convinced that your life as 'Sadao Maou' in Japan was a ruse, a cover for the Devil King's latest upcoming conspiracy. I was certain you continued to see humans as beneath you. That you would betray them, hurt them, the moment you were given a chance."

"Well, geez, that's mean. Though I s'pose most demons would take it as a compliment…"

"But that simply fails to mesh with reality. You fully adhere to the law of the land; you play everything fair and square; you maintain healthy relationships with your boss and coworkers and neighbors; you show nothing but respect for the very species you attempted to subjugate not long ago. And you are not the only one—Alciel and Lucifer are just as worthy of praise."

"Uh, has Urushihara talked to any of our neighbors before?"

"He has a rather close relationship with the Sasuke Express deliveryman by now, I would assume."

"Oh, for Pete's sake…"

Maou rolled his eyes. He suspected it all along—while he and Ashiya were away, Urushihara was still buying random crap off the Internet. How nice of Suzuno not to tell him.

"And yet all of you, to a man, remain adamant that someday you will conquer Ente Isla once more. You maintain that, yet you seem to bear no particular ill will toward Emilia, the woman who is by far the greatest obstacle between you and that goal. Even when I revealed myself to you, your reaction was more bemused than hostile. So does that mean…"

With a grunt, Suzuno stood up, staring down Maou—even though his back was still turned to the fire.

"Does that mean there is some benefit to all of you? In having myself, and Emilia, and Chiho close by?"

"Sure. To our finances, yeah. Adds a lot more variety to our diet, too. It's gravy all the way."

"You have transformed back into your full demonic self several times since traveling to Earth. Why have you never returned before now? Why have you never tried to eliminate us? Why do you remain 'Sadao Maou,' law-abiding citizen of Japan?"

"..."

"This journey of ours—would it not be the greatest chance you've gained yet to destroy us? You should have enough force to over-power even the archangels at this point. You have Alciel close by, as well as a seemingly infinite army of loyal demons. You could have killed me anytime here on Ente Isla, forgotten all about Japan and Earth, and returned to your home realm. Emilia is no longer free to act. The humans here can no longer forge a united front against your forces. What better time to make your move?"

"...You want me to do that?"

"Of the Devil King Satan pictured by the populace of Ente Isla," Suzuno bluntly replied, "I would expect nothing else. But instead here you are, with me, in this forest. You fear for Emilia's safety; you took action to calm Rika's nerves; you promised Chiho you would return to Japan; and you asked Amane to keep the land safe in your absence."

"Fear for her...? Nothing as big as that, really..."

Suzuno sighed again. Maou must've already forgotten what he'd blurted out inside his apartment before they'd left.

"If you add it all up, it looks to me that you say one thing, yet act the exact opposite. But over the past few weeks, I've come to formulate a theory. A theory that, assuming I am right, explains everything about your inexplicable behavior."

"...Can you knock this off? This ain't a science lab. Save your theories for someone else."

Suzuno ignored him.

"Devil King Satan."

"I said..."

Her voiced softened.

"Nothing has ever changed in you from the beginning, has it?"

"Knock it off..."

"Truly, Chiho is wise beyond her years. Or perhaps being exposed to you with no previous knowledge let her see what I could not. Devil King, you—"

"Ahhhhh, shut up!" Maou shouted, covering his ears. "I don't wanna heeeaaarrr it! Ahhh, la-la-la-laaa-la-la-laaa...!"

Suzuno's cold eyes easily bore through the interference.

"You... You were always a kind, sober-minded man. Almost strangely so, considering your demonic birth."

The sound of popping kindling from the fire echoed through the forest, almost interrupting her revelation.

"...Are you listening to yourself?" Maou countered. "You're embarrassing me."

"I am simply repeating what Chiho has said all along," Suzuno flatly stated. "She knows you are the Devil King of an alien world, but she never doubted your nature for a moment. Love may be blind, but in Chiho's case it seems to have only further sharpened her perception."

Maou found himself at a loss for words again.

"And there is something else she noticed. Something neither I, nor Emilia, nor anyone on Ente Isla could have seen."

Their small argument at the Shinjuku electronics store replayed itself again in her mind. He said it himself back there.

"You are, at the core, a true king. One who leads the people of the demon realms."

"...Um, yeah?" Maou sulked, back still turned. "That's part of my title. Devil King. What about it? And what's my past got to do with right now, anyway? We're both trying to get Emi and Ashiya back to Japan with us. What's so bad about that?"

"Everything."

"Why?!"

"To put it simply, it worries me. You may decide to have my head any moment you wish. You may decide to betray me the moment we regroup with Alciel in Heavensky. There is certainly a non-zero chance you will seize that moment to launch a new Devil King's Army."

"L-look, girl, aren't you the one who's saying one thing and doing the exact opposite right now?"

"I have made a career out of suspecting others, remember."

"Shouldn't a cleric believe in people a little more?"

Maou glowered to himself, facing the dark forest before him. Behind him, Suzuno smiled softly. "Indeed," she said, "they should. I may be a former inquisitor, but before that, I am still an acolyte of the Church... Oof."

"Whoa!"

Maou turned around at the sensation of something pushing against his back. Perhaps a few inches below his eyes was the sight of Suzuno's head lit by the fire. She was seated right behind him, back to back.

"Wh-what the hell?" Maou protested, a bit offended at the invasion of space.

"A Church minister," Suzuno quietly began, "never reveals what is stated to them during confession." Her voice was the picture of calmness. "This way, you will not need to see my face. If you like, you are free to tell me, O King of All Demons. Why did you lead your people on a conquest of Ente Isla?"

"What has gotten into you tonight...?" Maou buried his face in his hands and sighed deeply. "Look, it's not like I haven't talked much about this to anyone because I have some grandiose dark secret I'm hiding or anything. It's just that nobody asked me, in particular. That's all."

He lowered his voice a level.

"It's gonna sound all too familiar to you humans, too. You've probably heard it a million times before. So don't start whining if you think I'm just giving you a line, all right? I'm not treating this as some huge bare-my-soul thing for your sake."

"Very well. Duly noted."

"...Ugh. This is so stupid." Maou let another sigh out into the forest, feeling the warmth touching his back. "Where should I start?"

Then, as if recapping the past day's work to his friend, he started to speak in a natural, relaxed voice.

"I forget if I told you this before, but back when I was born, the demon realms were a real piece of shit. Violence was the only rule—if you were strong, you got to torment the weaker demons to death and bask in the gory results. That kinda place. I wanted to change all of that, so I started up an army. And once people like Camio and Alciel joined me, the ball really started rolling, y'know? And after a while, we had an actual civilization going. A kingdom, led by me. Got all that so far?"

"Yes."

"So that pretty much put an end to the weaker demons being doomed to a life of torture, at least. We put together a formal system of demonic magic, too. That made the kingdom stronger, and a hell of a lot more efficient, too. But that whole time, there was something that neither I, Camio, nor Alciel ever picked up on."

Suzuno could sense Maou's breathing quicken a little through her spine.

"Like you know, demons can siphon off people's fears and desperation to gain magical force. They can obtain the energy they need to survive that way. But my kingdom brought peace and order to the demon realms for probably the first time in ages. Fear and desperation gradually started to disappear, and that means the realms' supply of demonic force started to dwindle pretty damn fast. It dwindled, but after unifying the realms, we had a population boom on our hands. You see what I'm getting at? The demon realms used to teem with dark energy, and I pretty much swept all of it away. It's like it was just billowing away from the land, like smoke from a fire. We calculated that it probably couldn't last us another five centuries. I didn't know what the hell I was gonna do."

"...So you invaded Ente Isla? A rather shockingly logical motivation, that."

Maou couldn't see Suzuno's face, but from her voice he could tell he had her rapt attention. So he continued.

"Invading another country to colonize it...to seize the natural resources you've used up in your homeland...that's an all-too-typical motivation for war, isn't it? Almost makes you laugh, not that I had anything to laugh about back then. My people followed me because they believed in me. They were freed from the curse of lethal violence meted out by their fellow demons. I couldn't let them starve because I dropped the ball on my whole plan. So that's why we went here."

"To 'rule over' Ente Isla?" Suzuno asked, choosing her words carefully. "Based on your appearance and your overwhelming power, we all assumed you were here to destroy us all. But you say that was not the case?"

"Speaking of that, you think the humans could ever forgive me?"

"That is not for me to say. I am here to listen to your confession, not to cast doubt upon your words."

He could tell she was smiling a little.

"If we destroyed you all, it'd just be kicking the can down a few centuries. I already knew by then that humans live nowhere near as long as we do. If we exterminated the entire species, all we'd have were more demon mouths to feed in our new colony. So I figured we could rule over humanity by applying juuust the right amount of fear to their psyches. I strictly ordered my generals to show no mercy to those who defied them, but to fully accept the surrender of any human force that offered it. 'Course, how much they stuck to that order was another ball of wax..."

"I see. Is that why you spared the nobility of Ente Isla?"

Even before she arrived in Japan, Suzuno had known that some of the Great Demon Generals who ruled the islands had more of a reputation for cruelty than others. Beyond the Central Continent that played home to Devil's Castle, it was the Southern and Western Islands that bore the brunt of human casualties; by comparison, the northern and eastern lands had it somewhat easier. The Church's statistics spoke for themselves.

"Yeah, I s'pose you know the rest. Emi started freeing each of the islands, I fled with whatever forces I had left, and I wound up in Japan. Really not that interesting, is it?"

Suzuno smiled at how adamant Maou was that this was the most boring story in the world to him. "Oh, I would say otherwise," she said. "It has taught me a great deal. Now I know that you are not so much different from a king as we humans define it. There is still something I fail to understand, though."

"Oh?"

Maou turned around. Suzuno, by coincidence, apparently did the same, because their eyes came close to meeting dead-on.

"What did you do after setting foot on Ente Isla?"

"...Me?"

Maou was puzzled. It wasn't the question he was expecting—or, to put it another way, nobody around him had ever expressed interest in that before.

"Indeed," Suzuno replied. "You. You and your army ransacked Isla Centurum, the de facto capital of the Central Continent...and, truly, that was the last time I heard the name 'Devil King Satan' until your final battle with Emilia. Each of your four generals had their own invasion forces handling the other islands, yes? So I simply wondered—what were you doing, while the Devil King's Army did their dirty work for you?"

The campfire flickered in her eyes.

"If you even so much as snicker, Suzuno, I'm shutting up."

"Well! Rather timid of you, no? Are you that uncertain about your past behavior?"

"Of course I am," came the curt reply. "I failed spectacularly in the end, remember? So anyway, I...I was conducting research. On humanity."

The voice was almost a whisper now.

"They seemed so...strange to me. Humans had so many languages. They looked and acted so different from each other—not as much as demons, but still. But after they all got done fighting wars against each other, they kissed, made up, built new societies, and worked together to survive. It made me curious."

"...Hmm."

"If a demon from my realm encountered a wounded countryman lying on the road, it would be a blemish on his honor if he didn't trample over him. With humans, though, you'd always find someone who'd try to help him, to make him feel better. I just wondered where that difference sprang from."

"I would hardly say every human is as virtuous as that."

"Yeah, but they aren't all total assholes, either. That's demons for you."

Another light sigh. Maou looked up at the sky.

"I did a hell of a lot of things I'm embarrassed about now. Like, for example, I decorated my personal Devil's Castle chamber to look like the kind of reception room you'd see in a human noble's manor. I figured, hey, I'm gonna be the unquestioned ruler of the human world sooner or later, so I'll need someplace where I could gather all the nobility together and make them pledge their oaths of fealty to me. That kind of BS."

"Hm. I wish I could have seen it."

"Oh, yeah, I would've loved to show off my personal room to a total stranger like you. But that wasn't it. I took in and researched all kinds of stuff we salvaged from Isla Centurum—human language, human society, that kinda thing. That's in part, of course, because I wanted to know more about who I'd be ruling over soon."

"And did it bear any fruit for you?"

"No, and that's why I'm working fast-food in Japan right now." Maou shrugged. "But it's always better to act on something instead of worry about it, y'know? Between invading Ente Isla and having my ass handed to me by Emilia, I spent nearly every day trying to figure out what made us different from the humans. Once I wound up in Japan, though, I had it all worked out in three days."

"What was it?"

"It's the simplest thing in the world. So simple, it just makes me want to laugh at this point."

Maou looked over at Acieth, blissfully sleeping nearby.

"It's whether you have to eat or not. Period."

Suzuno lifted her head to face Maou again.

"Food?"

"Yep."

He deeply nodded. He doubted he would ever forget his third

night in Japan, when he fell asleep on the ground and then woke up staring at the ceiling of the hospital he was rushed to for dehydration and malnutrition.

"We demons didn't need to do anything to gain the dark force that kept us going. Sometimes demons devoured the corpses of their enemies, but that was more for their own amusement than anything else. There was no reason at all for us to eat anything. But humans can't get away with that. No matter how rich you are, you can never live by yourself."

He turned to face Suzuno, deliberately this time.

"I'm not talking in some kind of spiritual fashion, Suzuno. I just mean, you can live off your riches but it's not like money's the thing that directly keeps you alive. You turn money into food, and that's what does it. With money, you can have some total stranger make you something good, something healthy; something you like. You want to eat, so you work to make money for it. That's how all of human society works. It's completely different at the core from how demons worked…and I had no idea the whole time."

"…Devil King?"

"I had no idea…and that cost the lives of so…so many people who believed in me. I was so shallow. I thought I could rule over humanity through sheer force of demonic power."

His back shivered against Suzuno's.

"Wait. Are you…?"

Suzuno attempted to turn around. Maou sidled his body to one side to stop her.

"I'm not crying, man. You know who should be, though, are all the Devil King's Army men who followed that idiot. That, and Emi and all the other humans who got killed or traumatized by that moron. I messed up. I was king, and I messed up."

He was bent over now, his back now feeling very small against Suzuno's. The awe-inspiring force he wielded to crush both angel and demon after he breezed into the fray in Sasahata North High seemed like a long-forgotten lie.

"And yet," Suzuno offered in a whisper, "you still had to take action, no? Since you were king."

Maou shook again.

"You had to balance the human world against your own people, did you not...Devil King?"

She looked up, staring at the back of Satan, the Devil King.

"What is the sin that bedevils your heart?"

"My sin..."

"Is it all the humans you killed, the Ente Islan land that you invaded?"

"No," Maou sharply replied.

"So what is it?" Suzuno pressed.

"It's the way I...betrayed my believers. The way I led them to their deaths. How I made the wrong move as king."

"If that is what you regret, what must you do next?"

"I..." Maou paused, letting each of Suzuno's words settle into his stomach. "I need to keep living. Keep surviving as king, no matter what. Until the moment I'm not."

"Precisely."

Suzuno smiled, then slowly stood up and away from Maou's back. She looked up at the starfield above, choosing to ignore the face of her confessor.

"It is just as you say: A king must constantly strive to discover the path he deems to be just, as he leads his people. He must pull his people ever forward, until another, newer king takes his place. And you will become king of not only demons, but humanity as well, no?"

"...Oh, right. This is a confession, huh?"

Maou's voice sounded about ready to break. Whether because he was laughing or crying, Suzuno couldn't venture.

"You think the god you worship's willing to forgive a demon's sins?"

"I imagine not, strictly speaking. Certainly not a demon king's, at least."

"Wow, thanks a lot," Maou jabbed. "After all that, this is what you give me?"

Suzuno flashed a calm smile and shook her head.

"I, on the other hand, do forgive you."

"Suzuno?"

Maou reflexively turned around. He found a robed figure slowly turning to meet his gaze. Her smile was among the gentlest sights he had ever seen.

"Satan, ruler of demons...I have heard of your royal isolation, and of your royal sins. I recognize it all to be the holy truth, and by the name of Crestia Bell, my very own, your sins are now forgiven. Whether my god, or anyone else on this world, believes it or not...I am impressed you could tell me all of that."

Maou gaped at Suzuno for a moment. Then, regaining his senses, he winced.

"Oh, come on! What the hell was all that about?! Did you put something in my fish pie this afternoon or something?!"

"Perhaps. I am feeling rather...out of sorts at the moment myself." Suzuno's face, lit by the dancing light from the fire, looked ever so slightly flushed. "But it is a simple matter. I have already been saved multiple times by you—whether you meant to or not. I felt I needed to repay you for that, and also, quite likely..."

"Wh-what?"

"...No. Never mind." She shook her head lightly, shaking off the tension, and stepped away from Maou, settling down at the other side of the fire. "If I went any further, I would simply be spouting nonsense. It would hardly do to throw the confessor into further confusion, and if it were to come out, we risk incurring the wrath of Chiho."

"Wh-why Chiho?"

"...I can only imagine how much more anxiety it would put upon her." Her voice seemed strained, but her face in the firelight was still smiling. "I have become quite the believer in Chiho, as of late. But enough of that. I do not have the conviction that Chiho does...or the bravery."

"Uh...huh." Maou fell silent, befuddled and unsure of where to go from here.

"...Devil King."

"...Now what is it?"

It might have been his imagination, but there seemed to be a twinge of sadness to Suzuno's face.

"No matter what you may think, I swear by my pride as a Church cleric that I have accepted your story. I do not intend to relay it to anyone else. But...I think you should tell Emilia. When you—"

"Forget it."

"—are prepared to...um?"

"Emi's the last person I'd tell."

Suzuno blinked. He sounded so decisive about it.

"Like, how would that even be fair?" he said as he shook his head, his voice just as resolute.

"Fair?"

"One thing I've learned over the past few months of dealing with her," Maou rattled off, "is that despite all that Hero crap, she's got the mental toughness of a block of tofu. She's just barely recovered now. If she starts up with that wayward-little-girl act again, it's gonna drive me crazy." He looked down, spitting the words out. "To Emi, I'm the king of the invaders who screwed up her life. And I'm fine with that."

"But that—"

"Whether her dad's alive or not, what I did robbed her of some of the best years of her life. I put her and the rest of the humans on the balance against my own kingdom's people, and I chose my own kind."

The words came slowly, as he chewed over each one.

"I don't really care to dwell on what I did to her, I don't want her to forgive me, and it's not like I got any right to be forgiven, anyway. If I asked for it, she'd have no idea what to do. She's already putting us through all this, besides..."

"...Devil King, are you—"

"This whole thing's involving me, and Ashiya, and Alas Ramus and Acieth, and Nord, too. I appointed Emi one of my Great Demon Generals. I'm helping her because I have a responsibility to. That's something totally different from Hero or Devil or whatever."

He gave Suzuno a rueful glare.

"So even if we all get out of this in one piece, you know Emi's probably gonna be all whiny about failing to live up to her…whatever. You think she'll be in any shape to listen to my dumb old story, too? God, she'd never let me hear the end of it."

Suddenly coming to his feet, Maou turned his back to Suzuno and headed for his tent.

"If she gets all sarcastic with me when she sees me here, fine. That's perfect. Anything more than that, it's gonna throw me off way too much."

"Devil King—"

"…Oh, and that counts as part of my confession, too, okay?" he shouted as he crouched by the tent flap. "No telling anyone!!" Then, before any response could arrive, he crawled in and closed the entryway.

Suzuno, without thinking about it, hugged her body. "…"

The body that had felt Maou's heat a moment ago.

"How gentle do you have to be," she said, a self-chiding smile on her face, "and yet how cruel…?"

She looked up at the red and blue moons decorating the night sky.

"Emilia… How are you planning to live, going forward?"

"*Mpph*… Ham and melon…*mhh*…"

Crestia Bell, a mere human, involved with only a tiny footnote of the massive demon battle that changed her world, found herself lost. There was no telling what lurked beyond the truth behind that war.

"Shrimp-chili dumplings… Sunny-side-up egg and toast…"

"I doubt you have ever eaten those things before, have you?"

That was why the night babblings of the innocent little larva, so honest and faithful to her urges, were just the coolant Suzuno needed to calm her soul.

"For that matter…what will happen to me, going forward?"

She felt the speed of her pulse as she kept her arms close to herself, and sighed once more.

✳

The surrender of the trade city of Gwenvan was nigh.

Under the banner of the Hero Emilia's return, the Eight Scarves army that rode from Phaigan—now known to the world as the "Phaigan Volunteer Force"—had begun to battle against the Malebranche forces controlling the lands west of Heavensky. They had seized the initiative, conquering town after town under the control of the Malebranche officers who formed the New Devil King's Army upper brass, and now they were at Gwenvan, second only to Heavensky in size.

The volunteers had the clear upper hand. As a city of commerce, Gwenvan had no stout city walls or defensive installations. The wide road that led inside easily allowed a large force to travel across it. What foolish Malebranche fighters dared to remain were wiped out momentarily. Soon Scarmiglione, the demons' chief in Gwenvan, was cornered.

"Reporting! The Inlain Crimsons on the front lines are engaging the enemy leader! Battle is underway!"

Emi immediately rose to her feet at the report from the harried soldier who had burst into the volunteer force's camp.

"I'm going out," she said. "Their chief will be dozens of times more powerful than his foot soldiers. It'll take more than a few half-hearted swipes to beat him."

She was about to leave the camp—equipped not with the Better Half, but the ornate sword Olba gave her—when a voice stopped her.

"No need."

Emi turned around and glared at Olba, who was serving as one of the camp's staff officers. "Olba," she barked, "do you want the blood of the Eight Scarves knights on your hands? This will be over in the blink of an eye when I reach him."

"Indeed it would be, I suppose. But it is not the role of a general to simply stroll into battle at the drop of a hat. If we were struggling, that would be one thing, but the general appearing when we have such a clear advantage is far from advisable. It could even damage our soldiers' morale."

"...But!" Emi trembled, the grip of the sword in her hand.

"Emilia, you are both the supreme commander of this volunteer force and its most powerful symbol. Please do not engage in such rash behavior. That courage of yours is instilling all of us here with the will to go on."

"*Gnh...*"

Emi sized up the Eight Scarves generals stationed in the camp, the ones who traveled with her from Phaigan. They greeted her eyes with hope and bravery, unaware of what she held in her heart.

"Can I at least provide some advice, then? Victory is ours—that much is sure enough. There's no need to sacrifice any more than we must by now. We need to ask the Malebranche forces for their surrender. We seek to free the town of Gwenvan, not commit a massacre of..."

It was a faint hope Emi clung to as she pieced the words together. Unexpectedly, the suggestion seemed to surprise Olba. "Emilia," he exclaimed, "are you telling us to let the demons live?!"

"I...was..."

All eyes in the camp were on Emi. She failed to form an immediate reply. And before she could figure out why, another messenger stormed into the camp.

"I have an urgent Idea Link report from the front!"

It had been less than five minutes since the last message, but the pale grin on this soldier made Emi emit a desperate gasp.

"Reporting from our frontline force! After fierce combat with the Malebranche leader, our forces have successfully defeated him! The leader's death has been confirmed!! The city of Gwenvan is free!!"

"*Nnngh!!*"

Emi's face couldn't have been more tightly wound. None of the generals around her, overcome with joy and relief, managed to notice. The jubilant words the messenger brought to the camp were exactly what Emi feared the worst.

"It… It's just another demon gone… Another enemy of mankind."
As the frenzied celebrations began across Gwenvan, Emi sat in the officers' conference room in the camp. She was bent over, clutching her knees.

"It… They're just getting what's coming to them. The demon stragglers who tried to follow in the footsteps of the Devil King's Army… The horrid demons we have to kill… It's just another one down."

There was no color to her voice, no sense of human emotion. It was like she was reading the words from a slip of paper.

"The demons are…our enemies. My—Ente Isla's enemy. If we eradicate them, we'll have peace in the world…"

"*What…do you think the 'demons' truly are?*"

"*Ngh…*"

She shivered at the voice coming from inside. She balled herself up even more tightly, shrinking at the weight she felt pushing down upon her.

"The enemy. Our enemies. The enemy of mankind. The fearsome foes that threaten our way of life…"

"*It is like the Malebranche, back on that very day. Those foolish Malebranche leaders, who believed every word of it when I told them they could gain revenge against the foe who slew the Devil King and his generals.*"

"*Nnh!!*"

Emi grabbed her head, groaning. She should have known the whole time. For the past year or so, she had seen mankind and demonkind from a completely different perspective.

"Why…? That demon is dead, and why am I so…?"

She couldn't bring herself to say that the enemy had their own motivations. She was lost, certainly, but she still had enough confidence to state that Maou and his demons were enemies to her. And yet her guilt at the death of a single anonymous Malebranche leader racked her with torment.

If the Malebranche hadn't been defeated here, Gwenvan would be under demon control forever. They were freeing the people of Gwenvan from them. It should have been the right thing to do.

"...*Mommy?*"

Emi's heart was so exhausted with emotion that not even Alas Ramus could reach it, inside. She listlessly stood up, none of the feelings swirling within her resolved at all, and returned to the canopy bed prepared specially for her. She threw herself in, not bothering to remove her armor, and then began to sleep the sleep of the dead.

Alas Ramus materialized next to her, looked at the pained face of the sleeping Emi. She gently patted the cheek of her thoroughly spent mommy.

"Oo?"

Suddenly, the child felt something near—something familiar.

"Who's there?"

But it was for just a moment, and just as quickly it disappeared into thin air, like a grain of sand in the desert. It was still enough to make Alas Ramus bring a hand to her forehead and sit up in the darkness for a while, eyes darting around the room.

✳

"Ooh, man, what a mess."

"..."

"You heard me, didn't you? I tried to stop 'em."

"..."

"Hey, um, can we try to make this more of a back-and-forth kinda thing? It's not like we're strangers, yeah?"

"...What are you trying to do?"

"Ooh, he speaks!"

The Azure Emperor of the great land of Efzahan would normally be sitting there, on the throne that gilded his vast main chamber in Heavensky Keep. Instead, the chamber was chiefly populated

by piles of bodies—the bodies of the so-called elites of the Eight
Scarves. Their adversary was watching over them.

"Well, Ashiya? Or would you prefer 'Great Demon General Alciel'
for old times' sake? How d'you like Heavensky Keep's throne room?"

"...It disgusts me."

Alciel's forked tail twitched in the air distractedly as he sat atop
the throne, dolefully glaring at Gabriel gleefully leaning against a
column near the entrance. Even with the ripped-up pieces of cheap
UniClo clothing still stuck to his body, he yet struck a fearsome
presence.

"Archangel Gabriel...what are you trying to do?"

"Me? Oh, nothin'. You remember from back in Japan about how
we angels aren't sidin' with the humans, right?"

He flung his arms open wide in a feigned show of joy.

"Besides, just look! You're finally back in Ente Isla! All your
demonic force is back! All those days of scoping out supermarkets
to find the cheapest box of laundry detergent are behind you now!
Isn't it lovely?"

No reaction.

"...All right, all right. I'll quit with the jokes. Eesh. Tough crowd."

"...This is truly Heavensky?"

"Mm-hmm. Wanna see?"

"Hmph."

Alciel stood from the throne and walked past Gabriel. As if following him down the aisle, the fallen knights began to wail at him.

"Nn...hhh..."

"Oh, will you guys grow a pair? I thought y'all were supposed to be
the baddest hombres Efzahan could dish out, yeah? I told you he was
too much for you guys to handle, but then y'all freaked out so much
over his transformation that I didn't have time to stop you... Hey,
thanks for not killing 'em, at least!"

"...They have no value dead," Alciel called out from the throne
room's balcony. "It would be meaningless."

The sight of Ashiya regaining his original form as Alciel had sent
the Eight Scarves knights guarding him into a frenzied panic. The

demon showed no particular sign of attacking them, but the knights had stepped up to subdue him anyway. This was the result.

The sight of Efzahan's capital spread out beneath his vantage point did nothing to change Alciel's expression. He turned around, only to find Gabriel foolishly grinning at him.

"What kind of role are you attempting to push on me here?"

"Oh! Figured it out?"

"Emilia's father's presence in that apartment was sheer coincidence. Hatching a distraction in Chiho Sasaki's school would naturally cause Bell to rush to the scene. Thus, I was your only feasible target."

"Mmm? What about Lucifer and Satan?"

"If you wanted them, you would have appeared when they were present. You are hardly so tactless that you'd strike without making sure your target was there."

"Ha-ha! Okay, fair 'nuff. Your role here's pretty simple, actually: Just sit back on that throne and stretch your legs out. Take a load off! Everyone else'll take care of the rest."

"..."

Alciel fixated his eyes upon Gabriel's frivolous grin. Then he closed them.

"This is ridiculous."

"Hmm?"

"Why, in that case, did you show me the scene outside?"

"Oh, was that a problem?"

"If the role you envisioned for me was just to keep that seat warm for you, Gabriel, you would have never let me see Heavensky. This... Heavensky, almost completely bereft of Malebranche."

"...Ooooh."

His reaction was trivial as always, but Gabriel's expression suddenly grew far more serious.

"In fact, you should never have shown yourself to me in the first place, now should you? The kidnapping should have been carried out strictly by the Malebranche and the humans, no?"

"Uh, if you don't mind my asking, what makes you say that?"

"It is simple. Not even all the Malebranche leaders in a unified team could ever hope to scratch you. And I know you are not the noble, pure-hearted demigods praised to no end by the humans' scripture. With you in the picture, it is easy to imagine that this is all the work of heaven afoot. Olba Meiyer, Barbariccia—they are all here now, and it is thanks to your sweet words cajoling them so. Am I wrong?"

Gabriel kept watching him.

"Now that I see this angel is present, I realize that the Malebranche forming a new Devil King's Army and the Malebranche-supported Efzahan waging war against the world are nothing more than a cover. Your true mission is hidden behind all of that. That is why you should never have revealed yourself."

"Hmmm… Well, hell, if you put it that way…"

The archangel scratched his head, grimacing like a held-back student in algebra class.

"You read me like a book, I guess. I shouldn't have appeared in front of you, no. I needed to have Barbariccia at your side when you woke up, not me. That way, I could've—"

"You could have made me the great hero Alciel," he interrupted, "guardian of Gwenvan, back where he belongs?"

"That sounds like the next summer blockbuster more than anything else, y'know?"

"I am, after all, the only Demon General Emilia is not on record as having personally defeated."

"Would you mind letting me finish? …In fact, how 'bout I start interrupting you for a change? See how you like that, huh?"

"I have noticed how the final events in the Central Continent Devil's Castle are still the subject of unfounded rumors here. If the Demon General Alciel has returned to the Malebranche-ruled Efzahan, I suppose everyone would assume the return of the Devil King's Army is nigh."

"Oh-ho! And then?"

"And then…the people of Ente Isla would wait for the return of the Hero to slay this new threat to their existence. That is why you have Emilia here, yes? However you managed to do it?"

"Okay, go on. I'll let you have the floor."

"...First the Devil King's Army, then the Hero. With both resurrected, the people will pine for the Hero's final victory. I presume your plan is to have Emilia defeat Barbariccia and me. Thus, the revived Hero Emilia will defeat the evil Devil King's Army once more, returning the light of purity to Ente Isla. The script could hardly be easier to follow."

"Eesh, I don't think it's that easy...but I suppose it is for you, huh? Given that you're one of the participants."

"But two questions remain. One, why bring up Emilia again? Two, why are you angels going through all this trouble? Emilia's presence would help the Church publicly admit to Olba Meiyer's crimes and reform itself—that much I understand. But I still fail to understand what lies behind all this scheming."

"Yeah, well, I never showed you."

Alciel ignored the aside.

"But, hey, we're still angels, more or less, yeah? Inviting the demons and instilling a little hope in people would set the stage perfectly for weakening the demon realms and protecting the peace on this planet, mmm?"

"What are you prattling on about? Our Devil King's Army had four-fifths of Ente Isla in the palm of our hand, and you lifted not a single finger."

"...Nooooo, but..."

"It makes no sense, you going through all this trouble simply to swat away a few meddlesome Malebranche leaders. If you had that much of a drive to act, you could have assassinated me and His Demonic Highness in Japan far more easily... What are you after, Gabriel?"

"Hm? What d'you mean?"

"If we do nothing and enough time passes, Emilia will appear here, and the Malebranche and I will be pressed into battle. An untold number of powerful demons will lose their lives, and your mission to restore hope to the lives of Ente Isla's humans will be accomplished. But that is not your mission at all."

"What makes you think that?"

"Many reasons. You showed me the outside. You gave me the time and materials needed to grasp the situation. Even that is enough to tell that you wish to put Emilia and me in place to do...something. Something besides what the heavens called upon you to do."

"...Guess you're more than just a guy agonizing over what grade of eggs to buy at the store after all, huh?"

"You... Where did you see me doing that, you dirty little rat?"

That, for some reason, was what made Alciel's formidable presence crumble. Gabriel snickered, sat down on the edge of the balcony, and took in the sight of the imperial palace grounds below.

"Well, sorry to burst your bubble, but I'm not really expectin' a hell of a lot out of you and Emilia. Like you guessed, this whole charade's meant to show off Emilia defeating the Malebranche to the general public. Nabbing Nord Justina along the way was one heck of a winning lottery ticket, I'll admit. Now, not only can the Hero Emilia once again defeat her bitter enemy, this nefarious Great Demon General, and save Ente Isla once more...why, she'll be reunited with her long-lost father, too! We're gonna be showered in Oscars next year!"

Alciel steeled his gaze at the angel.

"Me, though," Gabriel continued, "I've already had enough of this two-bit farce."

"Oh?"

"Feel free to dis me for it, but I'm scared. Yesod, Gevurah... Y'know, those aren't the kinda things I'm s'posed to be messin' with. The 'dark' blood I ran into when I kidnapped you, in its complete form... Man, I thought I was gonna jump outta my toga. Life flashing before my eyes, the whole bit."

"Complete... What?"

"I'd kinda like to save heaven, yeah?"

"What are you talking about?" Alciel grumbled in a low, threatening tone. "The heavens are hardly under threat of invasion."

"True, true," the angel laughed. "But they are about to repeat a mistake they made in the past. They had a single chance, and you know what? They had to play it off as a 'cataclysm,' when it was all said and done. All so they can enjoy this lazy, listless peace they have. Sad to say, though, there ain't much I can do by myself. As intelligent and handsome—and did I mention modest?—as I am, not even I can fend off that kind of rabble up there."

A pause.

"...Um, you were supposed to chime in with one of your *bons mots* right then? Like, personally, I know that rabble's beyond saving, but they're my friends, yeah? I don't wanna lose 'em for nothing. No matter how stupid and lazy and arrogant they are, they're still the gang I spent the past ten thousand years with, y'know?"

"...You are truly the worst straight man in the world."

Gabriel exploded in joyous laughter. It made him fall off his balcony stoop. He stood up, stretching his legs out.

"...Y'know, there's really only thing I want from you: When Emilia shows up, try to keep the fight going as long as you can." He placed a hand on Alciel's shoulder. "Mm-kay? 'Cause with the kind of safety margin I need, a good forty-eight hours would be juuust about right."

"Um..."

Before Alciel could speak, the archangel slowly walked away. He watched him leave.

"When we first met," Gabriel called out, "I had no expectations for him whatsoever. Like, he was so ready to dish out his life for every stupid little thing. But...I dunno. All that time he spent in that other world... Must've made him think a little, hmm?"

"What do you mean?"

"I mean that I've been waiting two thousand years for this—for a new Devil Overlord to be born. And I think this is about the last chance we got."

His voice was just as fluttery and obnoxious as always, but soon it was gone, too far for Alciel's ears to pick up on.

✳

"Dahh!" the shrill voice echoed across the palace grounds. "Why did this have to happen, I ask you?! Where did Olba disappear to?! Why won't he come back?!"

It belonged to a figure perhaps a shade higher than your average grown man, but peeking out from his robe, one could easily spot the enormous curved claws on both sides—the telltale sign of a Malebranche. They were far longer than those of a typical tribe member, forming strong and beautiful scythe-like crescents in the air—and they could belong to none other than Barbariccia, leader of the entire Malebranche force.

"Please, Lord Barbariccia, calm yourself! Wailing about it will not help our situation."

"Silence, Farlo! How could anyone remain calm at a time like this?!"

The Malebranche called Barbariccia shot off his seat, almost knocking it to the floor, and slashed one of his mighty claws down. Farfarello, the young officer who had faced off against Maou and his new generals in Japan, was forced to watch as it tore through the table they were seated at. He sighed.

"Raguel!" Barbariccia shouted, not bothering to notice Farfarello's exasperation. "You were with him! Where did Olba Meiyer go?"

"...Can't say I know," replied the man with the Afro cut, not letting his superior officer's glare faze him.

"Like hell you don't! I cannot allow this!"

"Whether you do or not, man, I don't know. Ain't you kinda in enough trouble right now, though? It's not like losing Olba's gonna change a lot for you either way."

"Gnnnh..."

Barbariccia, who had taken the post of Malebranche leader after the death of the Great Demon General Malacoda, sized up the map of Efzahan strewn among the battered remains of the table. "What is going on in Phaigan and Gwenvan?!" he bellowed, tramping on the papers and debris like a movie monster.

"Something bad, I'd guess?" Raguel said, keeping his legs casually crossed as he watched the map get torn to shreds. "Whatcha gonna do, though? The way the Eight Scarves in the capital are putting it, you two are about the only Malebranche leaders left. You guys and Libicocco, and he ain't exactly in any shape for battle right now. Not after what happened in Japan."

There was hardly a trace of urgency to his voice, but Raguel's choice of words made Barbariccia's and Farfarello's faces visibly darken.

"I had thought," Farfarello sharply replied, "you were all here to counsel us during emergencies like these."

The punky-haired angel scoffed at him. "I think you and I got different definitions of 'emergency,' man. I thought you guys told me we were invading Ente Isla with your forces, and no one else's. Otherwise you'd never be able to live up to Devil King Satan, or whatever. Right? Ain't that what you said? And then I said I'd help set the table. I don't remember ever saying I'd come galloping in to the rescue."

"Youuuu..."

"Besides, haven't I earned my keep enough already? Alciel could wind up being your supreme commander by the end of this, and now he's right here. Right alongside Emilia's father, the guy with the other holy sword. I set everything up perfectly for you, and you're still cryin' about how you can't do anything by yourselves?"

The mention of Alciel's name, in and of itself, helped soothe Barbariccia's frayed nerves a little. It only made Farfarello feel even more depressed about his fate.

"Perhaps we should have listened to His Demonic Highness after all..."

"What, Farlo?!"

"...Er. Nothing."

"...So be it. Our first order of business, then, is to confirm Draghignazzo and Scarmiglione are alive. That, and find out what we are dealing with in the force invading Heavensky from Phaigan! Farlo, fly over and examine the front lines for me and—"

It was perhaps just as well that Barbariccia's not-so-well-thought-out orders were interrupted midway. The ponderous doors of the meeting room opened, revealing a figure that immediately made he and Farfarello sit straight up in their seats. It didn't affect Raguel's stance at all, although his face did stiffen a little.

"Ah…"

"Lord…Alciel…"

"Give me the situation," his low voice rumbled. "Be concise." He raised a finger, and instantly the smashed table and ruined map were returned to perfect condition.

"Ah, Lord Alciel! I have heard the particulars of your run-in with Farlo in the alien world of Japan. I certainly empathize if he has angered you in any way, but I promise you, we of the Malebranche would never dream of interfering with—"

"I said, give me the situation concisely."

Mown down by the Demon General's sheer force, the leader of the New Devil King's Army fell dumb.

"Let me present it, my lord," said the young Farfarello as he stood at his end of the restored table.

Alciel, looking at the demon's haggard face, nodded. "You are the one Erone serves, yes?"

"Yes, my lord. I regret that I was the one who treated His Demonic Highness and his new general, Her Excellency Chiho the MgRonald Barista, so rudely in Japan. I will gratefully accept any punishment you wish to mete out after this is over, but first, allow me to answer your question."

Farfarello saluted, then used a claw to point at the map of Efzahan.

"We, the Malebranche, have invaded and occupied Efzahan with the aid of Olba Meiyer and the angel Lord Raguel, an aide from the heavens. At one point, we had every major city in Efzahan under our control. From there, we intended to seize the site of Devil's Castle on the Central Continent, so we may be ready to provide Lord Satan his proper setting in the future. To achieve this, we needed to take apart the Federated Order of the Five Continents, the unified knight corps rebuilding the land. That is why we have bolstered the ranks of the Eight Scarves and declared war against the rest of the world."

"Mmm."

"Our move had the desired effect. The human knight corps returned to their homelands to prepare for war, leaving the Central Continent comparatively unguarded. We also made advances at the holy sword wielded by the Hero Emilia, which was being concealed by the Church on the Western Island. Doing so, we believed, would disrupt the balance of military power across the islands, stoking discord among the human race and preventing them from putting up the sort of unified front that so devastated us before."

Alciel stole a quick glance at the smirking Raguel.

"So why are you in this current predicament?"

"The cities under protection from our Malebranche forces and the Eight Scarves corps," Farfarello briskly replied, claw pointing at different marks on the map, "have been forced to capitulate one after the other in recent days."

"Hohh."

Alciel nodded briskly, but his eyes were no longer on the map. They were on Raguel, now a silent observer as events unfolded around him.

"We have lost contact with Scarmiglione and Draghignazzo, whose forces were garrisoned at two points between Heavensky and the naval port of Phaigan. The lands under the control of Libicocco, currently recuperating in Heavensky after being wounded in combat in Japan...I fear their seizure is a matter of time as well."

"I see." Another emotionless nod. Alciel crossed his arms, eyes still on Raguel. "So you fools let Olba and these rats from heaven sweet-talk you into ravaging the lands I worked so hard to conquer. And not only did you fail to take Devil's Castle, you let the lives of His Demonic Highness's people go to waste for little to no benefit."

"...I have no defense, my lord," Farfarello meekly replied.

"Y-yes, but Lord Alciel..."

"Silence, Barbariccia! You damned fool! There is no point in criticizing you for raising your forces at this point. You had every right to be stoked to anger after the cruel humiliation we were dealt. But! Why did you refuse to faithfully carry out the orders His Demonic Highness gave to you, Farfarello? He specifically instructed all of you to return to the demon realms!"

Barbariccia remained silent.

"We… I apologize for this disgrace, my lord."

"Aw, don't be so pissed off at 'em, man! They just kinda stuck their necks out a little too far, you know? It was lookin' pretty good for a while there, too."

"This is exactly what you wanted all along, no doubt, you scurrying little rats of the sky."

Alciel had no time for Raguel's advocation for his fellow demons.

"Rats? C'mon, bro. If anything, we're on your side here. I set the table for this whole thing!"

"I have had enough of you angels. You and your false pretenses. I have yet to discover what you are using us for, but I, Alciel, am not the sort of obedient demon willing to wag my tail and do as you say!"

Just as he finished, Alciel disappeared into thin air. The next moment, he was behind Raguel, claws poised to strike his head—not that he needed to be too careful with his aim, what with all that hair.

"*Ngh?!*"

But another arm stopped him—stopped the most powerful body in the demon realms. And the person doing it was as small as a child.

"Y-you…!" Alciel exclaimed as he turned around to see the ashen-skinned boy behind him. His hair was black, save for one streak of red.

"You… Erone… The one Farfarello used…"

For a moment, Alciel thought the Malebranche were rebelling against him. Raguel quickly set the record straight.

"Oh, uh, I was kinda lending him to the crew for this effort, so that guy isn't backstabbing you or anything. No worries, right?"

"Lending him…? Ngh!"

The physical strength of Erone—the boy borne from the Gevurah

Sephirah who sent Suzuno flying and deflected the Alas Ramus–infused Better Half—proved too much even for the fully powered Great Demon General to resist. Stony-faced, the boy pulled Alciel down, then threw him straight into the wall behind them.

"Erh!!"

Alciel managed to avoid plunging in headfirst, but the incalculable amount of force applied to his frame shocked him. Raguel breezily stood up before he could recover.

"Yeah, you can see how borrowing this kid for a bit kinda made 'em a little too big for their britches, huh? So go easy on 'em. Can you blame 'em?"

He gave Erone a pat on the head, nonchalantly walked up to Alciel—and there, his Afro-crowned shadow covering the Demon General, he smiled an evil smile.

"Not like the demon realms got any future. No matter which way you go."

"What...?"

"'Course, that's not necessarily true, either! Assuming you fight well enough in the battle comin' up..."

Just as the words echoed against Alciel's eardrums, Raguel and Erone were enveloped in a soft light, only to blink out of sight the next moment.

"Thing is, though, the demons have to die sooner or later. It's for our future, you know? Best of luck out there."

All Alciel, Farfarello, and Barbariccia could do was lie there and watch as the viciously conniving angel left.

"Wh-what is the meaning of this, Raguel?! We will have to let go of Efzahan if this continues, to say nothing of seizing Devil's Castle!"

"...What it means, you, is that the Malebranche were exactly the sort of dupes the angels needed." Alciel sighed as he rubbed the wrist Erone just wrestled behind his back. "I have yet to ascertain how many of them there are aside from Raguel, but even one of them might prove too much for us. You were deceived, from start to finish."

It was clear from Gabriel that the heavens wanted Alciel and

Barbariccia to do something for them. Barbariccia's forming the New Devil King's Army in the first place was likely all part of their scheme. None of the surviving leaders could even hold a candle to the late Malacoda—and given how readily they had danced for the angels in the face of their overwhelming force, Barbariccia's fate was likely sealed from the beginning.

"But...but Lord Alciel," Barbariccia continued to plead, "we were fully aware of the angels' power! The holy sword... If only we could obtain the holy sword, we would no longer have to accept orders from anyone. But that accursed Raguel... He rounded up this simple man off the street and claimed he was the father of the sword-bearer, Emilia..."

To Alciel, however, the mere idea of demons attempting to possess a holy sword was, in itself, unthinkable. "Fool," he began. "The Better Half Emilia wields is far more than merely a weapon. It is a holy presence, one with the jeweled Sephirah known as Yesod at its core—the fruit of the Tree of Life. We have no holy force—to us, it would be nothing more than a hunk of iron."

"Er...?" Barbariccia paused. "My lord, if I may, I think you are mistaken."

"...What?"

The Malebranche leader reached into his pocket. "I believe you know that Farlo once had Erone under his control," he said as he took something out. One look was all it took to shock Alciel all over again.

"The power of the Sephirah is not something restricted to angels or humans, my lord."

At the tip of one enormous claw was a small purple stone. A fragment from the Yesod Sephirah, the sort that Alciel—or Shirou Ashiya, to be exact—had seen many times before.

"This stone reacts quite strongly to demonic force, my lord. Let me show you."

Barbariccia murmured a word or two into the fragment, instilling it with dark power.

"N-no... How could this...?"

A shallow shade of purple began to erupt from the stone, a familiar sight to Alciel by now.

"When we first sent Ciriatto's forces to the land of Japan," Barbariccia quickly explained, "we attempted to use this fragment and a Link Crystal to search for Emilia's holy sword. Ciriatto failed to return in the end, sadly, but when we infused this fragment with dark power, it resonated with another fragment for a single instant."

Alciel wasn't around for that exact moment, but he knew that Ciriatto had a Link Crystal with him over the seas of Choshi. Up to now, though, he had only seen Emi handle Yesod fragments. He assumed it required the touch of a holy-force wielder to successfully handle Sephirah and holy swords. Barbariccia just blew that assumption out of the water for him. He struggled to link his thoughts together.

"So the holy sword... The Sephirah are not...holy in nature?"

Then it struck him.

"...!"

The thought that had escaped him this whole time. And with it, part of the other, more personal objective Gabriel hinted at on that Heavensky balcony.

"Barbariccia! Farfarello!"

""Sir!""

"Where is Nord Justina? Emilia's father? He should have been brought in here with me!"

"I-I believe he is being held in a room within Heavensky Keep... but he truly is Emilia's kin?"

"You bear a Yesod fragment, and you still doubt it that much...?"

Alciel's mind flashed back to a moment in Villa Rosa Sasazuka. Out from the pouring rain, Maou had just deposited the unfamiliar-looking Nord into the room. Nord, and a silver-haired girl who disappeared into the sky with Maou.

"Nord did not bear the holy sword with him, yes?"

"Y-yes, my lord..."

Barbariccia and Farfarello nervously looked at each other, unsure where this was going. Alciel, meanwhile, was juggling several thought streams at once. He took a moment to organize them in silence.

"His motives remain unclear to me, but I think I know what Gabriel is scheming for us now."

"Sir?"

Another moment of thought. Then Alciel mournfully snapped his tongue against the roof of his mouth.

"Pathetic. Absolutely pathetic. No way out, except to dance on top of his hand…"

"M-my lord, what is…?"

Alciel stepped up to the meeting table and began pointing at the map.

"I will be brief. The person defeating your leaders and storming Heavensky is none other than Emilia herself."

"E-Emilia?!"

"But I thought Emilia was in the other world! In Japan!"

"Emilia returned to Ente Isla several weeks ago. Olba Meiyer and the angels made her do their bidding—how, I cannot say—and now they have rallied an army with which to seize the capital. Their mission: to have Emilia kill us all."

"What?!"

"For…for what purpose?!"

"I imagine Raguel and his cohorts in heaven are hoping to further weaken the demon realms through this farce. That, and use our defeat to build more support for themselves from the devout humans of Ente Isla."

Alciel used his eyes to trace the path of the "mystery force" that had made its way across the map of Efzahan, slaying every Malebranche leader it came across.

"Curse you, Emilia… Acting so grand and self-important, and letting yourself be caught in this repugnant crisis…"

"Um, Lord Alciel?"

"Barbariccia, how many days has it been since my return?"

"Er? Oh. Um, approximately seven days, by this land's reckoning."

"Seven days…hmm."

Alciel did some quick mental calculation. Regardless of the wild card that Gabriel was proving to be, if Raguel and Olba wanted

Emi to defeat the Great Demon General for the public's edification, they would naturally have no reason to attack Heavensky until he had turned into Alciel. Now that he had, though, Raguel must have informed Olba about it and sent Emilia's forces their way.

As long as Alciel had no idea how many other angels were part of this conspiracy, not even he could afford to make any rash moves. And judging by now Emi seemed to be meekly joining the cause, she must have been in a similar position—all the power in the world, but no will to exercise it. And despite himself, Alciel couldn't help but direct his thoughts toward another objective entirely: a way out. How could he escape the clutches of heaven and get himself and Emi back to safety?

"...Lord Alciel..."

Farfarello's worried eyes began to gauge the silent general. Alciel felt compelled to address his Malebranche comrades, but he used an unexpected language:

"<My Demonic Highness's shift schedule last week had him leaving early on Monday. Tuesday was a night shift, Wednesday was all day, Thursday he had the afternoon covered, Friday noon 'til closing. He has Saturday off, works all day Sunday, has off the following Monday as well, then handles opening on Tuesday...>"

"Farlo, do you understand our lord's speech?" Barbariccia whispered.

"N-no, sir... It appears to be from the other world..."

"<The Sunday shift would be the main bottleneck, then—that, and finding a shift supervisor for Thursday. I believe they were low on staff on that day to start with. I must assume my liege could take action Thursday afternoon at the earliest, then...>"

Even before the confrontation at Villa Rosa Sasazuka, Alciel had made full preparations for Maou to follow the trail of Emi and Alas Ramus. If his message to Amane had been relayed over correctly, Maou was bound to make a move.

"<So...all that remains for us is to survive every second we possibly can. As naturally as we can.> ...Barbariccia."

"...Y-yes, my lord!" Barbariccia straightened up his posture.

"Where is the Azure Emperor? He is alive, is he not?"

During his entire stay in Heavensky Keep, Alciel had yet to set eyes upon the theoretical font of all power in Efzahan.

"Yes, sir. That old man's authority was a prerequisite in order to gain the support needed for our declaration of war. We are holding him in the Cloud Retreat, a smaller keep on the premises. He is being guarded by Regal Crimson Scarves holy-magic wielders to prevent anyone from casting demonic spells upon him."

"Hmph. A rare intelligent decision on your part." Alciel nodded. "Bring me to him. I wish to speak to him."

"Ah? B-but..."

"Do not worry about the angels," Alciel ordered, the confidence clear in his voice. "I will dance just as they wish me to. If he wants my choreography, he will certainly get it."

Gabriel, listening from the keep's roof as the two conflicted Malebranche leaders guided Alciel to the Cloud Retreat, stifled a laugh.

"Your choreography, hmm? Fair enough, fair enough. Just make sure you start dancin' when you get your cue, yeah?"

Then he clapped his hands and disappeared into thin air.

EXTRA CHAPTER
THE DEVIL BLOWS CHUNKS

The next morning, Suzuno awoke to the sensation of someone slapping one of her cheeks. She opened her eyes, concluding that Acieth had flopped over to her side of the tent yet again...

"?!!!!!!!"

...but when it was Maou's face she saw through the dim darkness, her heart almost leaped out of her throat.

"Mao—*mngh!!*"

Maou immediately put a hand over her mouth to stop the screaming.

"?!?!?!"

Her eyes turned into dots, her face flushed red at this sudden threat to her well-being. She knew she wasn't quite herself last night, but had she really driven him to do this? Panic began to set in, and Maou bringing his face close to her ear almost drove her to asphyxiation.

"Don't say anything. Someone's close."

But those few words were all it took for her blood pressure to fall back to normal. Maou's eyes had deep rings around them—he must not have slept much—but that mattered little to her.

"...Pickled meat chocolates, microwaved in oil and thawed sashimi...mngh..."

Then Maou leaned over to quiet down Acieth, the dreams of whom he could no longer imagine, as he used his eyes and a finger to point out a direction to Suzuno. She was still cocooned in her sleeping bag, but a few quick zips and her arms and legs were free. She took out her hairpin, waiting, her long hair spilling out from the top of the colorful bag, making her look more like a carnivorous plant than some insect larva. Either way, she was ready for battle.

Maou peeked out from a slit at the entrance.

"Enemies?" Suzuno whispered.

"If it's a friend, I'd love to know right now."

"I would have no idea who it is. A passing traveler, I would hope."

"…Doubt it."

Suzuno grasped her hairpin, ready to summon her magical hammer at any moment. The sound of footsteps was unmistakable now—somebody, through the morning mist of the forest, was approaching. A single person, at least—but few travelers would be curious, or foolhardy, enough to wander this far into the forest from the main path.

"Does Acieth work while asleep?"

"Apart from having her whine at me afterward, I think so."

Maou seemed no more optimistic than Suzuno was.

The owner of the footsteps made no attempt to hide the sound of their boots against the underbrush. They were making a beeline for Maou's camp. There would be a fight soon, no doubt. The scooters, and most of their camping equipment, would have to be abandoned. If their luck ran out in front of the capital…

Then a familiar rumbling voice muttered to itself:

"<This… They call it a…'scooter,' yeah?>"

Both Maou and Suzuno could understand it. It was an Ente Islan language—"scooter" being something of a recent new loanword.

"Ahhh… Ahem, who's there?"

Then, after clearing its throat, they found themselves being greeted in clear Japanese.

"The Devil King? Or Alciel, or Lucifer? That Sasaki lady, perhaps, or maybe even Crestia Bell?"

"Wha…?"

This surprised Suzuno even more than having Maou violate her personal space first thing in the morning. Not many people on Ente Isla or Japan could name those five people in the Japanese language.

"I have no idea what this is about…" Maou must have thought the same. He leaned away from Acieth, relaxing his body. "...But shock-ingly, I guess you're friendly, huh?"

He stood up and walked out of the tent, Suzuno hurriedly follow-ing behind.

The morning intruder was as broad and stout of body as the trees that surrounded them all, his skin tanned by the sun. They had to crane their necks upward to see his face—but when he looked down at Suzuno, his face scrunched up.

"Wh-whoa, what's that?" the figure asked. "Some kinda new race of demon?"

"A new race of what? How dare you!"

Maou rolled his eyes. Suzuno was still in carnivorous-plant mode.

"Yeah, I can't blame you. Freaky, ain't it? But you didn't just hap-pen to run into us, though, did you? Think we could have a friendly little exchange of information to start out, Albert Ende?"

"In...deed. And you are sure she's not a demon?"

"I am not!"

To Albert Ende, mountain sage from the Northern Island and one of Emi's companions on her Devil King conquest, the sight of Suzuno in a modern zip-up sleeping bag was far more bizarre than encountering the Devil King himself.

"But how did you home in on us with such pinpoint accuracy, anyway?"

After slapping Acieth awake from her dreams of transforming into fanciful dinner menu items and yanking the sleeping bag off Suzuno's frame, Maou turned to face Albert once more.

"It wasn't that difficult, I'll tell you," Albert replied as he care-fully eyed the newly awake larva in front of him. He pointed at the scooters hidden under the shadow of a nearby oak. "I heard tell of a woman in Church robes riding some strange manner of wagon, and I tracked them down to here yesterday."

"Uh, we're already the subject of rumors?" Maou and Suzuno exchanged glances. They had made an effort to keep away from the prying eyes of people and settlements, but remaining completely undercover proved even less possible than they had hoped.

"I wouldn't be too concerned," Albert assured them. "Y'all aren't standing out too much. There are thousands of rumors flowing across Efzahan at any given time. I just happened to pluck out the right one, y'see? Besides, everyone here's on the edges of their seats right now—far more than when you were invading, Devil King. It'd be one thing if it were all over and we were under demon control again, but all these vague rumors about Heavensky being taken over, without much else being affected... The anticipation is killing everyone."

It must have been. The tavern keeper from yesterday confirmed as much.

"The most common stories are eyewitness accounts of this-or-that demon, I'd say. Mostly animal sightings, if y'ask me, or cover stories for criminals. But that tale of the strange wagon being driven around—it reminded me more'n a bit of what I saw in your land. Japan, I mean. And since I had business in Heavensky anyway, I thought I'd just poke around to see what I could find, y'know?"

Albert settled down on a nearby fallen tree trunk, sizing up his audience. "So," he said. "Y'all here to help Emilia?"

"Indeed," Suzuno nodded, "but before we discuss that, I need to ask you what is happening to Emeralda. I sent an Idea Link to her the moment I lost contact with Emilia...but she never replied. Until certain events transpired in Japan to open our eyes, we had no confirmation that Emilia was being held captive."

"Ahh, well, that's a bit of a long story, innit?" Albert gave the side of his head a scratch. "The short of it, though, is that Eme received a summons from Saint Aile the day she was supposed to regroup with Emilia."

"A summons from the empire?"

"Yep. I guess Eme's cover story was that she was inspecting the area around Emilia's village so she could expose some of the corruption that's been goin' on, but..."

"Was she found out?!"

"Even worse, in a way." Albert pointed at Suzuno's Church vestments. "Your friends are on the move. She's finally been branded a renegade by the Church. They're doin' everything they can to keep Olba's crimes under wraps. They say she'll have to face an inquisition at the bishops' headquarters in the capital."

"...At this point?" Suzuno asked dubiously. "Why?" Emeralda, after all, had been in all but open rebellion against the Church since well before Suzuno had traveled to Japan. Why was the Church in a panic to prosecute her now, several months after the fact?

Albert's face darkened. "Me and Emilia were guaranteed some level of public safety mainly because of the power Eme wields. Whether I fight for her or surrender to the Church, I gotta go back to her sometime. And along the way, I could've helped Emilia get back home in Eme's place..."

He pointed his face southwest, toward Heavensky.

"But about half a day's travel from her village, I picked up on what musta been a zillion Gates opening up all over the area. Damn, was I afraid. So I made my way to the village, and I saw all these weird guys messing around with Emilia's village and fields and such."

"Demons? Or angels?"

If Albert thought them "weird," they must have been quite weird indeed. But Albert shook his head. "No, they were Church knights from the nearby walled city of Cassius."

"Cassius?" Suzuno jogged her memory. "There's a cathedral under direct control of the bishops there... What would their knights want with Sloane?"

Albert shook his head again. "That's what I wanna know. But I'm certainly in no position to act hostile at all toward the Church knights. I asked 'em why they had activated so much holy force to open all those Gates, and they said it was for a land survey. Part of the rebuilding work, or whatnot. It made no sense at all to me. First they send Eme to find out why rebuilding's been delayed so much, then they trigger all those Gates and start 'survey work' immediately after? And of course I caught neither hair nor hide of Emilia herself anywheres. I spent two days searching the area."

He flung his hands in the air in resignation.

"So if I can't make contact with Emilia, I figured, I might as well ask Eme for some instructions. So I go back to Saint Aile, and lo and behold, the whole Holy Magic Administrative Institute's been shut down by General Pippin from the royal guard. To keep Eme from destroying evidence before her trial, is how they put it. The whole building got put on lockdown, so I couldn't even retrieve the angel-feather pen I needed to open a Gate. That's why I took so damn long to get here."

"…And that is why you never contacted me?"

Albert nodded. "Yeah, well, you were in Japan on a secret mission from the Church, no? If someone spotted me communicating with you, I figured you'd have to pay for the fallout as much as I would. I got this from Emilia…"

From a coat pocket, he took out a smartphone, similar to the one Emi owned.

"But, man, I wish I'd bothered asking Eme for the number of your 'phone' when I had the chance. Biggest regret o' my life. And if I launched another sonar bolt toward Japan, there's no telling who'd find it."

"All right. Let's exchange digits now before we forget."

Oblivious to the situation, Maou and Suzuno both took out their cell phones. They were both, of course, long out of battery juice. So was Albert's. Not that they needed any to complete an Idea Link, but the lack of a physical number inside the phone's memory could affect the accuracy of the spell's connection. It still functioned as an amplifier, but without the number, it was an imperfect one.

But Maou was prepared. He took out the LED lantern he had argued so long with Suzuno about purchasing—the one with the radio, solar battery, and hand-cranked charger that actually worked with his ancient phone—and gave Albert's mobile phone a few percentage points of charge.

Given Albert's complete unfamiliarity with electronic devices, Suzuno's natural suspicion of machines, and Maou's inability to afford anything on the market newer than five years old, the phone-number exchange took far longer than it should have. But they still managed it.

"Ooh, nice! I want the phone, too!" Acieth said.

"...Maybe a kid's one. I got a feeling you'd run up the bill with in-app purchases the moment I gave you one."

"Aww," she said, ruefully staring at the three phones in their hands. "But okay. You buy it?"

"I didn't say I would yet, Acieth... So. Albert. What brought you to Efzahan, anyway?"

"Simple: I'm just checkin' up on the vast amount of holy force I picked up on. It's centered right on Heavensky, like all hell's about to break loose at any moment. I have some of my men deployed in the Northern and Southern Islands, but thinkin' about what I saw in Emilia's village when she got disappeared, I figured this is the spike I oughta be personally checkin' on. And with you guys all here, something tells me I'm right, eh?"

"You got it. Emi's in Heavensky right now...or she's supposed to be shortly, anyway."

"And what's your proof of that?"

"That's kinda rich, isn't it? After traveling the length of Ente Isla on a hunch? Luckily, the idiot pulling the strings behind all this was kind enough to tell us directly."

Maou used the thumb and pinky finger on his right hand to create a pretend telephone handset to demonstrate.

"Look, Albert, there's a lot I'd like to ask you later, but can you give us a hand for now? You probably guessed by now that this is about a lot more than rescuing Emi and waving see-ya to this world. I hate to bare my family drama to the world, but Ashiya... I mean Alciel... He's been kidnapped by the same guys who took Emi."

"Huh? Kidnapped? Alciel?" Albert's eyebrows rose in disbelief.

"And if you don't believe that one, try this on for size: Emi's dad, Nord Justina, was captured with him."

"Huhh?! Emilia's father?! Is that—"

"Oh, and you know that kid over there who's ready to steal my cell phone the moment I let it out of my sight?"

"Agh! Um, Maou, I am sorry! The apology for you!"

Maou grabbed Acieth by the sleeping bag just as she made an attempt at the phone in his hand. She hung her head in shame—feigned or otherwise—as Maou thrust her toward Albert.

"Well, guess what?" Maou proclaimed. "This is another holy sword."

"Huhhh?"

"Aieeee!"

There was Acieth the colorful insect larva, hanging from Maou's hand as Albert stared intently at her. Suzuno sighed. "I was hoping this could be a more solemn event."

"If my hunch is right," Maou continued, "the bastards behind this show are using Emi and Ashiya to make the world go the way they want it. And lemme tell you, I hate people who aren't willing to do the dirty work themselves."

"M-Maou, I want to go down nowww..."

"We have kind of a tough road to hoe by ourselves, but it'll be a hell of a lot easier with you around, Albert. How about it? Wanna mess around with this little farce before they make our friends do anything else?"

"Sounds fine to me, but...is that the girl Emilia said she 'fused' with, or whatnot...?"

"No. She's separate from Alas Ramus. She's the core of a completely new holy sword."

"A human forming the core of a sword? ...Yes. Well, let's just hope you go into a little more detail on that later, all right? If there's a second Better Half here, that's all I need to know. But...come on, Devil King, you can't use that, can you? Are you handling it, Bell?"

"Hmm? No, I...um."

The question from Albert was sensible enough, but it still threw Suzuno off enough that she looked to Maou for guidance. It was natural to expect that this so-called second Better Half would run off holy energy—which was exactly what the Devil King didn't have. But Suzuno had seen it herself—Maou wielding this sword with power that was neither holy nor demonic. He was fused with her, and there was no doubting that by now.

"Mm? Wait. This makes no sense."

"What, Suzuno?"

"No, I...I think I have been missing something important..."

Maou winced as he saw Suzuno bring a quizzical hand to her forehead.

"Well, how about I just show you? Acieth, let me see the sword."

"Um, okay! But, uh, I feel not too good. How it works, I don't know."

"Not too good? What, you eat too much?"

"No! Not that! So mean! But since I come to this country, I feel hungry a lot. Maybe I will not do so good?" She craned her head, still in the larval cocoon in Maou's grasp. "But, ooh, nothing ventured, nothing lost! I will go back."

"That's not how that saying goes, Acieth..."

Acieth's contours were already starting to glow before Maou could finish. The next moment, she turned into a swarm of purple light particles that streamed back into his body.

"Oh?" Albert leaned forward, surprised. "Emilia would do that, too, no?"

Maou imagined how much more surprised Albert would be in a moment as he raised his right hand into the air.

"Bring it out, Acieth!!"

He focused on his palm. The particles from before formed around in his hand, and then...

"...Huh?"

Maou, in his dramatic pose and everything, was the first to voice concern.

"Wow, you call that a holy sword?" Albert asked, eyes upturned.

"H-hey! Acieth! What the hell?!"

"Ooh, I don't know what happens," Acieth replied in his head. She sounded just as lost as he was. *"I was using almost the full power, too..."*

"You can't be! It was this huge...thing back at the school! This huge thing!"

"What is wrong, Devil King?" Suzuno asked, still musing over her thoughts. All Maou could do was give her a simpering look. Which was understandable. Because the "holy sword" in his hand looked to be just large enough to slice up an apple or an orange. None of the sheer power that shone from every atom of the "second Better Half" at Sasahata North High was there any longer. Even worse:

"Urrp."

Maou's face twisted. He covered his mouth with his free hand.

"Wh-what, Devil King?"

The blood drained from his face as he staggered back. Suzuno stood up to catch him, but it was too late. He fell to his knees.

"Oh, crap," he groaned, batting Suzuno's hands away. Then, out of nowhere, he ran off a distance into the forest.

"Devil King?!"

"What's gotten into him?" Albert marveled at the jackrabbit-like speed Maou exhibited when he leaped into the nearby undergrowth. After a moment:

"Bleaaaarrrrrggghhh..."

There was a mighty, heaving groan, wholly unbefitting the shaded forest grove they were in, along with the wet, rushing sound of something that should never come out anyway.

After witnessing Maou striking his action-hero pose, the butter knife he produced, and the "reversal of fortune" that struck immediately after, Suzuno and Albert were afraid to ask what came next.

A few moments later, after it was all done and accounted for on the ground, the ashen-faced Maou returned, supported by Acieth in human form once more.

"Are you...all right?"

"Do...I look that way?" the teary-eyed Maou muttered as he released his grip on Acieth's shoulder and fell to the forest floor.

"Acieth," Suzuno asked, ignoring the out-of-commission Maou for now, "what happened?"

"Umm, I don't know! It was like I say, 'come out, power,' and someone say 'no' instead."

"No...? You were denied it?" Suzuno looked at Acieth, then Maou. "Who could do that?"

"Ooh," came the chastised reply, "Maou, of course."

"Huh? Me?" Maou looked up at Acieth as he attempted to catch his breath. "I told you to come out! Why would I be the one holding you back?"

"I dunno! It is how I feel, in you. It is a shock! Before, we do so well together."

"You—*urrp!*"

Maou was about to lunge at the none-too-concerned Acieth, but his stomach wasn't done with him yet. It sent him back to the ground, hand over mouth.

"So I s'pose," a pained-looking Albert commented, "we can't count on this holy sword at all, huh?"

"It would appear so," Suzuno said. "Which puts me rather in a bind."

She had been going under the assumption that Maou, paired with Acieth, was all but invincible on Ente Isla—at least as powerful as the angel-dispelling Emi, if not more so if the times called for it. With that out of the picture, they could find themselves underpowered if the archangels of Efzahan decided to push the issue. It didn't make sense to her. He harnessed the sword's full power at first blush back at the school. It had no ill effects on him after that.

"Hmm?"

Once again, a mysterious alarm bell began to sound in Suzuno's mind. She sized up the queasy-eyed Maou, the carefree Acieth, and the silent but clearly perturbed Albert, as she fiercely attempted to piece her thoughts together.

It took the slowly recovering Maou to start griping at her to make it all click.

"Ahh, dammit, why's this happening now, of all times? I felt great up until now..."

"Ah!"

She finally had it by the tail. She knew it. She should have suspected it was strange from the start, but she never did. Why not? Because she had known this human, this Sadao Maou, for too long.

"Devil King. You have been back in Ente Isla for days. Why are you not in demon form yet?"

"...Um?"

"And beyond that...where is your demonic force? Not even a little of it has returned?"

"...Oh."

Maou gulped nervously at Suzuno's increasingly shaky voice.

"Uh...? Yeah, I...should? Wait. What?!"

His face went pale once more. Now he realized it. How important this was.

The demonic force wasn't returning to his body. Ente Isla was a human realm, yes, but it was a world with enough dark energy that the Devil King Satan never had an issue retaining his demonic form upon it. If it was there, Maou wouldn't have to think about it—it'd flow back into him, and *pop*, horn-and-hoof time.

Maou grabbed at his head and legs, double-checking to make sure nothing had changed. It hadn't. He was dumbfounded.

"Is this because of...Acieth's power...?"

"I dunno," came the out-of-hand reply. Maou didn't appreciate the attitude, but either way, it was apparently nothing she was doing consciously.

Then, watching him fall into full-blown panic, Suzuno realized something else. Something just as important.

"Devil King... You fused with Acieth on Japan, did you not?"

"Y-yeah..."

The question Suzuno posed next had the potential to shake the core of every human and demon involved in the Devil King's Army invasion of Ente Isla.

"Why was the Devil King, with his demonic force, able to fuse with a holy sword? With...with a Yesod fragment?"

THE AUTHOR, THE AFTERWORD, AND YOU!

Have you ever asked someone (or been asked) what you'd bring with you to a desert island if you were only allowed to pick one thing? I, Wagahara, have always had an issue with this question.

When most people hear the term "desert island," they probably picture a small, sandy little thing with a single palm tree growing in the middle. Maybe a little jungle, maybe a few animals or whatnot, but that's it. But wait—what if the island has a volcano? That would limit the plant and animal ecosystem pretty drastically. If the island was on a reef, securing a steady water supply could prove to be challenging. And they have desert islands up (or down, I suppose) in the polar regions, too. They're just as deserted as what you'd be picturing from the Equator, but the conditions are completely different.

All these question marks, and I'm only allowed to bring one thing with me? That's kind of an unreasonable thing to ask, isn't it?

You might say that I shouldn't be such a nitpicker over what's really nothing more than a fun way to strike up a conversation. But if you seriously think about this desert-island issue, it winds up morphing into a question more along the lines of "If I'm tossed into an unknown land, what should my priorities be?"

What I'm getting at is this: If all of you, my readers, were thrown into another world, one different from your own, what would be the most important things to you? It's a topic I had to give some honest thought to when writing this volume.

If the conditions of this world—the atmospherical makeup, the nonhuman creatures that lived on it, the composition of the ground soil—weren't suited for the tastes of Earth-dwellers like us, we wouldn't have much to look forward to apart from death. Let's assume, then, that there were no major obstacles to people like you and me from surviving in this strange land, and go from there.

The first thing you'd want to do is find out where you're located. It's surprisingly difficult for people to travel in a straight line, in any direction, if they have no landmarks to count on. In white-out conditions on snowy mountains, we'll famously travel in circles without any idea we're doing so. Gaining a grasp of directions and climate grants us a basic indicator of where we are, and where we should go.

Once we have this grasp of north, south, east, and west, the next item on the agenda is sustenance. Not every body of water is guaranteed to give you something drinkable—you'd prefer to have a spring or clear stream handy, or at least some kind of flowing water. Rivers provide another guidepost for directions, and people tend to live around them, giving you a chance at finding someone to help you. And that's not even counting the plants and animals that gather toward them, providing potential food sources (and the chances of encountering predators, but let's not make this too complicated).

So assuming you manage to live long enough in this world to seek help from others, that's where the adventure really begins. Much like the term "desert island" can be defined in a lot of ways, your starting point in this "other world" can be on the tundra, in the desert, or up in some alpine region. Even if you find a path to take in these areas, that's gonna make your survival rate plummet bigtime.

The level of civilization in the people you encounter in this world matters a lot, too. Even if you run into a large, concentrated area of humanity, if we don't share a common simian ancestor, dark clouds might start forming on the horizon.

So if your daily lifestyle commonly opens you up to the chance of being whisked to an alien planet, don't be so focused on bringing only the one thing. Wear pants and long-sleeved shirts at all times (with a coat if possible), have a compass handy so you can gain your bearings, and always have bug spray and some mineral water in one of your pockets. That alone puts the odds overwhelmingly in your favor. Long sleeves protect your body against both the freezing cold and the searing desert sun; the compass and water are self-explanatory; and there's no telling what kind of instantly lethal diseases the local insects might be carrying in your new home.

Having these basic tools on hand helps ensure that, even if you're in a world with a civilization of creatures evolved from otters or iguanas or whatnot, there's a pretty good chance they'll recognize you as an intelligent being. Note that Wagahara takes no responsibility for any curious stares you receive for carrying this stuff around in our world all the time. My clients are responsible for their own extraterrestrial-travel preparations.

Considering how my daily thoughts are filled with questions like these, it was only natural that the story of *The Devil Is a Part-Timer!* would eventually take me to the setting of Ente Isla, the Land of the Holy Cross and birthplace of Emi and Suzuno. Or, to be more accurate, I had to get there sooner or later. This volume tells the story of a litany of humans, demons, and angels, all struggling to live through their daily lives but often having a rough go of it as of late.

I do have to apologize to readers hoping to see what ultimately happens to Sadao Maou, Emi Yusa, and Chiho Sasaki as the *Devil* story delves into a new stage of development. Sorry to make you wait once more. This volume is still just a checkpoint along the way, and the next volume, the tenth, is a major turning point for the series—both because it's a nice round number and because our heroes still have this new world to fully explore. I hope you'll be kind enough to join the Hero, the Devil King, and all their companions for the trip.

Here's hoping I see you in the next volume. Until then!!

THE DEVIL IS A PART-TIMER! 9
SPECIAL END-OF-BOOK BONUS

RÉSUMÉ COLLECTION

NAME

Acieth Alla (TSUBASA SATO) —MAOU

~~DATE OF BIRTH~~	AGE	GENDER
	LOOKS ABOUT 14_{-ISH}	

We'd better look into her birthday. —Chiho

ADDRESS

VILLA ROSA SASAZUKA #201
SASAZUKA x-x-x, SHIBUYA-KU, TOKYO

↖ Inside Maou! —Acieth   *Acieth! You have to take this more seriously! —Chiho*

TELEPHONE NUMBER

I want one. ← HEY... —MAOU

PAST EXPERIENCE	
	None. ← — Same as me, dude. —Urushihara
	Isn't it sad for Acieth to be grouped with you? —Chiho
	As a Great Demon General, do you not
	find it embarrassing to be compared to
	a little girl who is practically a newborn?
	—Suzuno

QUALIFICATIONS/CERTIFICATIONS

I want a driver license! ← No! —MAOU

SKILLS/HOBBIES

LOOKING AT THE SKY/STARS, WALKING

REASON FOR APPLICATION

TO SEARCH FOR HER SISTER

PERSONAL GOALS

REUNITING WITH HER SISTER,
LIVING TOGETHER

IT'S THE OTHER WAY AROUND!
—MAOU

COMMUTE TIME	**FAMILY/DEPENDENTS**	**NAME OF GUARDIAN**
We're together all the time!	MAOU	HIROSHI SATO

STOP IT! —MAOU

NAME		
Emeralda Etuva —Yusa		

DATE OF BIRTH	**AGE**	**GENDER**
Ignora 1213, summer	Did you cross this out, Eme? —Emi	

ADDRESS
Secretary's Office
Holy Magic Administrative Institute, 1-1-1 Orleans, Saint Aile Empire

WHY DOES SHE HAVE ONE AND ASHIYA DOESN'T?! —MAou

Hopefully this translation works... —Emi
'Cause we're poor

TELEPHONE NUMBER —Urushihara
080 - ×▽■× - △○○△

PAST EXPERIENCE	
1-1223, Month of the Wing	joined Palace Magical Academy, Saint Aile Empire
1-1225, Month of the Tree	top graduate, Palace Magical Academy, Saint Aile Empire
1-1233, Month of the Wing	joined Saint Aile Holy Magic Administrative Institute — *Wow, she's an elite student...* —Chiho
~~____~~ Month of the Iron	general Secretary, Holy Magic Administrative Institute
Why're you erasing this?! —Emi	

QUALIFICATIONS/CERTIFICATIONS
palace sorcerer, holy magic doctorate, fluent in Centurient

SKILLS/HOBBIES
eating

REASON FOR APPLICATION
just happened to be here

Shut up! —Emi

PERSONAL GOALS
I want Emilia to live a happy life. ← WOW, GOOD FRIENDS, HUH? —MAou

COMMUTE TIME	**FAMILY/DEPENDENTS**	**NAME OF GUARDIAN**
0 min, half a day ↑	none	

What? —Suzuno ← *Apparently she sleeps at work a lot because she hates getting out of bed at home. —Emi*

NAME		
Sariel Mitsuki Sarue		

DATE OF BIRTH	AGE	GENDER
love has	no age,	no time

ADDRESS
My Future Palace of Love
Heaven's Chateau Hatagaya #302
X-X-X Hatagaya, Shibuya-ku, Tokyo

TELEPHONE NUMBER
080 - ♡♡♡ - XXXX

PAST EXPERIENCE	
	My time in heaven doesn't matter anymore.
20XX	infiltrated Sentucky Fried Chicken (current)
Future 1	sharing my heart with my goddess
Future 2	MgRonald and SFC merge, tearing down the walls between us
Future 3	a life brimming with love awaits us
Future 4	a life brimming with love continues

QUALIFICATIONS/CERTIFICATIONS
sales agent (level 2), bookkeeping (level 3), food hygiene manager, disaster preparation manager,
Handwriting Exam level (1B), Evangelist of Love, future companion of my goddess

SKILLS/HOBBIES
romantic eye for my goddess, ikebana, ability to sense Mayumi Kisaki's presence

REASON FOR APPLICATION
I wish to pierce Mayumi Kisaki's heart with my arrow of love

PERSONAL GOALS
a life brimming with love, spent with Mayumi Kisaki

COMMUTE TIME	FAMILY/DEPENDENTS	NAME OF GUARDIAN
10 min. on foot	planned for future	